NEVER TIL NOW

KIMBERLY CHANCE

FOX AND FLOWER BOOKS

• Cover Design by
www.emilywittigdesigns.com

• Interior Design by Tyffany Hackett
www.tyffanyhackett.com

Author's Note:

Hello, reader! I am so glad you're here and so excited for you to meet Callie and Jensen! I did want to mention before we get started that this book does contain some heavy themes and topics. I've done my best to handle these things with care, but they could still be potentially triggering. Please be advised this book features/mentions (spoiler alert) death of a spouse, death of a serviceman, struggles with infertility, dealing with grief and depression, and scenes that depict panic attacks. Additionally, this book contains mild language and while it is a closed door romance, it does have instances of implied intimacy. If that's not your jam, no worries—just be sure to skip most of chapter 25.

Happy Reading!

For anyone who's ever had to—in the words of Ross Gellar—pivot! to keep the dream alive.
This one's for you.

Chapter 1
Callie

I need to put on pants. Real pants.

Not the pizza-grease-stained sweats I've been living in for the last three days—something without an elastic waistband. Which wouldn't be a problem if everything I owned wasn't stuffed into the back of my 4Runner.

If I remove even one little item, there's a good chance the entire thing will explode like a piñata, burying me alive.

It would be poetic in a way, I suppose. Crushed to death by all the clothes Adam made me buy, all the boring business books he said I needed to read. All the little odds and ends he insisted were much more "me."

He'd already crushed my spirit, so why not let him crush the rest of me as well?

"Why did I even bring this stuff?" I grumble, fighting the urge to smack myself in the face as I stare into the open hatch. It's impressive really, the way I've managed to Tetris all the junk, but there's not much in this SUV that actually matters to me. But when your boyfriend of six years gives you an eviction notice instead of the engagement ring you were expecting, you get a little petty and take as much as you can from the apartment you two shared.

I eye the red duffle bag at the bottom of the pile and give it a good yank, but the duffle doesn't move. Everything piled on top of it, however, gives an ominous rattle. I try again. The duffle still doesn't move, but the pile sways this time, making me jump back.

"Fine," I declare, holding my hands up in surrender. "You win." I reach for the back hatch, slamming it shut, and walk back toward the bungalow. Mabel, my cousin and best friend, is in the kitchen, scrambling eggs like a pro and singing along to a Billy Joel song playing from the Alexa in the corner.

"Morning!" she chirps, pointing to one of the seats at the island bar where a plate waits for me. "Today's the day, right?"

"The day I binge season 12 of *The Real Housewives?*" I stuff a forkful of eggs into my mouth. "Mmhmm."

Mabel rolls her eyes. "Come on, Callie. You promised you'd get out of the house for a while. I don't care what you do, but you can't sit on my couch all day. You need fresh air!"

"No, I need Netflix to stop being all judgey." I counter, taking another bite of my breakfast. "It keeps asking me if I'm still watching."

"That's because it knows, like I do, that you're wallowing."

"I'm not wallowing!"

"You've been here for almost a month now, and the only person I've seen you interact with besides me is the pizza delivery guy."

"Yeah, well, people are overrated." I wave a hand. "Being a recluse is the new big thing, didn't you know?"

"You know I love you right? But as your cousin, I'm familially obligated not to let you turn into . . . ." She indicates my general direction and wrinkles her nose. "This."

"I'm perfectly fine with *this*," I retort, brandishing my fork like a pointer.

"Uh-huh. You're like one step away from adopting multiple cats and never going out into public again."

"Listen, if the cat distribution system chooses me, who am I to argue?"

"Callie," Mabel whines, drawing out my name into one long word. "I know what Adam the A-hole did to you has made you doubt everything about who you are, but you can't just throw in the towel forever. When was the last time you painted? Or did something just because you wanted to? Or at least showered on a regular basis?"

She pauses, waiting for me to give her an answer, but I can't. And my insides twist when I think about the feel of a paintbrush in my hand.

Painting has always been my *thing*. My passion. My outlet for when life was just a little too heavy to handle. It's one of the only things that helped me when my parents died, and it's the reason I worked my butt off to get into one of the most prestigious art schools in the country. It's what makes me, *me*. Or at least it did . . . until I met Adam.

He was everything I'm not. Polished and professional, and he had a plan. At first, I felt honored that he wanted to make me a part of it, privileged even. So when he began to make a few simple suggestions, it was easy enough to agree. Swap my favorite paint-spattered overalls for a matching gym set? Sure, I can do that. Dye my naturally golden hair a platinum blonde? Heck yeah, let's go!

But it wasn't enough. And before I even realized it, I became a frog in a pot of hot water.

Give up art school for a more respectable business degree? Well, if you really think it's for the best.

Learn to play tennis instead of painting so much? Yeah, I can give that a try, I guess.

I didn't realize at the time that I was being boiled alive. I was in love, after all. And someone you love could never hurt you like that, right?

Spoiler alert: Wrong.

"If you don't get it together soon, he wins," Mabel says as gently as she can. "You know that right?"

Ugh. She has me there. I can still picture Adam's smug, unfeeling face when he told me he was making Partner *and* that he no longer saw a future with me and wanted me to move out by the end of the week. He said he needed the time and space to focus on his career.

I sigh. "I did have a thought about putting real pants on today."

"Yes!" Mabel claps her hands together like I've just solved the world's energy crisis. "Real pants are good!"

"Except when they're buried at the bottom of your SUV and retrieving them means facing death by avalanche."

"Okay, that's probably true, but maybe that's your first step. Unpacking your car."

"And put my stuff where?"

"In the loft, of course."

I roll my eyes. "Mabel, we've talked about this. I can't stay in the loft much longer."

It's the same argument we've been having for days now. Despite being super cute and well-decorated, Mabel's tiny bungalow is only meant for one person. The one bedroom isn't big enough to share, and the small "studio" space that's really more like a glorified closet, is where she keeps all of her photography equipment. There's barely space for me on the couch, much less all the junk in my car—which is why I've been sleeping in the small loft apartment above the detached garage out back.

Mabel scrunches her brow. "Well, it's my house, and I say you can."

Her response, even though it's nothing but 100% pure stubbornness, makes me want to jump up and squeeze the snot out of my cousin. When I'd called her, all dramatic and tearful, to tell her that Adam dumped me and I was coming home, she hadn't hesitated to offer a dozen hugs, a pint of Ben & Jerry's, and the loft space she usually rents out for extra income.

With only four months between us, we've always been close, a bond that grew even deeper when my parents were killed in a car wreck when I was fourteen. I'd moved in with her and my aunt and uncle and we became inseparable. People even mistake us for sisters because we look so much a like—same blonde hair, same fair skin and dark green eyes. But Mabel's shorter than me and curvier, with a line of freckles across her nose that I've always envied. She's more confident than I am, too. She knows who she is and in the words of Dolly, "does it on purpose." She's my person, and even after I graduated and moved away from our hometown of Dayton Springs, Alabama, we'd never gone more than a day without talking.

There isn't anything Mabel wouldn't do for me and I for her. But occupying her loft space on a permanent rent-free basis would place a huge financial burden on my cousin's shoulders—and I'm not about to ask her to do that, especially after all she's been through the last few years. Let's just say, I'm not the only one with baggage when it comes to exes.

Mabel's photography business is still in the early phase, and she's worked so hard to try and build her portfolio but she hasn't had her big break yet. Instead of doing photography full time, she's stuck working shifts at the local diner to make the mortgage. The rental income from her loft used to help a lot, but now things are extra tight with me squatting up there.

"You could just let me pay rent." I say.

"Pssh," Mabel waves a hand. "You're family. Your money's no good here."

Tell that to the three overdue bills I saw you stuffing in the junk drawer the other day, I want to retort but don't. I've known Mabel my whole life, and she's not one to back down—especially when it comes to the people she loves. Arguing with her won't work. If I really want to help, I need to find my own place. And fast.

But finding the energy to even pick myself up off the couch lately has been tough.

"Now, stop trying to change the subject." Mabel lightly swats at my arm. "Are you going to get outside and touch some grass, or am I going to have to call the sheriff and tell him there's a phrogger in my living room?"

I crack a smile at that, even if the idea is a little

overwhelming.

"I want to," I admit. "I hate feeling like a depressed blob of patheticness, but this whole thing with Adam has just sucked all the wind out of my sails." I pluck at the fabric of my sweats. "My life revolved around him for so long . . . and now? I don't even know who I am anymore. I mean, look at me. I'm a mess."

Mabel comes around the island and throws her arms around me. "Aren't we all, though?" She squeezes me tightly and then pulls back, a smile lifting her cheeks. "It might take some time, but you'll find her again. That girl that I've always known and loved? She's still in there. You're still her. That man-baby may have stolen your shine for a while, but I know you'll find it again."

I swallow hard, trying to keep the tears welling up in my eyes from dripping down my cheeks. "I hope so."

"I know so," Mabel gives me another squeeze. "Annnnnd, in the meantime, I think I know what you need."

"Oh yeah?"

"Yup. You need something to boost your confidence."

The look in Mabel's eyes is one that I'm more than familiar with, and I immediately start shaking my head. "Oh no . . . no, no, no. I can already tell that whatever devious plan you're concocting involves a man, and I've decided I'm allergic to those."

"Oh, come on, not every man is a narcissistic douche canoe, Callie."

"Well, I'm a *fool me once, shame on you, fool me twice, shame on me,* kind of gal. And I do not want to be made into a fool, thank you very much. I'm officially done with dating. Gives me more time for the cats."

"You don't even have any cats."

I hold up a finger. "*Yet.*"

Mabel squares her shoulders and levels me with a stare. "Who's being stubborn now?"

"Call it stubbornness if you want. I'm calling it self-preservation. I'm not letting you set me up on some awkward blind date. Two hours in a restaurant, poking at a plate of overcooked salmon while some guy attempts to impress me? Hard pass."

"Well, I wasn't thinking of that, per se," Mabel waggles her eyebrows. "I was thinking of something a little more creative."

"Which immediately translates to us either being in jail or dead."

"Stop, it's nothing illegal or life-threatening." She tilts her head and bats her eyelashes. "Come on, it could be really fun!"

I snort. "You said that two years ago when you signed us up for that Warrior Women Mud Run."

"Oh, that was fun!"

"No, that was torture in the form of extreme exercise. I'm pretty sure my quads are still in revolt over that one."

Mabel props a hand on her hip. "Have I ever steered

you wrong?"

I open my mouth to give a dozen examples, but she holds up a hand stopping me. "I mean when it really counted?"

"No." The answer is automatic. Despite all the shenanigans we've managed to get into together over the years, Mabel is the one person in the world who has never let me down.

"Then, trust me. I think this could be really good for you. You wasted too many tears and too many years on Adam, the A-hole. You have to get back out there, Callie, and you might as well start now. So, what do you say?"

It's an absolutely terrible idea, and my gut instinct is to vehemently refuse. It doesn't matter that I'm getting a little sick of my own "drowning in the pit of despair" routine. History has shown me that love only brings pain. And I'm not sure I can handle that again.

So no, I don't want to entertain whatever harebrained scheme my cousin has concocted . . . but the hopeful look in her eyes definitely has me pausing.

I sigh. "I'm not agreeing to anything yet . . . but what exactly did you have in mind?"

Mabel squeals loudly and dashes over to the counter to grab her phone. "It's called a blind date shoot or a stranger session," she explains, swiping at the screen. "The photographer picks two people they think would have good chemistry, gets them together, and then captures the moment they meet on camera!" She points to a Pinterest board of saved photos. "Look how cute these are! I've been wanting to do one of these for forever!"

"A photoshoot?" I scroll through the images. The couples on the screen hardly look like strangers. I zero in on one pair who are wrapped up in each other's arms, sharing a passionate kiss. "These look like an engagement session or something."

"That's kind of the idea. The photographer poses the models like a couple, and if the chemistry be chemistry-ing, well, then the camera captures it all."

It's an interesting idea, and the photos are gorgeous, but imagining myself and some guy I don't know pretending to be a couple and posing romantically sounds super awkward.

"I don't know, Mabel. Maybe the overcooked salmon really is the way to go here. I mean, I'm like the world's most boring human. I highly doubt pictures of me and Joe Random would turn out even half this cute."

Mabel scoffs. "Then you seriously underestimate my skills." She presses a hand to her chest in mock offense. "And besides, you're also underestimating yourself. You're a babe and one of the least boring people I know. You light up every room you walk into."

"You know who they say that about? People who end up getting murdered by their blind dates. Do you seriously want me to end up on a true crime documentary?"

"See?" Mabel laughs. "How could anyone think you're boring when you say funny stuff like that."

"I don't know . . . I mean, what if we don't have any chemistry at all. What if this guy smells like hotdog water or something?"

"Do you have that little faith in me?" Mabel purses her lips. "I know you better than anyone. If anyone can find a new guy for you, it's me, don't you think? I promise he's not gonna be some basement dweller who 'puts the lotion on the skin', okay? He's gonna be great."

"You say that like there are actual decent men in this town. You do remember I grew up here, right?"

She completely ignores that part. "I promise to make it a really great experience for you, and I'll be there the whole time. I've seen photoshoots like this go viral—trust me, it's not as weird as it sounds."

And that right there settles it.

If there's even the slightest chance this will help Mabel's photography business, then that's my answer. Mabel has been my rock my entire life, and it's time I return the favor. I have zero interest in meeting anyone right now and even less interest in a relationship, but if her photos of me and Hotdog guy go viral, it could be a much-needed boost for her business. I know that's not why she's asking me to do this, but I can see the potential, and that makes it really hard to say no. And with my cousin looking at me like that, so hopeful and excited, I don't want to.

So, with as much enthusiasm as I can muster, I nod. "Okay, I'll do it."

Mabel squeals again and yanks at my arms, pulling me into a tight hug. "This is going to be amazing, you'll see!"

"I sure hope so," I deadpan. "Because if I end up on an episode of Dateline, you'll be the first person I haunt."

Mabel beams. "It's a deal."

"I guess I better go do battle with the 4Runner . . . " I say with a sigh. "I'm gonna need those pants."

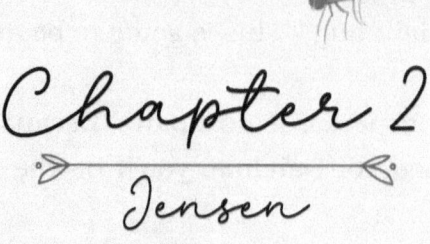

Chapter 2

Jensen

The mini tornado of gray-black water swirls toward the drain, the remnants of a long, exhausting day stark against the crisp white porcelain of the sink. I dry my hands with a few paper towels and turn off the light in the bathroom.

The shop always seems different without the din of customers asking questions, the clanking of tools, the cranking of engines, and the late 70s music old man Angus insists makes him a better mechanic.

Most of the time, I welcome the quiet and the emptiness after everyone else has left for the day. But not on days like today when the ghosts in my head won't stop taunting me. When the shadows lurk, their claws digging into me.

I'd known it would be a bad day from the second my eyes flipped open, heart pounding as the images from the same old nightmares faded into nothingness.

They aren't typical bad dreams—no creatures or gore, no life-threatening situations or violence. Instead, my subconscious likes to torture me with recollections of the life I no longer have. The smiling face of the wife who left me. The boisterous laugh of my now dead best friend. Happy, carefree moments that had felt infinite at the time.

It's the realization of what's coming that has me gasping awake, choking on the lack of air in my lungs. Even in sleep, the agony of what I lost finds me. This morning was no different.

I'd pulled myself out of bed, going through the motions to get through the day, but bone-deep exhaustion clung to my limbs, making every move feel like I was slogging through wet cement. With the workday over, all I want to do is turn off my brain and collapse on my couch, but it's not that simple.

Sighing, I head for my office to grab my keys. My phone buzzes just as I'm locking the main door.

Sutton:

> Hey! Swing by the diner on your way home from the shop.

> I'm locking up now.
> Everything okay?

Sutton:

> You worry too much :)

I roll my eyes, but the tightness in my chest eases a little. It happens a lot—the feeling of overwhelming dread that settles over me every time I get an unexpected call or text. Even though four years have passed since the worst moments of my life, I still walk around with my entire body tensed, bracing for impact.

Shaking my head to clear it, I finish locking up the shop and head toward my truck. The bright red letters above the door—*Bradford Auto Parts and Repair*— glow bright against the darkening sky.

I don't really feel like seeing or talking to anyone, but maybe that's all the more reason to head down to the diner. Sutton has an uncanny knack for knowing when the storm clouds are rolling in on me. So, I put my truck in gear and head for main street.

The parking lot is packed, which is the norm for a Friday night. The Silver Diner has the best burgers in town and everyone with good sense comes here once it's quitting time.

I push open the door and head for the counter, waving at Angus and a few other regulars who call my name in greeting.

Sutton Bradford is standing behind the counter, her cheeks the same rosy color as her uniform. Her dark brown hair is twisted into a bun atop her head, and she looks tired despite the smile on her face. The bright overhead lights glint off the silver chain she wears around her neck—the dog tags she keeps hidden beneath her clothes, but always close to her heart. Guilt, a long-time companion of mine, steps in closer, hissing in my ear.

I wince but recover quickly once Sutton's eyes land on me.

"Shep!" She calls out, waving me closer. "You made it."

"Like I had a choice," I growl, though there's no real bite to my words. "If I hadn't, you would've just kept texting me."

"True, but that's my job as your best friend, to pester you into doing things that are good for you. Kasey would agree with me, you know."

She says his name casually, but it damn near sucks the breath right out of my lungs. "Yeah, well that's because he knew better than anyone how bossy you are."

Sutton laughs, reaching across the counter to smack my shoulder. "Somebody has to keep you on your toes, Jensen Shepherd. Might as well be me. Now, you sit right there until I get back. I've got something for you." She holds up a hand in a "stay" motion and whirls around to disappear through the double doors that lead to the kitchen.

I sigh, slumping down against one of the barstools. Talking about Kasey always hits me like a ton of bricks, though I'm glad whenever Sutton brings him up. It keeps him with us for a little longer. But the fact remains, my best friend is gone, and that reality still leaves me as raw as the day we put him in the ground.

I try not to let it show, especially around Sutton and Ethan. I made a promise to Kase, that if anything ever happened to him, his wife and son would be taken care of—and that's exactly what I've done. As soon as my enlistment ended, I moved to Dayton Springs and took over the shop.

Kasey had magic hands when it came to mechanical parts. There wasn't anything he couldn't fix— which is what made him one of the best mechanics in the Army. It's also why Bradford Auto is so well-known across the state of Alabama and parts of Mississippi. I'm nowhere near as good as he was, but I do what I can to run the shop as he always did.

I keep things working around Sutton's house and play catch in the backyard with Ethan, but try as I might to be there for both of them, I know I'm a sorry replacement for what they lost.

"Here you go," Sutton's voice breaks through the spiral of my thoughts as she bursts through the kitchen doors carrying a steaming platter piled with food. She sets it down in front of me, pulling a set of rolled silverware from the front pocket of her apron. "All your favorites."

I eye the food. A patty-melt on rye, dripping with

extra cheese and caramelized onions, sits on the plate next to a bed of crisp sweet potato fries and a scoop of the diner's famous coleslaw. All my favorites, indeed—which immediately makes me suspicious.

"Alright, Sutton. What's going on?"

"What do you mean?" she asks, a little too innocently. "Can't I give my best friend a meal without there being a reason?"

I point at her with a fork. "You have the worst poker face in all of Clayton County, you know that?"

Sutton presses her lips together for a second and lets out a huff. "Ugh, fine. There is something I wanted to talk to you about."

I scoop up a mouthful of coleslaw. "Everything okay with Ethan? The house? I know I've been working a lot lately, but I'll come by tomorrow and—"

"Shep, stop. Everything is fine. I keep telling you that you don't have to worry about us so much, but you never seem to be able to get that through that thick skull of yours." Sutton reaches out and lightly taps her knuckles against my head. "And that's exactly why I'm about to say what I'm about to say."

There's something about the set of her shoulders and the determined look on her face that makes me tense. I grip the fork a little harder, trying to swallow both the coleslaw and the panic rising in my throat.

Sutton sucks in a breath and then lets it out quickly right before she blurts, "I think you need to go on a date."

It takes a second for the words to compute. "What?" I spit the word out along with my confusion. I'd been braced for bad news, but . . . this? Definitely didn't see that coming.

"Hear me out, okay?" Sutton leans against the counter, lowering her voice. "You're a good man. The best I know, actually. What you've done for me and Ethan . . . " Her voice catches and silver lines her eyes. "I don't have words for how grateful I am for you. But it's been four years, and I don't want you to waste the rest of your life on us."

"It's not a waste." The words come out sharper than I mean them. "You and Ethan are my family."

Sutton's face softens, and she covers one of my hands with hers. "I know, and you're ours, but you don't ever do anything for yourself. You spend all your time at the shop, and when you're not working, you're helping take care of Ethan or doing whatever list of random to-dos I give you. I know what you promised Kasey, and you've more than kept your word, but . . . God, Shep. You're such a golden retriever, sometimes. Loyal to an absolute fault. I'm not saying that you have to stop being there for us, but I think you need to take more time for yourself."

"I take plenty of time for myself. What about the RVs?" I point out. "I just finished up the airstream last week. I'm getting ready to list it." Restoring vintage RVs is something I've been doing pretty much my whole life, and it was what I'd hoped to make a career of once I got out of the Army. But that was before Kasey died. Now, it's more of a side gig.

"Think of how many you could actually finish if you weren't worrying about us all the time," Sutton counters, which makes me scowl. "All I'm saying is that I want you to work a little less. Do something fun. Take a beautiful woman to dinner now and then."

That was the last thing I needed. I start to argue, to explain that I do have fun—not a lot of it but enough—when Sutton's face changes, all the levity draining from it. "I'm worried about you. You're not happy and you haven't been since . . . well, since Anna left."

I don't wince this time, though internally, there's a sharp tug on my insides at the sound of my ex-wife's name.

"You deserve so much more, and I don't want Ethan and me to be the reason you never find it."

She's wrong. I don't deserve anything. I know it's pointless to argue though, so I say nothing.

Sutton takes that as her cue to keep going. "That's why I did what I did."

"And what exactly did you do?"

"I volunteered you . . . for a blind date."

A groan erupts from my throat, and I shove my plate away. "So, all this is just a bribe to get me to take some random girl out for drinks?"

"Not exactly."

I let out another groan. "I do not like the way you said that."

"Do you remember Mabel Callahan? She works the day shifts here during the week."

I nod, recalling her face. "That's who you want me to go on a date with?"

"Hush, and let me finish," Sutton chides, pushing my plate back across the counter. "Eat while I talk." She waits until I scoop up a fry and pop it into my mouth before she continues. "Mabel is actually a photographer. She's been trying to get her business off the ground for a while, and she only works shifts here to help pay the bills. Anyway, she's got this really cool idea for a photoshoot, and she needed a guy for it, so I told her you'd do it."

I finish chewing my fry. "Wait . . . so it's not a date?"

"No, it is, but it's a photoshoot, too." She quickly fills me in on the concept of the shoot, her face brightening as she speaks.

I still don't fully understand, but I know enough to know there is no way in hell I want to be involved.

"I don't think this is a good idea. I appreciate what you're trying to do for me. Really, I do, but—"

"Jensen."

That word, my own name, stops me from saying more. Sutton only ever calls me Jensen when things are serious.

She reaches for the chain around her neck, her fingers curling around Kasey's dog tags. "We only get one life, and we never know when the sand is going to run out. Don't you want to make the most of the time you have?"

I don't think she means to do it on purpose, to fling Kase's death at me like a knife, stabbing at all the places inside of me that still ache, but pain lances through me just the same.

"I know what I'm asking you to do is a little unconventional, but it's just one afternoon. A few photos. What could it hurt?"

Everything. I learned a long time ago that stepping outside of the lines I carefully draw around myself only leads to heartbreak.

But as I look into Sutton's hopeful eyes, her fingers still clutching Kase's tags, I know there's no way I can deny her.

"Fine," I huff. "I'll do it."

Chapter 3

Callie

"Stop fidgeting. You look like you're about to jump out of your own skin."

I groan, itching to rip away the folded bandana Mabel has tied around my head just so I can roll my eyes at her. "Is it too late to cancel?"

Mabel doesn't bother responding, but her camera starts clicking, and I know she's snapping pictures of me . . . which only makes me squirm more.

"Oh my god, Callie. Relax." Her voice gets louder as she walks closer. Her hand lands on my shoulder. "Breathe. You look absolutely beautiful, and today is supposed to be fun, remember? No pressure. Just fun."

"Says the one not wearing a blindfold," I mutter, trying to ignore the way my chest is tightening. I don't want Mabel to know how close I am to freaking out, so I suck in a deep breath and slowly blow it through my lips.

I want this photoshoot to go well, if for no other reason than I think it might be good for her business, but I'm already counting down the seconds until it's over. People Magazine's Sexiest Man of the Year could show up and I still wouldn't be interested. I just want to get today over and done with.

Mabel pushes the hair off my shoulder and repositions me. "Stay just like this, okay?" The camera clicks a few more times. These are the "before" shots and in just a few minutes, Mabel will be heading off to do the same with the guy I'm shooting with today. She arranged to meet him in the parking lot and once she blindfolds him, she'll drive him to this spot in her Jeep. Then we'll meet and pretend like we're some couple in love while my cousin takes a thousand pictures of us. Because that's not weird at all.

"So, where'd you find this guy again?"

"He's a friend of a friend," Mabel tells me. "He comes into the diner all the time."

My brain immediately supplies me with a mental picture of all the regulars that frequent the diner, and it's mostly a bunch of old, hunch-backed men or good ole boys who peaked in high school and still get together on Friday nights to relive "the big game."

"Great," I mutter. "Mabel, I swear to all that is holy

that if you're trying to hook me up with one of the Tom-lin brothers or—"

"Calm down," Mabel cuts me off. "He's not from around here, okay? He's a transplant. Moved to town a few years ago."

Not a local, then. Interesting.

I open my mouth to ask another question, but a short three-note chime interrupts me.

"Okay, he's in the parking lot. I'm going to go get him. You—" Mabel's hand finds mine and gently tugs. "Sit here and don't move." She helps me sit down on a worn, wooden bench. "And no taking off the blindfold."

"Fine," I grumble, listening to the sound of her boots crunch in the grass as she hurries over to where she left her Jeep. She starts it up and drives off, leaving me alone, blindfolded, and feeling like this whole thing is a very bad idea.

Sighing, I rub the pads of my fingertips along the hem of my skirt. I'd swapped the ratty sweats I'd been living in for a pretty, floral sundress. It's an old favorite of mine, one I haven't worn in years. I was surprised to find I even still had it. My hair is hanging in loose waves around my shoulders, and I've paired the dress with a pair of dark brown cowboy boots. It's the most *me* outfit I've worn in a long time, which makes me feel good even if I am about to do the world's most awkward photoshoot.

This is fine, I tell myself. *Totally fine.*

I'm way more nervous than I thought I would be when I agreed to this. I have no interest in dating right now, but I also don't want to embarrass myself either. It's been years since I've been on a date or even looked at another man. I don't know if I even remember how to talk to one. Most of the men I've interacted with in the last year were Adam's stuffy lawyer friends, and they never really took the time to talk to me beyond casual pleasantries.

My heart clenches a little at the thought of just how much time I've wasted the last few years, and I take a breath to steady myself. Maybe, if I'm a little more open to the idea, something good will come from this. Not just for Mabel but for me too. I don't mean a relationship, of course, but maybe this is just what I need to help me shake things up, to propel me in a new direction. Sometimes you have to take a step outside your comfort zone, right?

Even though it's early out, the spring air is warm and fragrant. The field Mabel chose to shoot in today is just on the outskirts of town near the river. It's a popular spot for picnics and swimming during the summer, but this time of the day, we're the only ones here. Mabel insisted the lighting was better first thing in the morning, which is why she dragged me out of bed before the sun had even come up to help me curl my hair.

When I hear the Jeep pulling up, I stand on shaky legs and flex my fingers, trying to expel the anxiousness through my fingertips. *For Mabel. You're doing this for Mabel.*

My cousin's laugh draws my attention, as does the deep rumble of a man's voice as they come closer.

"Be careful, it's a little uneven right here," Mabel instructs, and I know she must be leading my date toward me. I have about five seconds to decide if I'm going to rip the blindfold off and bolt or if I'm actually going to go through with this.

A hand lightly grips my elbow. "You okay?" Mabel whispers.

Here's my out if I want it. I know she won't force me to do this if I really don't want to, but that's all the more reason to stay put. "Yeah," I whisper back. "I'm good."

She lets out an excited little chirp and walks me forward a few paces. "Almost there," she says, but I'm not sure if she's talking to me or him.

She pulls me a few more steps and then carefully spins me around, pushing me backward until I hit something solid. My date. The warmth of his back pressed against mine permeates through the cotton of my dress. "Um . . . hi," I say, trying not to let my nerves get the best of me. "I'm Callie." I feel ridiculous introducing myself with a blindfold on, but it feels even weirder to not say anything at all.

"Hey," my date replies, his voice deep. "I'm Jensen."

Before we can say anything else, Mabel comes close and adjusts our position. "Okay, I want to get a few shots with the blindfolds on and then we'll take them off," she tells us right before she starts snapping photos.

I have no idea what to do with my body or if I'm even supposed to be smiling, so I just stand there hoping I don't look as awkward as I feel.

"Hmmm," Mabel moves close again, assessing us. "You two sorta look like a pair of bank hostages."

I guess I'm not the only one who's feeling a little weird about this whole thing.

"Why don't you try holding hands?" Mabel throws out the suggestion. "And smile, okay?"

I sigh and move my hand slightly behind me. There's a deep rumble of . . . nervous laughter maybe? And then I feel a large hand slide across my open palm and long fingers interlock with mine.

As our palms press together, I'm surprised by how good it feels.

Physical touch has always been a love language of mine, but Adam . . . well, he hated any public display of affection. He never held my hand in public, never rested a palm against my lower back as he led me into a room, and certainly never kissed me when people were around. Even when we were alone, there was a chaste distance between us. I'd gotten used to it over time and even convinced myself that I didn't need such things, but there's something so comforting about the feel of this stranger's hand holding mine. The intimacy—as simple as it is—is more than I've felt in a very long time.

I like it more than I want to admit.

"Okay!" Mabel declares after another minute or two. "I think we're ready. On the count of three, I want you both to turn around and remove your blindfolds. Ready?"

My heart flutters so wildly I'm sure it's about to fly right out of my chest, but I shake my head.

"1 . . . 2 . . . 3!"

I don't wait for my brain to even consider all the ways this moment could be a disaster, and instead, I spin quickly, ripping the blindfold over my head.

It takes a second for my eyes to adjust to the bright sunlight, but when they do, every thought in my head goes silent. I stare at the man in front of me.

He's tall with broad shoulders and tan arms that appear to be covered in colorful tattoos—at least from what I can see peeking out from under the shoved-up sleeve of his Henley. He's got dark brown hair that's short on the side, longer on the top, with strands that hang just a little over his forehead, and there's a line of stubble that covers his lower jaw. His eyes are a dark, radiant blue. There's a solemness about him that I notice instantly, but his expression is kind as he scans my face, his lips curling in a small smile. He's handsome in a way I'm not sure I could accurately describe, and I tear my eyes away from his as the blood rushes up into my face.

Mabel isn't saying anything from where she stands

nearby, but I can hear her camera whirring and clicking.

My date takes a step closer and a warm woodsy scent with just a hint of citrus floods my nostrils. "Hi again," he tells me. "It's nice to meet you, Callie."

His voice is one of those deep gravelly ones, the kind you hear singing some soulful ballad in a bar, and my eyes lift to find his. And there's something about the way Jensen says my name that makes me shiver. "Hi." The words come out a little breathy. I clear my throat and try again. "It's nice to meet you too."

"You ever done anything like this before?"

"No, never. You?"

Jensen shakes his head. "My first time."

"And is this as weird for you as it is for me?" The deadpan words pop out of my mouth before I have a chance to catch them. "I mean . . . not that you're weird or anything, it's just this whole situation is weird and . . . like who goes a blind date like this? We've could've just gone for burgers or something, but we're here and my cousin is taking pictures of us and it's kinda weird that she's doing that, and now I'm rambling because I called you weird, but not *you* per se, and oh my god, I need to stop because I'm just making things worse, aren't I . . . " I suck my bottom lip between my teeth and bite down hard to keep anything else from spilling out.

Jensen's mouth twists into an adorable half-smile. "No, I get what you're saying. This is definitely the most unconventional date I've ever been on." He shoves both of his hands in the front pockets of his jeans.

He seems a little shy, and there's a quiet seriousness about him that I find really endearing. Adam was always putting on a show, always had to be the focus of any room, but Jensen doesn't seem like that at all. And when he gives me another tentative smile, my nerves settle even more.

Mabel takes a few shots of us as we walk to a new spot she points out and then positions us in a few poses that I can only assume are the warm-up poses. One with Jensen's arm around my shoulder, another with us sitting next to each other on an old picnic table, and a few more simple poses that feel very low pressure. Jensen and I move around each other politely, following Mabel's directions, but I find myself sneaking glances at him. I swear I can feel his eyes on me, too.

"Ah, this is already so great!" Mabel squeaks from beside me as we take a short break. "You guys are naturals." She flips her camera around to show us one of the frames in which she's captured my laughter and Jensen's wide smile. The glowing morning light in the background makes the focus on our faces even more prominent. It's stunning.

"Wow," I lean closer to the display screen. "Mabs, it's stunning."

"Thanks!" She beams. "But, we're just getting started. Are you guys ready?"

I know what she's asking. The whole purpose of this shoot is to capture our chemistry, to put us into close, intimate positions like she would a real couple in love. No one wants to see pictures of us just talking or making jokes.

I'm still nervous, but Jensen gives a confident nod that makes the rest of the tension in my shoulders disappear, so I nod too. "Yeah, let's do this."

Mabel leads us closer to the river and positions us facing one another. I have to tilt my chin up to look him fully in the face, he's so tall. He must stand at least a foot if not more over my 5'3 frame.

"Callie, can you place your right hand on Jensen's chest?"

I reach out, my fingertips meeting soft cotton and a wall of hardened muscle beneath it. He's as solid as an oak tree.

"Oh, sorry," I say, realizing I just poked him in the stomach. I glide my hand upward until I feel the gentle thud of his heartbeat beneath my palm.

"Good, now, Jensen, will you put your hand on her waist?"

There's a light touch as his fingers brush against the bare skin of my arm. He finds my waist and when he wraps his hand around me, the weight that's been sitting on my chest ever since my horrible break-up lightens. It makes no sense, but there's a surety in his touch that relaxes me, makes me not only feel comfortable, but safe.

What is happening right now? A tiny voice whispers in my mind. But I don't have an answer.

"Can you guys move toward each other just an inch or two?"

We follow Mabel's instructions, our toes bumping into one another which makes us both laugh. "Yes! Now, lean toward each other. Get close. Don't be afraid to get into each other's space. If it feels weird then that means you're doing it right."

I roll my eyes at my cousin, but do as she says, leaning into Jensen. My nose nearly skims the fabric of his shirt, and he smells so incredibly good I almost let out a laugh. Definitely no hotdog water here.

Jensen leans down, bringing his face closer to mine, and I instinctively tilt my chin up and to the side to make room.

The hand on my waist tightens and Jensen's other hand finds the small of my back. He pulls me in, and I wrap the hand that isn't pressed against his chest lightly around the back of his neck.

"Is this okay?" he whispers, his brows lifting.

Even though we both agreed to this, I appreciate that he's asking, making sure I'm okay before we proceed to the "act like you're in love" part of the photoshoot.

"Yes," I whisper back, my fingers curling in the hair at the nape of his neck.

Jensen's lips brush against the shell of my ear and

my skin immediately heats. A nervous giggle bubbles up in my throat. I try to swallow it, but instead it comes out as a snort.

Jensen pulls his head back a little bit, his eyes finding mine. "Did you just snort?"

"Yeah . . . sorry, I'm a little ticklish."

"Me too, but don't tell anyone. Can't have everyone knowing my weakness."

"Your secret is safe with me," I promise, nearly melting into a puddle on the grass when the corners of his mouth lift and an easy smile emerges.

I tuck a loose strand of hair behind my ear but the wind near the water has picked up and almost immediately the same strand flies free again, unwilling to stay put.

"I got it," Jensen says, chuckling at the way my nose has scrunched in frustration. He reaches for the strand, trapping it between his fingers and then carefully placing it behind my ear, his thumb brushing lightly against my cheek.

He hesitates slightly, not pulling his hand back, but instead trailing his fingers down to cup my neck. The feather-light touch heats my skin and as I lean into it, the realization that I don't want him to stop touching me slams into me hard.

What is happening right now? The voice in my head demands again, a little louder this time, but I shove the thought aside. A lump rises in my throat as this man's gentle touch makes my battered and bruised heart beat in a way I'd long forgotten. A way I'd sworn I no longer wanted or needed.

His eyes find mine, a slight worry in them, which I try to smooth away by reaching up to grasp the wrist that's holding me. For a moment, something else flickers in the depths of those ocean blues, so deep I swear I could drown in them. It's surprise and . . . sadness, maybe?

Jensen slowly lifts his other hand, his fingertips sending tingles down my back as he touches me. And when he gently leans down, pressing his forehead against mine, I can't move or breathe. I don't want to.

Yes!" Mabel practically squeals with delight. "Oh my gosh whatever you do, don't move."

I couldn't if I tried.

Chapter 4

Jensen

Callie's eyes are green. A deep, rich shade of green that makes me feel some kind of way, even though I can't name it. She stares back at me for a moment before her eyelids flutter and she closes them, a sigh escaping her full, pink lips.

My own eyes shut and the tension in my shoulders eases, my entire body relaxing as I run my thumbs across the smooth plane of her neck—something I can't seem to stop doing. Callie's skin is soft and smells like vanilla, and there's an aching need deep inside my chest, one that wills my arms to wrap around her body, pulling her flush against mine. It's been so long since I held a woman, *really* held a woman, and the desire to do so now overwhelms me.

I didn't come here expecting anything.

I only showed up to appease Sutton and to hopefully quell any further conversations about me needing to date more. I never expected to have such a strong reaction to a complete stranger. But the moment I touched Callie's hand, something unraveled inside me. An easiness washed over me, soothing out the jagged edges I try not to let anyone else see.

Then, when the blindfolds came off, I could barely breathe. To say she's pretty would be an insult. She's beautiful, and not in the way that most people think of beautiful—solely based on physical features alone. No, it's more than that. It's the brightness in her eyes, the genuineness of her smile. The pink flush in her cheeks. She's stunning in a way I'm not sure I have words for, but it's not just that. It's not just her loveliness that has my entire body relaxing in a way that's been damn near impossible for a long time now. It's *her.*

You deserve so much more, Shep. Sutton's voice floats through my thoughts, a fragment of our conversation from the diner. I hadn't argued with her then, even if on the inside I was recoiling at her words.

But standing this close to Callie, with her soft, warm body leaning into me, there's a tiny part of me that wants this—a bit of happiness. A small reprieve from the bone-deep aches that wear me down each day. She feels so good underneath my hands, and I realize now just how much I've missed this. This closeness. I don't want to let her go. At least not yet.

I know it won't last, it *can't* last. But maybe . . . maybe I can let myself have this. This small break. An hour with a beautiful girl in the glowing morning light—where the shadows can't find me. A chance to pretend.

"Amaaaaazing," Mabel trills, popping up next to us. "Okay, let's try something else."

I open my eyes and pull my hands away from Callie's neck, as much as I don't want to, and wait for instructions. Callie's eyes linger for a moment before flicking over to Mabel.

"Callie, I want you right here, facing me." Mabel points to a location a little closer to the water. "Jensen, can you stand behind her and put your arms around her?"

We move into position, and when Callie's back presses into my chest, I cross my arms over her, pulling her even closer. Mabel walks around us, taking pictures from different angles while the sun slowly stretches its glittering arms across the sky.

Callie relaxes against me, her hands coming up to rest atop my forearms. I nearly groan at how incredible she feels in my arms, and without even thinking about it, I drop a kiss to the top of her head.

The camera clicks and I stiffen, realizing what I've done. "Sorry," I hurry to say, fearing I've crossed a line or made Callie uncomfortable. "I didn't mean to, it was . . . " *habit.* The word hits me like a freight train but stays stuck in my throat as a sharp stab of pain lances through me.

"No, that's perfect!" Mabel squeals from where she's standing a few feet away, which makes Callie laugh as she looks over her shoulder and up at me. Her sweet smile is like a lifeline, and I cling to it to bring me back from the edge.

Her eyes linger on me again and for a second, I swear I see concern in them. Or worry maybe? I break eye contact and force myself to take a deep breath. Her fingers on my forearm tighten—a little squeeze that lifts my chin, and the reassurance I find in her gaze steadies me.

"So, tell me something," she says. "Something about you."

"Alright, what would you like to know?"

Callie adorably scrunches up her nose. "Since this is our first date and all, we should probably stick to the easy stuff . . . buuut considering the unconventional conventions of this date, I think we should skip all that and get to the deep stuff, don't you?"

My insides freeze. "Um . . . sure." The words come out hoarse. I brace myself for what she might ask. Talking about "deep stuff" isn't something I do. Ever. And as much as I'm enjoying this moment, I don't want to start now.

She pantomimes thinking particularly hard about something and then snaps her fingers. "Okay, I've got a good one. When you make a peanut butter and jelly sandwich, do you put peanut butter on both sides of the bread or just one?"

A laugh erupts from my chest. "That's what you want to know?"

Callie nods, her face all seriousness. "I couldn't possibly go on a second date with someone who doesn't understand the exact perfect ratio of a PB&J."

"So, you want to go on a second date with me, huh?" I tease, hardly recognizing myself. The laughing tone, the wide smile . . . they're not me. At least not the me I usually am. But in this moment, I don't mind.

Callie's cheeks flush with pink. "Well, I . . . um . . . " she stammers.

It's so damn cute, I laugh again. "I'm a grape jelly one side of the bread kind of guy," I tell her, letting her off the hook. "With a smooth, but not too thin, not too thick layer of chunky peanut butter on the other side."

"Ooh, I like your style." She beams at me as Mabel calls out, directing Callie to face the camera.

I settle back into our pose, my arms still wrapped tightly around her petite frame, and I sink into the feeling of her in my arms. *A chance to pretend,* I remind myself and shove away any last, lingering tendrils of shadow, giving myself full permission to do just that.

I lean over Callie, resting my chin on her shoulder, our cheeks nearly touching and flash the camera a smile.

A few seconds later, Callie leans to the left slightly so

she can look at me and then plants a kiss on my cheek.

Mabel squeals and rushes closer. "Don't move!" she shouts, focusing her camera. "Oh my gosh, that is so cute!"

Callie freezes, her lips soft against my skin. Heat rushes up the back of my neck, slowly spreading through the rest of me. It feels like the sunshine on my skin has seeped through my pores, warming me from the inside out.

Mabel is chirping praise at us like a bird as she circles, getting different angles. "The camera is loving you two!" She steps closer, flipping her camera around to show us another of the photos. It's one of the shots with Callie kissing my cheek, and I look content, happy even. It's strange to see myself like that, but at the same time, it's kind of nice, too.

"Now, I want to get some movement shots," Mabel directs, backing up to test the lighting. "We've probably only got another half hour before the light quits cooperating." She points toward the edge of the lake. "Why don't you walk that way together?"

Callie gives Mabel a little salute and then turns to me, her smile so bright it nearly knocks me over. "Shall we?" She drawls in a funny little accent, like a stuffy old butler or something.

The mischievousness in her eyes triggers my own and before she has time to react, I sweep her legs out from under her and throw her over my shoulder, making sure to keep a hold on her skirt so it doesn't fly up.

Callie lets out a whoop of surprise, but then she's laughing hysterically. Mabel lets out her own squeal of delight, her camera flashing like a summer storm.

I walk a few more feet and then set Callie down. Instead of letting go of her hand, I twirl her around. She follows my lead easily and then we're dancing, our boots kicking up dust that swirls around us. It's not a smooth or eloquent dance, but as we twist and turn, our arms and hands gliding over each other's, we're both laughing. I know I'm supposed to be pretending, but this warmth in my chest is real. The peace that floods my senses is real. The pounding of my heart every time this girl smiles at me is very, very real.

Callie collapses against me. "I'm dizzy," she breathes out, swiping at the hair that's fallen into her face.

"These have a mind of their own," I say, reaching for the locks that refuse to stay out of her eyes and brush them back.

"Tell me about it," she jokes with a grumble.

I realize how closely we're pressed up against each other. One of my hands is cradling her head, and the other is on her back, holding her to me.

Her hands are pressed against my chest, and I wonder if she can feel the thunder reverberating through me.

I'm absolutely lost in her eyes. Everything else has faded away. I don't hear Mabel or her camera, even though I know she's close, moving around us like a satellite does the moon. I don't see the sun or the river or the trees around us. It's just Callie and the way she's looking at me right now.

An overwhelming urge to kiss this woman surges through my entire body, so electric that I can feel it in every pore, every cell.

Don't do it. Don't go there.

But Callie is staring up at me, her eyes deep pools of green that I could absolutely get lost in, and I lean down, my nose skimming hers. My other hand finds her neck, and god, she's so soft against my fingertips.

I wait for her to pull away, to put space between us, but she doesn't. Instead, she lifts her chin. It's a tiny movement, almost imperceptible, but I see it.

So, without second guessing, without giving a single damn or bit of caution, I close the last bit of distance between us and press my lips against hers.

Chapter 5

Callie

I wanted Jensen to kiss me but now that he is, I know without a doubt that I wasn't prepared for this. I wasn't ready for how poetic the touch of this man's mouth would be.

Each brush of his lips is a perfectly crafted bit of prose in a language that I desperately want to understand. When his fingers tunnel through my hair, holding my head with such gentle care, all I can do is lean my neck back slightly, giving him more room to explore my mouth.

The taste of peppermint explodes on my tongue as the kiss deepens with a tender thoroughness that I know is going to absolutely ruin me on some level. I've been kissed before, but never like this. And certainly never by a man I've only known for an hour.

I slide my hands up his chest and around his neck, my fingernails lightly grazing the soft skin at the nape of his neck as I push up on my toes. Jensen's hands slide down my back, holding me to him in a way that makes tears prick at the corners of my eyes.

All the noise in my head goes silent. It's as if my day-to-day thoughts are the booming brass section of a symphony, but this moment, this kiss, is a smooth, velvety violin solo. There is nothing but this sweet, sweeping melody that says everything that words cannot.

Click. Click. Click.

Mabel's camera reminds us of its presence, breaking the spell. Awareness of where we are and what we're doing seems to smack into us both. Jensen drops his hands, and I step back out of the circle of his arms, my cheeks burning.

I let out a nervous laugh as my eyes find his, but there's no amusement in his gaze. His eyes are wild, and the emotion burning in them twists my heart. It's devastation and heartbreak and pain.

Jensen rips his eyes away from mine, studying the boots at his feet for a moment. When he looks up again, his expression is more even, but also guarded in a way that it wasn't before.

What just happened?

Mabel pops up next to me, camera in hand, with a triumphant grin. "Oh my word, you guys!" She squeals. "That was amazing. I cannot wait to get home and start editing. These shots turned out beautifully."

"We're done?" Disappointment replaces the butter-flies fluttering in my stomach.

Out of the corner of my eye, I see Jensen let out a low breath as if he's relieved. It stings more than I want to admit.

Mabel nods, looking from me to Jensen. "I think I got it. You both made my job so easy." She walks a few feet away to where her camera bag sits in the grass and begins removing her lens. "It'll take me a little bit to go through everything, but would either of you mind if I posted a preview of the shoot to my socials? I know everyone is going to go wild for you two!"

"I'm okay with that."

"Sure," Jensen adds, his tone a little flat.

I study his face, the hard lines that seem etched into his features. The man in front of me now is night and day different from the one who just kissed me, and I don't understand.

Mabel doesn't seem to notice. She claps her hands together now that her camera is safe in its carrying case. "Great!" she says as she heads over to the Jeep to load her equipment.

Jensen and I follow her, neither of us saying any-thing. There's an awkwardness that wasn't there before that's settled over us, and even though I keep trying to catch his eye, Jensen won't look at me—which really bothers me, especially when I can still taste him in my mouth.

We load into the Jeep and Mabel drives to the parking lot, pulling up next to a black truck that I assume is Jensen's.

"Well, this is me," he says.

I open my mouth to . . . say what exactly? But Mabel beats me to the punch. She swivels around in her seat and gives him a pointed look. "You should give Callie your number. That way she can let you know when the photos are ready."

I know exactly what she's doing. The over eagerness in her voice makes me want to groan. I give her a look. One of those "Girl, what the hell?" looks but she ignores me.

"Oh . . . sure," Jensen says, although the hesitancy in his tone makes me wish a sinkhole would open up right then and there and swallow me whole.

With my face burning, I grab my phone and open up a new contact. "Here," I say, handing it to him.

Mabel is starting to resemble the Cheshire Cat from *Alice in Wonderland* from her perch in the front seat, and as gleeful as she is about this whole thing, I'm back to feeling panicky.

Jensen hands me the phone back, and I dip my head in thanks, praying he can't see how mortified I am.

"Callie, you should text him," Mabel pipes up. "That way he has your number too."

If there was ever a moment in our lives where I was

close to decking Mabel right in the nose, this was it. But I keep my composure and make quick work of opening a new text thread and typing out a short message. "Yeah, that's a good idea."

Jensen's phone dings. "Got it."

"Great," I say back, though the sound is a little strained. "Um . . . it was really nice meeting you." I give him what I hope is a genuine smile and not a grimace.

He dips his head. "It was nice to meet you, too."

My eyes meet his, and I feel it again. That thing between us, that connection that shouldn't exist but somehow, it does. It's warm and comfortable and so inviting I want to get lost in it. Then I'm thinking of his lips, of the way they felt against mine and the touch of his hands on my skin. Jensen's gaze pierces through me, but sadness flashes across his expression so intensely, it makes my chest ache.

Before I have a chance to say or do anything else, he tears his eyes from mine, gives a quick, "Ladies," and then pops open the door, getting out so fast you'd think the Jeep was on fire.

I wait until he's safely reversing out of his parking space before whirling on my cousin.

"Seriously?" I all but yell. "What the hell was that?"

Mabel bats her eyelashes, the epitome of innocence. "What was what?"

"Mabel Evangeline Callahan," I punch each syllable. "You know exactly what I'm talking about."

"You mean when I secured his number for you?" She grins. "You're welcome."

"Ughhh," I fall back against the seat and cover my face with my hands. "Could you not see how awkward things were? He practically leapt from the Jeep while it was still moving."

"I don't think so, babe."

"What do you mean you don't think so? It's obvious he was more than ready for the photoshoot to be over and the only reason he gave me his number is because you practically forced him to. He was too polite to decline."

Mabel shakes her head. "That's not what that was."

"Then what was it?"

"Some of the most incredible chemistry I've ever seen. I mean, my god, Callie. Did you not feel it? I was only behind the camera, but good gravy, I sure felt it."

My brain immediately supplies me with moments from the photoshoot, little snippets of memory that swirl around my thoughts and warm my blood. "Of course I felt it, but . . . " I think about the look on his face after we kissed and his rigid posture a few moments ago. "I don't think Jensen felt the same way."

"No, no, no," Mabel scoffs, reaching for her camera from the passenger seat. "Don't even go there. I can guarantee you that man felt it."

"Oh yeah?" I challenge.

Mabel scrolls through the images on her camera before flipping it around to face me. "Uh-huh."

The picture she's chosen is one of us kissing. It was taken from an angle behind me, so it's Jensen's features that are highlighted and a gasp bubbles in my throat at the sight of his face, the way his eyes are squeezed tightly, but not in a "let's get this over with kind of way," but more in a "god, I don't want this to ever end kind of way." The way he's holding me to his body, the way his lips claim mine, the way the entire image screams intimacy and passion. It's undeniable.

Tears well up in my eyes before I can stop them.

"Oh Callie," Mabel's entire demeanor shifts from smug to Mother Hen. "Don't cry, it's okay."

"Is it?" I swipe at my cheeks, hating the heavy weight of insecurity that's dropped over me. "I don't even think I've fully processed what happened back there, but this—" I point to the screen. "That kiss was incredible."

Mabel nods. "The chemistry between you two was really something. I wanted the photoshoot to go well, but I didn't think you'd connect like that. I mean, I *hoped* you would, but I wasn't sure."

I think about my years with Adam. Even in the beginning, things between us had always felt more sensible than passionate. Our relationship was never a Fourth of July fireworks show, more like a single birthday candle, quickly blown out.

"I've never felt like that with anyone," I admit, still taking in the image on the camera screen. I'd long convinced myself that I didn't need that ever-encompassing, all-consuming want of another person. But my lips still tingled from Jensen's kiss, and a small, hopeful voice is in my head already whispering, *again?*

I shake my head and carefully hand Mabel back her camera. "But afterwards, things were . . . weird. You saw how he acted. It was like he was being held hostage or something."

"I think he was just a little surprised. I don't think he expected the photoshoot to go like that either. From what I hear, he's not the type of guy who lets his walls down easily."

"What else do you know about him?"

"Not a whole lot," she admits. "I met him a while back at the diner. He comes in a couple of times a week to eat and see Sutton."

"Sutton?" Alarm bells start going off in my head as I think about Mabel's cute, perky blonde co-worker. "They're dating?"

"No, nothing like that! They're best friends. They have been since . . . " Mabel's face drops a little. "You remember Kasey Bradford, right? We went to high school with him? Sutton is his widow."

"Oh . . . " I remember now, hearing about the helicopter crash a few years back. I was in New York with Adam when the news broke on social media. He hadn't understood why I was so upset, but Dayton Springs is a small town, and losing one of our own always hurts. "I forgot he was married."

"He has a little boy, too. Jensen was his best friend. After it all happened, Jensen moved here to help Sutton run the auto shop. I don't know him very well. I think he keeps to himself when he's not with Sutton and Ethan, but he's always been really nice, and I mean, let's be real. He's pretty easy on the eyes." Mabel gives me a wink. "I mentioned the shoot to Sutton last week at work, and she volunteered him."

I let out a groan. "She volunteered him? So he wasn't even here by choice?"

"I highly doubt Jensen Shepherd would have shown up today if that were true," Mable scoffs. "Sutton told me she was going to tell him about the shoot and see if he was interested. If he wasn't he wouldn't have come."

I'm not sure I buy that, but I nod anyway. "So, what now?"

Mabel lifts a shoulder and lets it drop. "I think that's up to you. You have his number—you're welcome, by the way—so why don't you just text him?"

It's the worst idea in the world. There may have been an unexpected moment of magic between us, but it's long gone now. Which, the more I think about it, suits me just fine. I don't need more complications or heartbreak in my life. I need to stick to my plan. No men, no relationships, no dating. I got a little caught up in the moment for a second, but that's over now.

"I don't think so."

"Why not?"

"Because we were just playing the part." I can tell from Mabel's frown that she wants to disagree with me, so I keep going before she has a chance. "It wasn't real, and it doesn't mean anything."

Mabel arches a brow. "You don't believe that. I've known you my whole life. I can tell when you're full of it."

"I'm just being practical," I say in defense, thinking again of Jensen's reaction to our kiss.

"No, you're playing it safe," Mabel counters. "Because you're scared." She says the words gently, but they punch through my chest just the same. Adam took a lot more from me than just my apartment.

"Just think about it, okay?" Mabel squeezes my hand.

Nope. There's no way I'm texting Jensen. Not going to happen.

But as resolved as I am, a tiny kernel of *something* opens up in my chest. I don't know if it's hope or idiocy or just sheer determination to prove that Adam didn't break me completely, but it's there.

"Fine," I say, against my better judgment. "I'll think about it."

Chapter 6

Jensen

There's hardly any traffic on the road since it's so early, but I'm still gripping the steering wheel of my truck like my life depends on it. Every muscle in my body is tensed and not even George Strait's *Oceanfront Property* playing from the radio—a usual favorite—can distract me. There's nothing running through my head except for her. *Callie.*

I'd convinced myself that I deserved a reprieve, a single hour with a beautiful woman and then I would return to life as usual. That was the plan. Once the photoshoot was over, I was supposed to walk away, check that box so Sutton would be happy, and move on. But now?

I drag a hand down my face and groan. How can I forget the way Callie felt in my arms, how perfectly she fit against me, how somehow despite knowing very little about her, she managed to crack something open inside my chest that I thought was long gone? She made me feel things I swore I'd never feel again. And kissing her had felt like breathing after being underwater for a very long time. Four years ago, the waters had opened up and swallowed me whole, and I've been a drowned man walking ever since. But when her sweet, strawberry lips touched mine, clean, crisp oxygen-rich air flooded my windpipe, and my swollen, suffocated, waterlogged lungs sputtered to life.

And it absolutely terrified me.

I pull the truck onto the drive that leads up to my property, the tires crunching the gravel as they roll down the path. Sutton's car is parked out front of my place and while I'm usually happy to see her, I know exactly why she's here.

I sigh as I pull up next to her car. I contemplate making a beeline for my neighbor Mrs. Dorothy's house, but there's no way Sutton didn't hear the dual exhaust from my truck as I came down the road, and if I don't go inside soon, she will most definitely come looking for me.

I push open the door and the first thing I see is Sutton perched on the couch—prime ambush location— waiting for me. The second thing is my dog, Peaches, who happens to be looking in the direction of the door when I walk in. Then there's a massive ball of white fur hurtling for me. Peaches practically does a front roll in an effort to get to me, tail wagging a mile a minute.

"Easy, girl," I tell her, giving her a flick of my hand, alerting her of the command. She immediately plops down into a sit, but her entire lower half wiggles uncontrollably as she waits for another signal. She's so precious, I don't keep her waiting longer than a second or two until I give her another hand signal to let her know it's okay. I bend down and she practically leaps into my arms, making me laugh. When I'd adopted Peaches two years ago, I'd walked down the line of the dogs at the shelter not really having a particular dog or breed in mind. But when I saw her face peering back, I knew she was destined to be mine. It didn't matter that she was deaf and that there'd be some extra training challenges. She was my dog. I knew it right then and there. We've only gotten closer since I brought her home. She makes me smile on the days when the shadows are near, and it helps knowing I'm not coming home to an empty house.

Sutton waits until I'm finished giving Peaches a thorough belly scratch before she blurts out, "Well? How'd it go?"

"Good morning to you too," I tell her. "I did sleep well, actually. Thanks so much for asking."

I dodge the pillow Sutton chunks at my head. "Come on, Shep! Tell me about the photoshoot!"

"Did you really get up at the crack of dawn on your day off to break into my house just so you could pepper me with questions?"

"Excuse me, it's not breaking in if I have a key." Sutton rolls her eyes.

"Where's Ethan?"

"He spent the night with a friend from school. I'm picking him up after lunch. Now come on, tell me."

I plop down on the couch, Peaches jumping up to curl up next to me. "There's nothing much to tell."

"Oh yeah?" She raises a brow.

"Yeah."

I should just tell her, should just let all the thoughts swirling inside my head tumble right out of my mouth. Sutton is my best friend, my family and there are no secrets between us, but telling her about what happened makes it *a thing*, you know? And I can't let it be anything other than what it was—a momentary encounter.

"Mmmhmmm," Sutton purses her lips. "How long have I known you?"

"Long enough to call me family."

"Okay then, don't you think I know when you're lying?"

"I'm not—"

"Yes, you are." She cuts me off. "I can see it all over your face. Now *spill*."

She levels me with a stare.

"Fine, it was . . . " I pause, rolling words around, trying to find the right one. For a split second, I think of brushing it off again or at least downplaying the whole thing. That's what I should do . . . but there's also this need burrowing in my chest to talk about it so that it doesn't just become some figment of my imagination. Momentary as it may have been, I want it to be as real as it felt. "Incredible," I whisper the word.

Sutton's eyes widen for half a second and then she's grinning. "Tell me *everything.*"

So, I start from the very beginning when our backs were pressed together and the blindfolds were still on. I'm not usually someone who talks this much or feels the need to dissect every little detail, but apparently today I am. I tell Sutton everything.

"And then," I suck in a breath as the memory of it hits me like a brick wall. "I kissed her. And I'll be honest, it was the best kiss I've had in a long time, maybe ever. There was just something about her. Something different. But kissing her didn't feel weird or awkward, it felt . . . right."

Sutton doesn't say anything, but when I look up, tears line her blue-gray eyes. "Oh stop," I groan, throwing my arm around her and mussing up her hair. "You're such a sap, I swear."

She pushes against me, laughing. "What do you expect? You're my best friend in the whole world, and I want you to be happy."

"Well, don't get too ahead of yourself. It was just a photoshoot. It's not like we're getting married." I mean the words as a joke, but I wince a little, which Sutton very much notices.

"Shep," she begins.

"You know what I mean," I wave her concern away. "You asked me to do the photoshoot, I did the photo-shoot. Was it enjoyable? Yes, way more than I thought possible. Callie is an amazing woman but . . . that's it."

"What do you mean that's it? You have to call her. You have to ask her out again."

The thought of taking Callie out on a date makes everything inside me warm, but seeing her again isn't a good idea. Dating. Relationships. Truly opening my heart to someone—I'm just not up for it. Not again.

"I can't do that."

"And why not?"

"You know why."

Sutton shakes her head. "You have to stop that." She reaches for my hand and gives it a squeeze. "You are worthy of being loved, do you hear me? I don't care what your evil ex-wife made you believe. I swear if I ever see her again, I'm going to give her a piece of my mind."

"It won't change anything."

"No, but it would make me feel better," Sutton sniffs. "To leave you the way she did, because you can't have—"

"It's fine," I cut her off, not wanting to go down that road.

Sutton frowns. "It's not, though. You came out of all that believing that you're not worth the ground you stand on, but you're a good man, Jensen. The best actually. And you deserve to be with someone who sees you and loves every part of you. No matter what."

I swallow against the rising ache in my throat. "You're biased," I attempt to tease. "You only love me because Kase did. We were a package deal."

Sutton's eyes go misty again. "That may have been true, initially, but that's not why I love you now. After Kasey . . . " She huffs out a breath, pain flashing across her features. "When Ethan and I lost everything, you were there. You took care of us both, and you still do. You're a good man," she repeats. "And even though I know you don't want to believe it, you deserve good things in your life."

A vehement need to argue rises so swiftly it almost comes out as a shout, but I force the words that have been screaming in my head for years back down.

"I know Anna broke your heart," Sutton says softly. "But I think it's time you finally let yourself heal and move on. You deserve happiness, and if Callie has the potential to make you happy, then you need to do something about it."

Anna. Usually just the mention of her name sends me into a spiral that can take days to pull myself out of. Somehow though, hearing Callie's name right after has softened the blow a bit.

It doesn't change anything, though. I have nothing to offer a woman like Callie. I'm broken beyond repair, and there's no future with me. What I do or don't deserve doesn't matter.

My phone chimes, startling me out of my thought

spiral. A text notification. I fish my phone out of my pocket. Sutton and I both see the name that appears on the screen, and she immediately squeals. "It's her!"

I swipe, opening the text thread.

Callie:

> Hi! I just wanted to say it was really nice meeting you today. Not weird at all. :)

I stare at the screen. The little inside joke makes me smile, but it also makes my chest tighten. This can't happen. I can't let it.

"Well?" Sutton asks, clearly reading the text over my shoulder. "What are you going to say back?"

One hour, one perfect hour—that's all I gave myself. And the hour has come and gone.

I click my phone back off.

"Nothing."

Chapter 7
Callie

The cover of my brand new sketch pad is flipped open. I've got a freshly-sharpened pencil in my hand, but the sheet of crisp white paper is totally empty. There isn't a single mark or scribble on it, nothing to show for the near hour I've been sitting on this park bench.

Groaning, I tap my pencil on the page in time with the knee I'm bouncing up and down. There's honestly nothing worse than a blank page. Some might see the blank space as potential, but it just feels like it's mocking me—that is, until I manage to start something. That's the problem, though. It's been a long time since I tapped into my artistic side and even longer since I started a new project. The thought of picking up a paintbrush felt a little overwhelming, so I thought I'd start small, maybe do a few sketches of trees or something since landscapes and nature scenes are my favorite, but so far I've got nothing.

It's not that there's a lack of inspiration. This park is one of my favorite places in Dayton Springs. It's lush and green this time of year, and all the dogwoods and magnolias are blooming. Pink and purple azalea bushes line the fence, and just beyond that, a patch of wild honeysuckle fills the air with its sweet aroma, attracting at least a dozen honeybees. The birds are chirping, and several squirrels are scurrying about, darting between the branches of the trees. It's a beautiful, peaceful place. In theory, it should be the perfect spot to do a few simple line drawings, but apparently, I've got artist's block. Or, more specifically, I've got *my stupid ex made me believe art was a waste of time and I believed him because I was in love* block.

I start scrawling random swirls on the corner of the page just to fill the empty space with something. I try not to think too hard about it, just let my hand move on muscle memory as my mind wanders. I don't realize what I'm doing until a pair of eyes stares back at me. I flip my pencil around to stub out the lines, but I barely swipe the eraser before I'm flipping the pencil again, the granite tip gliding across the page to add more depth and clarity.

When I'm finished Jensen Shepherd's eyes pop off the page. I've managed to capture the exact expression he wore when the blindfolds first came off, and even though it's not the real thing, my heart gives a pathetic little jolt.

"Stop," I murmur, chiding myself. "Don't even think about it." I hate that I'm still thinking about him. It's been three days since the photoshoot, three days since I mustered up my courage and sent Jensen a text against my better judgement. A text that got no response. Zilch. Nada. Literally nothing.

It had stung a lot more than I'd expected. I should've listened to my gut, to the voice in my head telling me that relationships are a complete waste of time, but a tiny kernel of possibility had wormed its way into my system, and I took a chance. Crashed and burned in the end, but at least I tried. A mistake I've sworn I won't make again. At least, not anytime soon.

Yet, I can't stop thinking about Jensen's warm hands gliding across my skin, almost reverently. I close my eyes and it's all too easy to imagine the way his strong arms made me feel so safe and secure. And that kiss? Oh sweet magnolias, it's living rent-free in my mind. How is it possible that a man can kiss like that and then completely ghost someone all in the same afternoon?

"Because that's just how they are," I mutter under my breath, covering my sketch with thick, dark lines. "Men like Adam and Jensen just . . . " I can't finish the sentence. As annoyed and frustrated as I am about the unanswered text, it feels wrong to put Jensen in the same category as Adam.

Huffing out a breath, I finish camouflaging the rendering of his eyes and turn the page to a fresh sheet. As I look around, I'm hoping something inspiring will leap into my peripheral or at least call out, "*Sketch me! Sketch me!*" Nothing does.

I scoop up my cell phone and do what every artist does when they're blocked: procrastinate by checking social media. The mindless scrolling is just that, my finger swiping quicker than my brain can process. But then I see something that makes the blood in my veins ice over.

The picture was posted a few hours ago. Adam's overly whitened smile is wide, and his arm is wrapped around the shoulders of a busty redhead in a blazer. It's pretty clear from their body language that this isn't a work colleague or friend. Nope, this is the hard launch of these two as a couple. Which is funny considering the reason Adam broke up with me is because he said he needed to give all his focus to the firm. I didn't realize he meant the new paralegal that started working in the office two weeks before he kicked me out.

I screenshot the picture and fire it off to Mabel with a WTF gif and then decide I'm officially done with social media for the day. Ignoring the unusual number of notifications at the top of my screen, I swipe to close the app. I toss my sketchbook and my pencil into my bag.

So much for finding inspiration today.

By the time I've made it back to my car, Mabel has sent me multiple texts in a row.

Mabel:

> OMG! ARE YOU KIDDING ME RIGHT NOW? 😡

Mabel:

> You know what? The next time I see his smug, stupid face, he's getting a junk punch from me. No questions asked.

Mabel:

> I hate him so much!

Mabel:

> Are you okay? On a scale of "I need a pint of Ben & Jerry's" to "I'm ready to rage smash"?

I snort and fire back a quick reply.

> Definitely rage smash, though I could go for a pint of Phish Food.

Mabel:

> YES GIRL. Grab me some Chunky Monkey and come home. I was just about to text you anyway. Did you see?!?

> ???

Mabel:

> THE PHOTOSHOOT HAS GONE VIRAL!!

> What? Seriously?

I re-open my app, tapping on the red notification button. Hundreds of comments fill my screen. "Whoa," I do a quick scan, my cheeks lifting.

> Ahhh! I'm coming right now!

Mabel:

> Don't forget Ben & Jerry! This calls for ice cream!

The Piggly Wiggly grocery store isn't far from Mabel's bungalow, and I pull into the closest parking space and grab a buggy from the corral.

Energy buzzes through me as I hurry down toward the freezer section. I grab our pints and some whipped cream and then aim my buggy down the savory snack aisle. We might as well go all out if we're celebrating.

I snag a box of Cheez-It and toss a bag of pretzels

into my buggy, pushing it without paying attention to where I'm going. I yelp when it smacks into something hard—another shopper's cart.

"Oh my gosh," I rush to say, "I am so sorry, I was just . . . " The words die in my throat.

Jensen Shepherd's hands are curled around the handle of the buggy I've just rammed, and his eyebrows are high, clearly surprised to see me. The same eyes I'd been sketching at the park are staring back at me in the flesh.

"Hi," I manage, my tone going flat.

"Callie, hi." Jensen reaches up and rubs at the back of his neck. "Uh, how are you?"

I'm fine, Captain Kiss and Run. How are you? Ghosted anyone else lately? I resist the urge to roll my eyes. "Good. You?"

"Fine, thanks."

There's a long pause, both of us waiting for the other to say something.

Good gravy, could this be any more awkward? I mean, three days ago this man had his tongue in my mouth and now he can barely look at me.

It doesn't help that he looks amazing. His face is slightly flushed, which brings out the deep blue of his eyes, and the stubble on his chin is a few days old, making him look rugged and handsome in a way that isn't fair at all. The collared Bradford Auto shirt he's wearing is a bit dirty, and there's a grease smudge on the side of his neck that my fingers are itching to wipe away. I force my hand to stay where it is.

I want to ask him so many things, the least of which why he ghosted me, but I decide it doesn't even matter.

"Well, sorry about almost mowing you over." I pull my buggy back and re-angle it so I can move around him. "Have a great night."

"Callie, wait." Jensen side-steps into my path. "I . . . "

I don't give him the opportunity to spin a lie or offer up some lame excuse. "I gotta get going, I'm heading to Mabel's. The photos from our shoot went viral." I point to the ice cream at the bottom of my buggy. "We're celebrating. But uh, yeah. Nice talking to you."

I whip my cart around in the opposite direction and speed walk down the aisle. I checkout in record time, and once I'm safely back in my car, I breathe out, low and slow. My reflection in the rearview is all red and splotchy. I crank up the air conditioner and adjust the vent until the cool air is blowing directly in my face.

To say I'm flustered is the understatement of the year. Seeing Jensen was awkward, but also electrifying. My entire body is covered in goosebumps. Despite the weird vibes and the text message snub, there was still a moment where my stupid heart leapt at the sight of him. For that split second, all I could think about was how nice it was to be held by him and how much I wanted to be held by him again—which is absolutely infuriating.

"We're not doing this," I hiss at my reflection. "We

are *not* going there. He's just another Adam waiting to happen." But even as I say it, the words don't sit right with me. Adam wasn't capable of emotional connection. He frowned upon it. The man I met during the photoshoot, the one who held me in his arms and kissed me senseless isn't in the same category. Whatever Jensen may be, I know in my gut that he's not like Adam at all.

Annoyed—with myself above all— I crank the keys and steer my car toward Mabel's.

Ten minutes later, I'm pulling into the bungalow's driveway. I slam the door to my 4Runner and hurry to the front door, flinging it open. "Mabel?"

"In here," she calls out from the living room.

I kick the door shut with my foot and heft the grocery bags of snacks a little higher on my arms.

Mabel waits for me in the living room, perched on the end of the couch and practically vibrating with excitement. "Did you see?" She hops up, rushing over to help put the bags on the counter.

"I saw my notifications blowing up, but I haven't had a chance to look at the post."

Mabel whips her phone out of her back pocket and taps the screen, flipping it around to show me the post she made about the photoshoot.

"I posted a teaser yesterday," she explains. "The response was so strong, I made another post this morning with more images and . . . " She points to the tiny number at the bottom of the screen. "Callie, look!"

My jaw drops. "Oh my god!"

She clutches my arm. "I know! I posted it and honestly forgot about it, but while I was at work today, my phone started going nuts with notifications and I opened it up to find this!" She takes the phone from me and taps on a different app, bringing up another platform. "I posted it here too." The post on this new platform is performing even better than the first one she showed me.

"I've already gotten a handful of inquiries about my services." Mabel bounces up and down on her toes. "Can you believe it?"

I reach for my cousin, wrapping her in a huge hug. "Well, of course I can believe it! You're amazing and now the whole world knows it!" We both let out a squeal, jumping around in a little circle as we squeeze each other as tightly as possible.

I take another look at the post. It has at least fifteen photos attached, and each one is more stunning than the last. Mabel's talent is undeniable, but that isn't what makes me suck in a ragged breath. It's the tenderness that leaps from each photo, the warmth, and the undeniable connection between me and Jensen. It's in the way our hands are linked, the way my smile brightens when it's him I'm smiling at, the way he touches me in every single frame. And oh my god, the kiss photos have my entire body feeling like the ground is shifting under my feet.

Then there's the comments. Mabel is right, people

aren't only gushing about her incredible photography skills—they're losing their minds over Jensen and me.

"Listen to this," I read aloud.

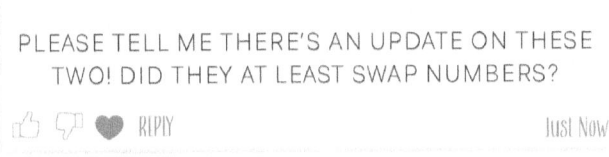

PLEASE TELL ME THERE'S AN UPDATE ON THESE TWO! DID THEY AT LEAST SWAP NUMBERS?

👍 👎 ❤️ REPLY   Just Now

I roll my eyes. "It's written in all capital letters."

"That's because it's a serious question," Mabel tells me, pointing to another one. "I like this one."

Someone get me some water because these two are on FIRE!

👍 👎 ❤️ REPLY   Just Now

"They're not wrong, you know."

"Yeah, well, tell that to Mr. 'I'm going to ghost you and then act like you have the plague when I run into you at the Piggly Wiggly'," I deadpan.

"Wait," Mabel holds up a hand. "What?"

I quickly give her the lowdown on what happened at the store. "It's fine, though. It's not like I'm interested, I mean, I've got my cats to think of."

"You mean the cats you don't have?"

"Yet," I remind her. "The cats I don't have *yet*."

Mabel rolls her eyes and continues scrolling through the comments, reading the good ones out loud and making us both laugh. When her phone rings, the sound of the Imperial Death March from *Star Wars* blasts from the speaker. Mabel's face immediately drops as the contact name shows up on the screen.

"Not today, Satan," she murmurs, silencing the call. She hastily returns to the viral post, but her enthusiasm is noticeably less.

"He's calling again?" I ask, treading gently. The topic of her ex is usually a forbidden one.

"Yeah, but I just keep sending it to voicemail."

I hate how small her voice sounds, so full of pain and anger. I throw my arm around her shoulder and squish her to my side. "You want to talk about it?"

"Nope." She makes a little popping sound on the P consonant. "I just want to keep pretending he doesn't exist."

"And so we shall," I tell her as I shove any lingering thoughts of Jensen far from my mind. "How about we focus instead on the two men who never let us down."

Mabel grins. "I'll get the spoons."

Chapter 8

Jensen

"Hey, Uncle Jensen!"

I glance up from the laptop I'm balancing on my lap. Ethan is standing just beyond the porch steps with a neon green ball in his hand, wearing a mischievous grin that would worry me if we weren't already outside.

Peaches darts back and forth between us, her afternoon case of the zoomies kicking in.

"Yeah, bud?"

"Watch this!" Ethan waves the ball at Peaches, getting her attention, then pretends to hurl it out into the front yard. Peaches takes off, running as fast as she can toward where she thinks the ball will land. Ethan tips his head back, laughing maniacally as he shows me the ball still in his hand.

I snort, shaking my head as Peaches

comes hurtling back, nearly tackling Ethan, which only makes him laugh harder. "Peaches, sit," Ethan commands, giving her the hand signal, and this time when he throws the ball, they both go chasing after it.

It's nearly dinnertime, and even though the afternoon seems intent on holding on to the day's sunlight as long as possible, I promised Sutton I'd get Ethan fed, bathed, and into bed at a decent hour. She's working the late shift tonight, so it's a sleepover Saturday for Ethan and me.

Sutton offered to come and get him on her way home, but I try to give her as much free time as I can, and after working a long shift, I figure she deserves to go home to a quiet house where she can take a hot bath or sip a glass of wine in peace. She's the hardest-working single mom I know, and besides, I love having Ethan here.

He reminds me so much of Kase. They have the exact same sense of humor, and sometimes when Ethan cocks his head, looking at me with that curious expression of his, I swear it's like my best friend is standing right in front of me.

I eye the empty rocking chair adjacent to mine. What I wouldn't give to have Kase here with us right now, sipping on a beer while we shoot the breeze and watch his kid play with my dog.

That's what was supposed to happen. We talked about it all the time. Moving back to Dayton Springs, raising our kids together. A lot of people assume men don't think about that kind of stuff, but Kasey and I talked about it often, what life would be like after we got out of the army. It was easy to see back then, a bright future full of possibilities, but those possibilities died right along with Kasey. Watching Ethan now is as close as I'll ever get to the real thing.

An ache, deep and sharp, squeezes my heart. I never realized just how badly I wanted kids of my own until the doctor told me I couldn't have any.

It still feels like yesterday. Sitting in that lumpy, faux leather chair while a white-haired, very direct man with decades of experience calmly ripped away a piece of my future with words like "severe oligospermia" and "OAT Syndrome."

Not impossible, he'd said, but also not probable.

It was as if he had taken a scalpel and sliced away a quintessential part of me, removing it like some kind of organ that they swear you can live without. You only really need a single kidney, and you can have your appendix and your gall bladder removed and be just fine. But when they take your future, the one you never even got to fully realize, it's a wound that doesn't heal. It's like a phantom limb that you never stop missing, never stop mourning.

And the look on Anna's face when she realized the big family she'd always dreamed of probably wasn't going to happen was like pouring salt into an open, gaping wound. The doctor had tried to give us hope, listing out the various treatment plans, all very expensive and not guaranteed, but he'd also very strongly suggested we keep our expectations in check. With every word, the light in Anna's eyes faded.

I knew then what was coming, and I was powerless to stop it. All I could focus on in that moment was the walls of the doctor's office. They were painted a dark, desolate gray. Not some cheery, optimistic color, nothing bright or calming like most people might expect in such a place, but the kind of gray that traps you, suffocates you. If agony were a color, it's undoubtedly the same shade as those walls.

And that's what the last four years have been like . . . gray.

Sure, there are some pops of color—Ethan, being one of them. My cheek lifts as I watch him chase after Peaches, the two of them rolling around in the dirt. They're both going to need a bath before bed. Ethan is yellow. Bright and happy.

There's Sutton, too. Her friendship is a lifeline, a calming, soothing blue that makes me feel like I can get from one day to the next.

My RVs. Peaches. A joke told at the shop. A warm patty melt with sweet potato fries—all small bright spots of color.

And Callie?

The voice that whispers in my ear isn't mine, and I glance over at that empty rocking chair. "Yeah, and what about her?" I swear I can hear Kase's laughing response, can see the expression he'd give me so clearly in my mind. *You know exactly what I'm talking about.*

My eyes land on one of the tabs I have open on my laptop browser. It's a tab that's been open for days now, ever since I ran into Callie at the grocery store. I tap on it, bringing the images full screen. Mabel's post about the photoshoot has indeed gone viral, but I couldn't care less about the number of likes or shares, and I haven't read a single comment.

It's the pictures that keep me coming back to this page.

I click on one to enlarge it and let out a breath as Callie's beautiful smiling face fills my screen. "She's all of them," I whisper, looking over at the empty chair. "Every single color of the rainbow."

I know what Kase would ask next if he were here: *Then what the hell are you doing, man?*

"What I have to," I mutter, closing the tab.

I'd hated how weird things were when she ran into me—literally. Part of me wanted to run after her and apologize for not returning her text the other day. It had taken everything in my power to stand there, gripping the handle of my buggy as she fled, more like sprinted, down the aisle to get away from me.

I don't blame her, though I wish she understood. It wasn't that I didn't want to answer her text. It's not that I don't think about her more times than I should because I do.

It's just that my life is gray. And it always will be.

I pull up another window, the one I was on before Ethan distracted me. For the last forty-five minutes or so, I've been working on getting my latest RV project listed on a rental website. The airstream I bought from some old guy down in Florida was in pretty bad shape when I brought it home, but I've spent the last eight months restoring it, and I have to say, she's a real thing of beauty now.

I could probably sell it quickly, but I'm in no hurry to see it gone. Working on an RV is like therapy for me. There's something really cathartic about taking something broken and in ruins and putting it back together piece by piece—if only my own life were like an RV. But I'm not fixable and I'll never run right again.

Just beyond the edge of my driveway, down a small lane that curves beside the lake on my property, the 1957 Airstream sits gleaming in the fading golden light. Two of my other projects, the 1953 Spartan Manor and a 1966 Gulf Stream Cruiser, sit a few feet away. I snort when I see the neon pink string lights, Ms. Dorothy has strung along the doorframe of the Spartan. Pink—that's her color. Sweet but sassy.

I never imagined myself with a tenant, but one day this spunky little old lady came waltzing into the shop to get her oil changed, and we got to talking. She told me she'd fallen on some hard times and needed a place, and it wasn't long after that I mentioned the Spartan. I'd recently finished it and wasn't sure yet what I wanted to do with it, but renting it to someone in need seemed like a worthy cause. That was a year ago, and she's the best neighbor anyone could ask for. She's also the one who made me realize the potential of rental income.

The salary I take from the shop is more than enough to live on, but restoring vintage RVs can be expensive. Renting the RVs once I'm done with them gives me the best of both worlds.

I return my focus to the rental application, enter in a few lines of information, and press save. I'll need to take a few pictures in the morning when the lighting is better, and then I can finish up the listing. Closing my laptop, I let out a long, deep breath. Of course, my mind drifts back to Callie.

"It's better this way," I murmur, my eyes drifting again to the empty rocking chair. "This is the way it has to be."

I wait, but this time, there's no voice that whispers back. No joking word, no teasing bit of advice. Just the empty chair.

Sadness rolls over me like a wave, but thankfully, I'm saved from drowning in it by the thumping of sneakers tromping up the wooden porch stairs.

"Uncle Jensen, I'm hungry." Ethan rubs at his tummy. "Peaches told me she's hungry, too."

"Oh, did she now?" I tease, standing up. "Well, how

about we head inside and get cleaned up? Then I'll make you two some dinner." I sign the word "eat" to Peaches which makes her bark and wag her tail. Ethan grins and dashes for the door, Peaches trailing behind him.

I follow, but I'm a little slower, my steps—and my heart—heavy.

Chapter 9
Callie

My pancakes are exactly how I like them—warm and fluffy, with a big ole glob of butter melting in the center and homemade syrup dripping down the sides—but it seems that not even they can make me smile today.

I shovel a forkful into my mouth and swallow, barely even tasting any of the maple sweetness, as I switch back and forth between the Zillow app on my phone and the Dayton Springs classified ads.

I'd gotten up early this morning with a mission: find a new place to live so I can stop mooching off my too-big-hearted-for-her-own-good cousin. But after spending all day driving around town looking at potential rentals, all I have to show for my troubles is a nearly empty gas tank.

A little comfort food seemed like a good consolation prize, but apparently not even the diner's pancakes can make me feel better.

"Ugh," I grumble, tossing my phone on the table and shoving it away. No matter how many times I check that stupid app, the perfect rental isn't going to magically appear—a fact that annoys the ever-living crap out of me.

I stab at my pancakes, scooping up another mouthful.

"How you doing over here?"

I quit glowering at my food long enough to see Sutton standing beside my table, a tray with a pitcher of sweet tea in hand.

I'd noticed her when I walked in, but thankfully she'd been busy delivering food to a table full of football players so another waitress grabbed my order. It really shouldn't feel weird or awkward seeing her, but it does. All thanks to Jensen.

Just the thought of him makes me want to put my head on the table and groan loud enough for people in the next county to hear.

It's been a little over a week since the photoshoot, and it feels like every time I turn around, Jensen is there. The likelihood of running into someone in a small town like Dayton Springs is pretty high, but the amount of times I've run into Jensen is getting ridiculous. It's like the universe keeps shoving us together just so it can have a good laugh. First, it was the Piggly Wiggly. Next, it was Maude's Bakery. Don't even get me started on how we both ended up at the drug store pharmacy counter on a day that the pharmacist was working solo with a drive-thru full of people.

He's always polite, but it never goes beyond the basic pleasantries—which, of course, is totally fine by me. Despite the way shivers ripple down my back when he says hello and the heat that flushes my skin at the sight of him, I am not interested. Even if my stupid body hasn't gotten the memo, my brain is pretty solid on that fact.

The check engine light is on in my 4Runner, and I'm at least 500 miles overdue for an oil change, but there's no way I'm taking it in to Bradford Auto. I'd rather have to cross state lines than do that. Nope, I'll pass. Take that, Universe.

Eventually, I'll stop thinking about him so much. I'll stop going over every detail of every interaction we've had in my head, and I'll finally stop obsessing over the photos of us I have saved on my phone.

Whatever my issues are, none of them are Sutton's fault. So, even though it feels weird seeing her after her best friend gave me a big ole NOPE, I do my best to put on a normal expression.

"I think I'm good," I tell her.

"Are you sure? Cause you're hacking up those pancakes like they've personally wronged you." She gives me a sheepish smile, and it's pretty obvious that it's one of those, *"sorry my stupid best friend made you feel all the feels and then left you on read,"* kind of smiles.

"I guess it's not their fault I've had a crummy day." I trace a finger around the edge of my plate and sigh. "Their one job is to be delicious, which they are. I may not be able to find a place to live, but at least there's that, right?"

Sutton's brows scrunch. "Wait, I thought you were staying with Mabel?"

I glance around for my cousin, who's due to arrive for her shift any minute before I answer. "I am, but I'm staying in the studio over her garage, which she usually rents out. Her last tenant got a job and moved to Atlanta, so it was vacant when I showed up. She insisted I take the space, but now she won't let me pay any kind of rent. She keeps saying we're family and that means my money is no good to her, but I know she's struggling to make ends meet. She has been for a while now, ever since . . . well, I'm sure she told you about her ex."

Sutton nods. "Oh, I've heard the stories."

"She was finally starting to get back on her feet, you know? Then I came home, and she's too pig-headed to let me help with the bills. I don't have a job yet, but I have plenty in savings. I could help if she let me, but she's determined to prove that she can stand on her own two feet—even if it means the electricity is about to be cut off." I reach into my bag and pull out the envelope I'd snagged from the mailbox this morning. The big, red bolded "Overdue" stamp on the front is hard to miss. I'd gone to the electric company and paid the bill in person, but I was sure there were more like it. The quickest way to help Mabel was to move out so she could find a tenant she'd actually let pay her.

"Oh man," Sutton winces. "She told me she needed to pick up some extra shifts, but I didn't realize she was struggling like that."

"She's more stubborn than a mule, I swear. Getting her to admit there's a problem usually requires an act of congress," I tease, shoving the envelope back in my bag. "I've been looking at rentals all day, but everything I've found is either some hole in the wall or comes with a questionable roommate." It was one of the "perks" of small-town living. There weren't any condominiums nearby, and the one apartment complex in the area had no vacancy.

"I've looked at everything from a shed in someone's backyard to renting a room from a woman whose entire house was decorated with frogs. And I don't mean the cute cartoon kind."

Sutton and I share a shudder.

"I need to find something soon. Mabel's been there for me when no one else has. I just want to make sure I'm looking out for her the way she's always looked out for me."

"Sounds to me like you already are," Sutton says, reaching across the table to refill my glass of tea. "I'm sure you'll find something soon. And . . . I get the whole too stubborn for their own good thing." She gives me a pointed look.

It doesn't surprise me that she knows about my text to Jensen and his non-existent answer. She probably knows about our awkward run-ins too.

I wave a hand. "It's fine, don't worry about it."

"I just don't want you to think that he didn't have a good time at the photoshoot, Callie, because he did. He told me all about it, about how incredible it was. It's just, Jensen is . . . complicated."

I can tell from the way she's pursing her lips that she's trying not to say too much. I admire her loyalty, even if it does feel kind of like a sucker punch to the gut.

I thought I was doing better, that I was finally starting to recover from what happened with Adam, but Jensen's rejection, as minimal as it was, brought back a lot of feelings I don't want to feel anymore.

I was never good enough for Adam—which is why he spent the majority of our relationship changing everything about me. The saddest part about it was that I let him.

And I have to live with that.

"It's okay, I get it," I tell her, even though I really don't get it at all. It's probably for the best anyway. The last thing I need is complications, and if anything, it's solidified the fact that I don't need any kind of relationship right now. I'm better off on my own. "Seriously, it's fine."

Sutton nods, not pushing the issue. "Alright, well, I hope you and me and Mabel can still hangout some time. Maybe do a girl's night? It's been a really long time since I had one of those."

"For sure, I would love that."

Sutton beams. "The next night Mabel and I both have off, we're planning something!" She taps the corner of my table. "But for now, I'll let you eat your pancakes in peace."

She finishes topping off my sweet tea and then disappears back into the kitchen. I take a few, less aggressive bites of my pancakes and pick up my phone again. It's not ideal, but there might be some rental options in the next town over. I type in the new criteria and hit search.

The prospects aren't great, and I'm contemplating whether I should circle back and reconsider Frog Lady, when Sutton returns to my table, a wide smile on her face.

"I can't believe I didn't think of it earlier, but I know a place that you can rent!" She hands me her phone which is open to a website called RV Share. The listing is for a newly renovated vintage Airstream.

"Oh, wow," I say, swiping through the pictures. "It's so cute!" The RV isn't very large, but the inside is bright and clean, with black and white accents that are absolutely adorable. There's a small kitchen, a bathroom, and a dining area that converts to a bed. According to the listing, the rent is more than affordable. It's exactly what I've been looking for.

"I know the owner," Sutton says, "and they mentioned a few other folks are coming to check it out tomorrow afternoon. I bet if you headed over there today, you could get a jump on it if you're interested."

"I'm definitely interested." I scan the listing, noting there isn't a phone number included. Just an email. "But it doesn't look like there's a way to call the owner? Do you have the number?"

"Oh, you can just show up," Sutton waves a hand. "I'll give you the address." She reaches for a napkin off the table and pulls a pen out from the pocket of her apron to jot down the information.

"You don't think I should call or something first?"

"Nah, I know the guy. He's more of a face-to-face type anyway."

I chew on my bottom lip, mulling things over. I don't love the idea of just showing up at a stranger's property, but I also don't want to miss out on the opportunity to rent the place—especially if Frog Lady is my only alternative.

"I mean, it's up to you," Sutton shrugs, "but places like that don't last long around here. I bet it goes pretty quick."

She confirms what I'm already thinking. I make note of the address. "I could swing by now on my way home, if you think that's okay?"

"I think that would be fine," Sutton rushes to say, a gleam in her eye. "But you better get going. Want me to bag up your food?"

I eye the mutilated pancakes and shake my head. "That's okay. I'm finished."

"Well, good luck with the rental," Sutton tells me, as she walks me to the door, practically shoving me out of it. "Let me know how it goes, okay?"

—

The napkin Sutton wrote the address on flutters in my lap as my 4Runner bounces down an unpaved road, the warm breeze blowing in from my open window.

Once you get outside the main drag, Dayton Springs becomes a little more rural. I've always had a soft spot for the Alabama countryside, and I missed it terribly while I was living in New York. Now, driving down this road, it feels a lot like finding something you thought you'd lost or remembering you put something away for a rainy day and now it's a rainy day. It's comforting.

The road widens a bit, opening up to a clearing, where an old, but charming farmhouse is nestled next to a sprawling grove of trees. There's a large barn situated off to the side and beyond that, about a half mile down the road, sitting next to a small pond are three RVs.

I turn down a smaller, more narrow lane that will

bring me around to the pond. One of the RVs, an older Spartan Manor style, looks like it might already be inhabited. There are several potted plants tucked just outside the door and there's a colorful carpet and rocking chair set up under a small awning decorated with pink solar string lights. There's even a sign posted by the door that says, "a spoiled rotten cat lives here."

The second RV is a vintage Gulf Stream Cruiser, and I can't help but admire the faded, mint green accent paint that gives it a cheerful demeanor despite its age.

The last RV is from the listing Sutton showed me. I immediately fall in love with its bulbous shape and the silver metal siding that has been polished so much I can see my reflection in it.

I pull my 4Runner up next to the Airstream and get out, my breath catching as the golden afternoon rays of sunshine glint off the surface of the pond, making it sparkle. I feel that old familiar itch and wish I had a paintbrush in my hand.

It's beautiful here and peaceful. I can imagine myself sitting out near the water's edge at twilight, my mind already thinking of what colors I'll need to mix to perfectly capture the rolling green of the hills, the glint of the sun on the water's surface.

It catches me by surprise how quickly my mind paints the image in my thoughts. Tapping into my artistic side hasn't been easy lately, but here, inspiration beckons.

The door to the RV is locked—which I expected. No matter, I have a really good feeling about this place, and I can already tell it's the perfect spot for me.

I get in my car and head back down the lane toward the farmhouse. The sooner I introduce myself to the owner, the sooner we can, hopefully, get the rental process started.

Parking under the shade of a looming silver maple, I open my car door. There's a streak of white as a big fluffy dog jumps off the porch, runs over, and practically leaps into my lap.

"Hello there," I coo, scratching behind the dog's ears. "Where'd you come from? Do you live here, too?"

The dog gives my cheek a sloppy kiss in response which makes me laugh. I get out of my car and the dog immediately flops over on her back, exposing her tummy for belly rubs.

"Aren't you a sweetheart?" I bend down and oblige her, rubbing my fingertips back and forth.

Behind me, there's the familiar squeak and slam of a screen door opening and shutting and then heavy footfalls growing closer. I give the dog one last belly rub and stand, wiping the dirt off the front of my jeans.

I whirl around, excited to meet the owner of the RV and ready to sell myself as their new tenant. "Hi, I'm—"

The words die in my throat as I realize "stupid, hot, kissed the hell out of me and then ghosted me" Jensen Shepherd is standing there looking just as shocked as I am to find me standing in—*oh sweet magnolias*— what is apparently *his* front yard.

"Callie? What are you doing here?"

The words are gruff, and I bristle at the tone. I open my mouth to answer, but the white dog, clamoring for more attention, takes that exact moment to jump up on me, catching me off guard. I step backward, tripping over my own two feet, and down I go, like a tree in a thunderstorm, nearly taking the dog out with me.

Chapter 10

Jensen

It happens fast. One minute Callie is standing there, shock that mirrors mine etched in her features, and the next, she's on the ground.

I'm moving before my brain has a chance to catch up, shoving Peaches out of the way as I lean over her. "Are you hurt?"

I reach for her arm, helping her gently into a sitting position. Her skin is warm underneath my fingertips, and I'd be lying if I said I didn't feel the pulse of electricity that shot through me when I touched her.

"I'm fine," she says quickly, searching behind me. "Is the dog okay?" Concern lines her eyes as she rakes them over Peaches. "I think I may have landed on her."

Peaches, who's at least 60 pounds and

as solid as an ox, answers for herself by trotting over and plopping down in the dirt next to Callie. I give her the eye and quickly sign "place" which she is fully aware means for her to go back inside and lay down on her bed. She ignores me.

"Peaches," I practically growl, though she can't hear me. I wave my hand in front of her face to make sure she's watching and then give the sign again. She responds by nuzzling herself even closer to Callie and shoving her snout up under Callie's palm.

She's always been a social creature, but she's clearly taken with Callie.

That makes two of us, pup. The thought rockets through my brain, but I swallow, shoving it away.

"Sorry about that." I meet Callie's eye, trying to ignore the magnetic pull I feel toward her. "She knows better than to jump on people."

"It's okay." Callie rubs both hands over Peaches's belly, making her leg move back and forth when she gets to a ticklish spot. "I'm just glad she's not hurt." She leans down a little further addressing Peaches. "You're lucky you're cute," she tells her. "You know that?"

I see the blood then, dripping down Callie's forearm. "*You* are hurt."

She waves a hand. "It's nothing."

It might be nothing to Callie, but the sight of her injured in front of me twists my insides. I stand up and stalk back inside to the bathroom where I keep the first aid kit and return to her side.

"It's just a scrape," Callie tells me, holding her injured arm. "It's not a big deal."

I ignore her, opening the kit, and pulling out supplies.

"Really, I'm fine," she tries again. "Jensen, you don't have to—"

"Will you just let me help you?" I growl, the words coming out way gruffer than I intend. I can't help it though. This close to her, I can smell vanilla and honey on her skin, and it's driving me crazy.

She purses her lips in annoyance but nods, watching me with narrowed eyes as I tear open a little packet containing an alcohol wipe. I carefully clean the scrape just above her elbow and cover it with a band-aid. "You're all set." Again, the words are like sandpaper. I know I'm being a jerk, but this is the way it has to be.

"Thanks," she mumbles, running her finger over my handiwork.

I stand up and hold out my hand to help her up. She takes it and I pull her to her feet. She's so close to me now, it takes every ounce of strength to stop myself from wrapping my arms around her. Just the thought makes my pulse quicken, but it also has my stomach flipping over. I step back, putting ample space between us. Annoyance flares through me at my own lack of self-control.

Callie crosses her arms over her chest and huffs.

"Look, I didn't mean to catch you off guard or anything. I didn't even know you lived here." Her body language matches mine, and my immediate reaction is to do something to make her feel more at ease. That only annoys me more.

"So why are you here then?" I scowl, not understanding at all how the very person I've been doing my best not to think about has somehow landed in my front yard.

"I came to look at the RV," she explains as if it's obvious. "Sutton said . . . " She trails off. "She said . . . " Her face pales. "Oh, biscuits!"

I almost laugh at her adorable albeit ridiculous exclamation, but realization smacks into me.

"Sutton sent you," I echo. It's not a question. Her face says it all, and honestly, I'm not surprised. Sutton is one of those people who loves hard, and she loves me like a brother. If she thinks something is for my own good, she'll do it without a single apology. Apparently, that includes sending unsuspecting, beautiful women to my house to be love-bombed by my dog and gruffed at by me.

"Listen, Callie . . . " This time it's me who trails off. As strongly as I feel about shutting down anything that might even halfway resemble catching feelings, I don't want to be unkind. It's not who I am, and I especially don't want to be unkind to Callie. She's done nothing wrong. In another life, she'd be exactly the type of woman I'd want to hand over my heart to.

But that's just it. My heart shattered a long time ago, and whatever's left is hardly worth much these days.

"Mabel tells me you two are best friends."

I can't quite understand the look on Callie's face, but it's an easier topic than what's rolling around in my thoughts, so I nod.

"Yeah, we're more like family though. We have been since . . . " I swallow as the familiar claws of grief dig into me. So much for an easy topic change. You'd think after four years I'd be okay talking about it, but the words still don't want to come out. I try again. "Since Kase."

Callie's eyes soften. "I knew Kasey in high school. He was really funny. And kind. That's what I remember the most about him, what a genuinely good guy he was."

"He was."

"How did you two meet?"

"In Basic. We were both fresh out of high school and thought we were badasses because we enlisted. We learned pretty quickly that the Army doesn't care what sort of bravado you think you have, they're gonna beat it right out of you." The memories from Basic Training pop up, and for once they don't make me sad. "I remember this one time I fell asleep when I was supposed to be on watch and had to do a ruck march as a punishment. Kasey smart-mouthed our Drill Sergeant so that I wouldn't have to do it alone. He was always looking out for me like that."

"And you for him." She states this not as a question, but as fact.

"He was my best friend. I would've done anything for him." Sadness swells in my chest, but for once, it feels good to talk about it, to talk about him.

"You run his auto shop now, right?"

"Yeah, just until Ethan is old enough to decide what he wants to do with it. Kase was so proud of his shop and so excited to teach Ethan everything he knew about cars. I'm no guru like he was, but I'm doing my best to make sure Ethan doesn't miss out."

Callie gives me the sweetest smile. "I'm sure you're doing a great job."

The back of my neck warms, and I lift a hand to rub at it. Sutton says similar stuff all the time, but when Callie says it? Well, it just hits different.

"So uh . . . " I clear my throat, needing a subject change. "Sutton sent you to look at the RV?"

"I don't want to overstep." Callie holds up both hands. "Clearly, you weren't expecting me, and I don't want this to be some weird thing. I'll just go live with Frog Lady. Really, it's totally fine."

"Frog Lady?" I can't tell if she means literally or not. "Is that some weird nickname for your cousin?"

"No," Callie snorts. "It's what I call the lady whose room I guess I'll be renting." Her shoulders drop. "To say the pickings around here are slim is putting it mildly.

Just trust me on that one."

I don't fully understand all the details, but one thing is clear enough. "You need a place to live."

She nods. "I do. Unless I want to bankrupt my cousin, which is definitely not on my bingo card for the year."

I know I should tell her that the RV isn't available. I should probably just feed her some kind of excuse or make something up that will get her back in her car and on her way into town, but the look on her face has me sucking in a breath instead. There's a heaviness to her shoulders, like there's a weight sitting there. A weight that she tries her best not to let people see. But I see it. And I understand what it's like to carry heavy things around with you.

"Come on then," I tell her, heading for my truck.

"Excuse me?"

"Come on," I repeat, opening the passenger side door for her. "I'll take you down there to give it a look."

She walks over to me, the corner of her bottom lip sucked between her teeth. "You sure?"

Sure this is a bad idea? Yes. Absolutely. 100%. "Yup."

Peaches saves me from having to elaborate by following Callie to the truck, her tail wagging a mile a minute. "You stay," I tell her. Giving her the "place" sign again.

I can tell she wants to ignore me, but she's too much of a good girl for that. Though, her ears droop as she begins the slowest walk in the history of dogs toward the porch.

"Oh, let her come," Callie calls out. "She's so sweet, and I just love dogs."

Despite myself, this makes me smile. "You sure? She nearly gave you a concussion."

"Nah, her love language is just intense snuggling." She returns my smile. "I don't mind that so much."

I chuckle, turning to jog after Peaches. I catch up to her and touch her back. When she looks at me, I give her the sign for "go" and she whips around so fast, she nearly knocks me over.

Callie squeals as Peaches runs at her, zipping back and forth in excitement. At the last possible second, she swerves around Callie and jumps into the cab, parking herself down in the middle seat, tongue hanging out the side of her mouth.

Callie laughs as she sits next to Peaches in the passenger seat, and I can feel the corners of my mouth lifting. Her laugh is contagious, and it's a sound I doubt I could ever get tired of.

Which is why this is a bad idea, I tell myself as I get inside the cab.

"What kind of dog is she?"

"She's mostly a mutt, but I'm pretty sure she's got lab and golden retriever in her."

"And she's deaf right?" Callie scratches Peaches behind the ears, clearly not minding that my dog is completely invading her personal space.

I nod. "Yeah, since she was a pup. The shelter isn't

sure if it was a congenital thing or if it was some kind of infection from before they found her, but they're pretty sure she's been unable to hear most of her life."

"Was it hard to train her?"

"Not too bad. She's really smart, and we bonded pretty quickly. Sometimes I think that dog can read my mind."

"Well, I think she's amazing." Callie beams at my dog. "What's her name?"

"Peaches."

Callie's smiling brightens. "Cause she's so sweet right?" She leans down and kisses Peaches on the top of the head. "Well, if that just isn't the perfect name for you."

Another chuckle slips from my throat, which makes me frown. There this woman goes disarming me again. I swear, talking to her is too easy.

"So, um . . . " I grasp for another safe topic. "You just moved back here, is that right?"

"I was born and raised in Dayton Springs, but I spent the last few years in New York City. I came home a few weeks ago."

I tend to avoid big cities—I much prefer the peace and quiet of country life. Probably a result of growing up in the hill country of Texas. It surprises me a little to hear that Callie lived in the city for so long. "I bet life moves at a much faster pace up there than it does here."

"It does," she confirms. "Sometimes so fast it moves

right past you and there's nothing you can do to stop it."

Callie says it casually, but there's a tiny tug that threatens to pull down her mouth, as though she's trying not to let a frown show. I shouldn't ask—there's clearly a story there—but I'm curious.

"Is that why you came back home?"

Chapter 11

Callie

It's an innocent enough question, one that most people tend to ask while they're making small talk—the whole, *where you from? What brings you to town?* sort of thing. I highly doubt Jensen knows it's a loaded one.

Still, he's waiting for an answer. I do a quick run-through of the options and decide to just go with the truth.

"My boyfriend of six years, who I thought was going to propose, dumped me and then kicked me out of our apartment," I rush the words out with a shrug. "So, I came home."

Jensen's eyes widen slightly as he processes the information.

"But don't feel sorry for me or anything," I hurry to add. "He wasn't the one. It just took me way too long to figure it out."

"He dumped you, and then kicked you out?" He repeats the words slowly.

"Mmmhmm," I confirm. "You know those pathetic country songs where you lose your house and your wife and your dog all in one shebang? Well, turns out that really does happen. I'm a walking, talking stereotype over here."

"He took your dog, too?"

"Not exactly, no. I'd been begging for him to let me get a dog for years, and he always said they were too much work. When he told me we needed to talk, I thought he'd changed his mind about the dog. But turns out, he changed his mind about *me*."

My laugh falls flat. I quickly drop my eyes to Peaches, who has her head in my lap. I hate how pathetic I sound.

Jensen pulls up next to the RV and puts the truck into park, but he makes no move to get out. He turns to look at me, giving me his full attention and clearly wanting to hear the rest of my pitiful little tale.

"He was nice enough to give me until the end of the month to find another place to live," I add dryly. "But I couldn't wait that long. The next time he left for work, I threw everything I could into my 4Runner and got out of there." I let out a sigh. "I ended up back here. It's where I should've been all along. Adam hated everything about this place, which in hindsight, should've been a big clue, but I guess I was just too dumb to see the signs."

"Don't say that," Jensen says gently. "I know I haven't known you very long, but 'dumb' isn't a word I'd use to describe you. Now him, on the other hand, I'd say that word—and a few choice others—describe him perfectly."

His sweet defense of me is a stark contrast to the grumpy demeanor he's been displaying ever since he found me in his front yard, and I'm not entirely sure what to make of it. Still, a warm shiver skips down my spine, and oh Sweet Caroline, do I love the way he says my name. There's something about the timbre of his voice, deep and low, that makes my insides feel like cooked spaghetti.

"You and Mabel are of the same opinion."

"Smart woman, that Mabel Callahan."

"She's the best," I agree. "I don't know where I'd be without her honestly. She's like an anchor in my life, always keeping me steady. It's why she's letting me stay in her studio right now, even though she can't afford it. I think she'd rather end up without a single cent to her name than let me spend another minute with someone like Adam the A-hole." The sudden urge to hug my cousin hits me pretty strong. "But that's also why I'm hoping this works out." I point to the RV through the windshield. "Mabel's been through a lot and she deserves nothing but good things. So, I really need to find my own place."

Jensen nods, though his face is impossible to read. He seems so much more closed off than he did at the photoshoot, and I hate how much I hate the weird distance between us. Despite the fact that he's clearly not interested in me, my heart still speeds up every time his stormy eyes meet mine.

It doesn't help that he's one of the most attractive men I've ever laid my eyes on. He's wearing a baseball hat today, and I have always been a sucker for a guy in a hat. His plain green tee stretches across his chest and his broad shoulders and the short sleeves show off more of his tattoos. The sleeve starts at his wrist and then moves up his forearm and bicep and, I suspect, his shoulder as well. The swirling black ink is rich and dark, and if I weren't such a chicken, I'd reach out and trace the patterns with my finger.

"Well, let's see what you think." Jensen pulls the keys from the ignition and opens his door. I follow suit, holding my door open long enough for Peaches to jump to the ground.

"It was made in 1957," he tells me. "The original owners kept it in pretty good condition, but after they passed, it went from owner to owner and eventually ended up at auction. It wasn't in the best shape by then, but I spent the better part of last year restoring her." Jensen unlocks the door to the Airstream and holds it open for me. "She's got all the vintage charm of her prime with a few modern upgrades."

I step inside and my mouth drops open. It looks exactly like the pictures on the listing, but it's even better in person. The space isn't huge, but roomy enough for me to be more than comfortable.

"You did all this yourself?" I ask, spinning in a slow circle so I can take it all in.

"I did," Jensen leans in through the open door. He's got one hand above his head, braced on the doorframe, and the other shoved into the front pocket of his jeans.

"That's . . . " For a second, I forget that I'm supposed to be admiring the RV and not its owner. "Um, that's amazing." My cheeks burn as heat floods through me. "You've done a really incredible job. Seriously, it's beautiful."

"Thank you. I run Kase's shop—that's where I spend most of my time, but whenever I can carve out some free time I work on RVs. Brings me a little bit of peace."

The way his voice curls around that last sentence, and the obvious pain in his tone, makes me pause. That's how I feel about painting. When life is too hard to face, I lose myself in the swirling colors across my canvas. It's the only thing that silences the noise in my head.

"What about you? What do you do?" His question catches me off guard. It's another one I'm not sure how to answer.

"Well, I'm not employed at the moment, but I spent the last four years working as a receptionist for an investment firm." I already sound super pathetic, I don't want to make it worse by explaining that Adam basically gaslit me into getting what he considered a "respectable" job, instead of doing what I actually wanted to do with my life. The longer I'm home and the more layers I peel back, the more I realize just how much of myself I let him change, and I hate it. "But don't worry, I can pay my rent and all that. I have savings and I'm looking for a new job. I'm sure someone in this town needs a receptionist."

Jensen must see something on my face because he scoffs. "What do you *want* to do?"

"Paint." It's an automatic response, I don't even have to think about it. "I've always wanted to open up my own studio, teaching painting classes or something. I did two years of art school before . . . " I trail off, not wanting to finish the story of how Adam had talked me into quitting school to be with him in New York, to admit that I'd allowed someone to talk me out of my own dreams. "Anyway, I'd love to do something with art or something that allows me to be creative. But I'll take anything at this point. Is the auto shop hiring?"

I say the last part with a smile, needing the joke to take some of the pressure off.

"Can you build a transmission?"

"Oh absolutely, 100%."

"Well, then, consider yourself hired," Jensen replies, playing along. "In all seriousness though, I might have a solution for you."

"You're not really offering me a job, are you? I was totally kidding about the transmission thing. I don't know the first thing about cars. I'm the kind of girl who waits 'til the light comes on to put gas in the tank. Trust me, you don't want me anywhere near an engine."

"No," Jensen laughs, "Not at the shop, but I did overhear Stephanie Smith saying they needed some help at the elementary school when she came in last week to get her oil changed. Apparently, the paraprofessional who helps the art teacher decided to retire."

"Really?"

"Really. Not sure if they've filled the position yet, but it's worth looking into."

"Definitely! Thank you."

Jensen gives me one of those half smiles of his, and I quickly turn my attention back to the RV to keep from blurting out all the things I'm thinking in my head, like how attractive he is and how much I like his beard and his eyes and his whole face really and—

My phone dings with a notification, and I swipe at the screen. "Mabel told me this morning she scheduled a post with more pictures from our shoot since everyone went nuts over the last one. Looks like it just went live."

I pull up her account and gasp. Three new photos of Jensen and I pop into view, and I'm blown away by how incredible they are. I'd seen some of the raw footage, but Mabel edited these in her signature style. They look even more amazing than they did the first time I saw them.

You all begged for more! The caption reads. *Ask and you shall receive! Check out these photos from Callie and Jensen's stranger session. I think it's safe to say there was some chemistry. Want to see even more? Let me know!*

One of the pictures is of us standing back-to-back with our blindfolds on. Another is one where Jensen is standing behind me, bending down so his cheek is touching mine. The third is one of us kissing.

The artistry in the photography is evident, but the chemistry leaping out of the photos is even more undeniable. I can't help but zero in on the one of us kissing, my skin heating at the memory.

"Wow," I say, passing my phone over so Jensen can see. "I knew my cousin was awesome, but I think she outdid herself on this one."

"She's a hell of a photographer," Jensen agrees, handing me my phone back. "And it looks like I'm not the only one who thinks so." He points to the comment section, which is already starting to fill with people gushing over the photos.

When I look up from my phone, Jensen's eyes are on me. I meet his gaze with my own, letting myself get lost in those deep blue irises of his. Electricity crackles through me and every bit of connection I felt during the photoshoot slams into me with such force it makes me breathless.

We stare at each other for far longer than is normally appropriate before a familiar wail fills the air.

It almost makes me laugh, the metaphor of it all.

"It's the first Wednesday of the month," I sigh, as the tornado siren—the town's monthly test of the emergency system—continues its shrill song.

Growing up in the South, especially a town that's smack dab in the middle of tornado alley, you get used to hearing the sirens on the first Wednesday of every month. But still, it's an eerie sound, especially now that the weather is warming up. Spring in Alabama means tornadoes, and I shudder at the reminder.

Jensen and I continue to stare at each other, but it's more awkward than heated at this point, and once the siren finishes blaring, Jensen tears his eyes away from mine and clears his throat. "So, what do you think?" He indicates the trailer. "You interested?" The words are brusque, and his expression has darkened. "It's yours if you want it."

My stomach sinks at the look on his face. Is he offering because he feels obligated? Is he just a nice, sometimes grumpy, and very confusing guy with a spare RV to rent? Or is it something else? I have absolutely no idea what's going on in his head, and I'd wager to say that Jensen Shepherd is one of the hardest people to read that I've ever met.

I need a place to live, but saying yes to this place

means saying yes to seeing Jensen every day, to being near him. Can I handle that? Do I want to?

All it takes is the thought of my cousin's overdue bills to make up my mind for me.

For Mabel, I would do anything.

So even though I know deep down that this is probably a very bad idea, I push my hair off my shoulder and steel myself. "I'll take it."

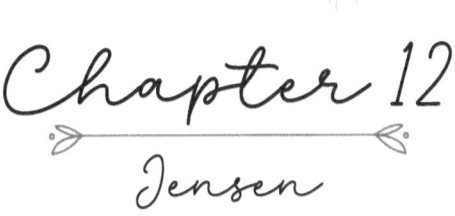

Chapter 12

Jensen

Ethan's cheeks are bright red, both from the warmth of the afternoon sun and the frustration that's been building for the last half hour.

"Okay, we're going to try it again. This time lift that back elbow up." I keep my voice calm, not wanting to heap any kind of pressure or expectation on his shoulders. "Keep your eye on the ball and swing hard, okay?"

I wait till Ethan nods and adjusts his grip on the bat. When he's ready, I throw the ball. He swings hard, but the ball still sails past him, landing with a thud a few feet behind our makeshift homeplate.

His face falls and his shoulders droop as the bat hangs loosely from his hand. "I suck at this," he whimpers, his eyes welling up with tears.

"That's not true." I hurry over and bend down in front of him so we're eye level. "You're doing a great job. Sometimes, these things just take a little practice."

"But we've *been* practicing, Uncle Jensen. It's been like ten hours!"

I crack a smile at that. Gotta love a seven-year-old's concept of time. "More like a half hour, bud."

His brows scrunch together. "Well, it feels like ten hours, and I'm not getting any better. How am I ever going to score a homerun if I can't hit the ball?"

He stares into my eyes, looking for an answer, and for a second, it's like looking in a mirror. Frustration has been a companion of mine ever since a certain green-eyed, beautiful woman became my neighbor two weeks ago, and every time I see my own face, my eyes ask the same question, *"what are we going to do about this?"*

I give Ethan the same answer I've been giving myself. "I know it seems impossible right now, but you're going to get through this. You can do this, buddy."

Ethan scrunches his nose, unbelieving. "You're just saying that to make me feel better."

This makes me laugh. *Touché, kid.*

"Well, you know what your daddy used to say?"

Ethan's face lights up at the mention of Kase. "What?" He looks so much like Kase, with his face all bright and animated that it takes me a second to recover before I respond.

"He used to say that when things got tough, you

might as well stop for a snack break. So how about we take a little break and get something to eat?"

Ethan cheers, tossing the bat to the ground and taking off for the back door that leads into the kitchen.

If only a handful of goldfish crackers and a juice box could fix my frustration as easily as it fixes his.

I take a second to grab the ball and the bat we were practicing with before following Ethan into the house.

I get him a snack and help myself to some sweet tea when the front door opens and Sutton walks through carrying a handful of grocery bags.

"Mama!" Ethan leaps from his spot at the breakfast bar and dive-bombs Sutton's legs. She squeals, nearly tripping over him, but then laughs. "Hey baby, did you have a fun afternoon with Uncle Jensen?"

Ethan untangles himself from Sutton's legs, while I reach out to take the grocery bags from her.

"We practiced baseball!" Ethan definitely sounds less glum about it than he did in the backyard. "I'm still working on my swing, but Uncle Jensen says I'll get better with practice."

"I'm sure you will, buddy." Sutton pulls Ethan in for a hug. "Why don't you go finish your snack in the living room? You can watch TV for a little while if you want."

I laugh as Ethan practically catapults himself into the living room, whooping as he scoops up the remote.

Sutton shakes her head, but she's smiling as she moves to the counter and begins unpacking the bags.

"Thanks for watching him for me."

"You don't have to thank me. You know I love spending time with him."

"I know, but I appreciate all that you do for us." Sutton lets out a sigh, her expression morphing into the one that she only wears when she's thinking about Kasey. "I'm not sure what would have become of us if it hadn't been for you."

A shadow crosses her face, and I know we're both remembering those early days. I shake my head to clear the images of Sutton practically comatose in her bed, staring at the ceiling for hours on end. Of Ethan's broken cries when he realized his daddy wasn't coming home.

"Well, the feeling is mutual," I mumble as more images flood my thoughts. The endless doctor visits, the way Anna looked at me when we heard the news. The empty closet.

Sutton lets out another breath and for a minute, we sit in the type of silence that only we can understand. I think grief is a lot like the ocean. Some days it can come crashing down on you, relentless and unyielding, but other days, it's just a gentle ebb and flow that you feel pushing against you even though you've found your footing. In moments like this, I know we're both feeling its pull.

Sutton turns away to put groceries in the pantry, and when she faces me again, her expression is bright.

The waves have passed. "Did you talk to that guy over in Macomb County today?"

"Yeah, he offered me a decent price, but I'm not sure it's the best move right now."

"What? Why? You've been looking for a Silver Streak to fix up for months now."

She's not wrong, I have been looking for one. But things at the shop have gotten really busy, plus as we move further into the spring and summer months, business is only going to increase. As much as I want to take on another RV project right now, I'm not sure I have the time.

"I've just got a lot going on right now. The shop is more than busy, and you know it's only going to get worse as the summer tourists start coming through."

"That's not a reason not to pursue the deal," Sutton counters, looking at me like she's just given me the most obvious solution in the world. "You'll regret it if you don't."

"There's no point in buying it if I can't work on it right now. I need to keep my focus in the right place."

"You mean the shop?"

I don't answer her, but we both know that's exactly what I mean.

"Shep," she starts, "we talked about this. You know how much I appreciate you stepping in and taking over the shop. You've not only kept it running, but you've made it better and you've preserved Kase's legacy for

Ethan. But it was never supposed to be a permanent thing. You need to just let me hire someone."

It's the same argument we have every few months, so I give her the same answer I always do. "You know no one can run that place like me."

"That may be true, but the shop was Kasey's dream, not yours. Don't you think it's time to let it go?"

I open my mouth ready to spit out the same ole rebuttal, but before I can, relief flickers to life in my chest at the thought of being able to walk away from the auto shop for good. But it's quickly extinguished by the same gut-wrenching guilt that keeps me walking through those doors every day.

"If I hadn't . . . " I can't finish my sentence. I try again. "Kasey can't be here to do it. He's my best friend. I'm doing it for him." My chest tightens, and I paw at the ache.

Sutton's eyes track the movement before lifting to mine again. "It's not your fault," she says softly. "When are you going to get that through that stubborn skull of yours? You don't have to keep working at the shop because you feel guilty about what happened."

She makes it sound so simple. Just walk away from the shop, just let it go. But that's just it. I can't. I can't just walk away.

I wasn't there for Kasey the day he died, and I should have been. That's something I have to live with for the rest of my life. So no, I can't just let Sutton hire someone to take my place. No matter how much she tells me that's what needs to happen, I know better.

I don't want to argue about it, so I clear my throat and steer the conversation back to neutral ground. "I told the guy over in Maycomb that I'd let him know this weekend if I was still interested."

It's a clear deflection, but thankfully, Sutton doesn't call me on it.

"Well, for what it's worth I think you should go for it. You've been looking for one for months. You could always put it in storage until things die down at the shop."

"I'll think about it," I tell her, and I mean it, even though I already have a feeling what my answer will be. The RVs will always be there. Sutton and Ethan are the priority. I won't let Kase down. Not again.

"Speaking of RVs," Sutton whirls around from the pantry, pointing a box of spaghetti noodles at me. "How are things going with your new tenant?" She presses her lips together in an obvious attempt not to smile.

Immediately, that same frustration that's been eating me alive for the last two weeks flares to life in my chest.

"Fine," I throw the word away, hoping we can just move past this particular topic of conversation, but Sutton's smirk just deepens.

"It's *fine*," I repeat. "She seems settled in well enough. I don't really notice her to be honest."

It's a bald-faced lie. Every time I step out onto my front porch, my eyes go straight to the RV, hope stirring inside me that I might catch some glimpse of her. And when I do? I notice everything about her. Like the way, she always wears her hair in a braid while she drinks her coffee in the golden glow of the mornings or the way she likes to sketch and paint in this one particular spot by the water. I can't help but notice that I can't help noticing her.

Sutton just keeps staring at me with that "yeah, okay, buddy" expression that she always gives me when she knows I'm full of it.

I have two choices really. I can keep pretending I'm not about to go out of my mind over this woman, or I can fess up and actually talk about it. I'm not one for spilling my guts, but the frustration coiling inside me is making me cagey.

I drop my shoulders in defeat. "I've been avoiding her mostly. I don't want to get too close."

Sutton's face brightens, knowing she's won. "And why's that?"

I roll my eyes. Of course she's going to make me say it. "Because being around her makes me . . . it makes me want to be around her all the time. And . . . " I let out a low breath. "I can't be around her, Sutton. I just can't."

I'm not explaining it right, but I can tell from the way Sutton's expression turns serious that she gets it.

"I know what you're going to say," I rush to get the

words out before she does. "But we both know that it's better this way."

Sutton sets the box of pasta on the counter and lets out a long sigh. "You may not want me to say it, but I'm going to anyway because that's what friends do. So, here it is: You have got to stop punishing yourself for things out of your control. It's not better this way, it's just *safer*. But that's no way to live, and if Kasey were here, he'd tell you that himself. Stop standing in your own way."

But he's not here, and that's part of the problem. I press my lips together, but Sutton reads my mind easily enough. I swear, she knows me better than I know myself sometimes. A fact that can be super annoying. Like right now.

"You like Callie. I know you do. I saw it in your face right after the photoshoot. There's a connection there, and you know what, you dummy? She feels it too."

The words send warmth through my entire body, and my stupid, stupid heart starts thumping the way it does every time I look out the window at that RV. "Did she tell you that?"

"No, but Mabel did."

I scoff. "You two hens have nothing better to do than try to play matchmaker."

My argument is weak, but I cling to it even though Sutton looks very much like she wants to punch me in the face.

"Listen, there's something to be said about small-town boredom. And gossip for that matter. This is neither of those things, and we both know it. I'm stepping in for Kasey as your wingman. Mabel's doing the same for Callie. Again, it's what friends do."

I start to argue, to tell her that Kase would never push for something like this, but that's not even halfway true. Kase was a risk-taker, and he always pushed me to step out of my comfort zone. He never let me settle for less, for mediocre. If he were here, well, he'd be standing next to Sutton looking at me the exact same way she is.

"I hear you, but it's not that easy. There's no future with me, Sutton, you know that. Anna's leaving proved that."

"Not every woman is like Anna. You can't go through life making assumptions about people and never giving them a chance to make up their own minds. It's not fair to them, and it's not fair to you."

Her words crack through some of my defenses. "When I'm around her, all I want to do is keep being around her. It's easy, you know. Just being near her. And when I'm with her . . . I can breathe."

There. I admitted it. What I feel when I'm around Callie terrifies me, but I also crave it. It's what drives me to my front windows every morning. Even the smallest glimpse of her fills my lungs. "For the first time in a long time, I can breathe when I'm next to her."

Sutton's eyes are all glassy. "Then breathe, Shep."

Those three simple words unlock something inside me. A lump rises in my throat as I reach for Sutton, wrapping my arms around her. She hugs me back in that fierce way of hers, and I let myself get lost in it for just a second.

I still don't know where to go from here. Being with Callie isn't a good idea—my thoughts on that haven't changed. But maybe, just maybe, I don't have to avoid her completely. Maybe we could be, I don't know, friends or something.

It doesn't have to mean anything. It doesn't have to go anywhere.

I can just be around her now and then. Just enough to take a breath once in a while. Would that be so bad?

"I'll think about it." I say, pulling back. "I promise."

"Good. You do that," She smiles before turning back to the groceries. "You want to stay for supper?"

"Nah, I gotta head home and check on Peaches. Thanks, though."

I give Sutton another quick hug and pop into the living room to tell Ethan goodbye. "Hey buddy, I'm getting ready to head out. You feeling any better?"

Ethan nods, his cheeks lifting in a bright smile. "You and my daddy were right. The snack helped a lot. Think we can practice baseball again soon?"

"Sure thing, bud." I return his smile and ruffle his hair.

Walking out to my truck, my steps are lighter than they have been in a while, and I steer for home with Sutton's words replaying in my head.

Then breathe, Shep.

I resolve to try.

Chapter 13

Callie

My paintbrush slides across the canvas. The golden streak of amber isn't a perfect match, and I wrinkle my nose at it. I lean back on my stool, studying the sky above me. The sinking sun has turned the sky into a breathtaking kaleidoscope of saffron and persimmon, but try as I might, I can't quite replicate its exact hue. Still, it's nice to have a paintbrush in my hand again.

I've been painting most afternoons since I moved into the RV. Nothing fancy, just me getting reacquainted with an old friend, but it's quickly becoming my favorite part of the day.

Something wet nuzzles against the palm I have resting on my lap, and a laugh bubbles up in my throat as I look down to see Peaches sitting next to me, her sweet little snout wiggling to get underneath my hand. "You are such a little love bug," I murmur, even though I know she can't hear me. I use both hands to scratch behind her ears, which makes her tail wag back and forth so fast, it's like she's one of those electric toys you wind up. It makes me laugh again.

I move off my stool and plop down in the soft grass next to her. Peaches immediately flops over, exposing her belly, and I give her all the scratches and rubs. She rewards me with several slobbery kisses.

"Oh you," I tell her, booping her on the nose. "I wish you could stay, but you know if he finds you down here again, he won't be happy."

Jensen's face fills my mind, and my smile fades. The knotted feeling in my stomach returns—the one I've been fighting for days now. Peaches must sense the shift in my mood because she lets out a little whine and practically crawls into my lap. "I know, I know," I tell her, running my fingertips along her back.

Jensen and I haven't spoken much since I moved into the RV two weeks ago. We've only seen each other a handful of times and every occasion has been more awkward than the last. Two days ago, he'd come home from work expecting to find his dog waiting for him. Except she wasn't. She was here at the RV with me.

It hadn't occurred to me that he would mind. It wasn't the first time I'd opened my door to find Peaches standing in the grass beside the door, tail wagging.

It also hadn't occurred to me to take her back to the house.

But when his truck pulled up, the look on his face made it very clear that he did mind. He'd minded *a lot.*

I thought maybe we'd turned some kind of corner when he agreed to let me rent the RV, but every time he looks at me, his expression is guarded. Not exactly unfriendly, but definitely standoffish.

It's more than that, too. There's something else behind his stiff posture and the way his cheeks always tug downward when he looks at me. Something much deeper in the way his stormy eyes stare into mine.

Even though I shouldn't, I can't help but want to know what it is, and thinking about Jensen takes up way more time than it should—especially given my official proclamation to swear off men in favor of becoming a cat mom.

I don't want a relationship. I don't want to put myself in a situation where I could end up heartbroken on Mabel's couch again, but despite what my brain is saying, my heart keeps reminding me of the way Jensen held me during the photoshoot, so tenderly. I can still feel his fingers tugging at my waist, pulling me closer. And sweet magnolias, I still think about the way his lips felt against mine. The way Jensen kissed me was unlike anything I've ever felt before. It was perfect, but poignant in a way that I don't understand. It was a hello and a goodbye all mixed in one, the opening of a door but the firm shutting of that same door. It was free-falling, totally weightless, and then having your feet touch the earth again, solid and defining. It was beautiful but sad at the same time, and I don't know why.

Maybe that's how it should stay. Adam took so much of me during our relationship, and now that I'm free of that and finding my way back to myself, the last thing I need is to be attracted to some broody, grumpy, impossible man.

"It's time I listen to my brain for once," I tell Peaches. She responds with a sneeze and a wag of her tail. I take that to mean she agrees.

"Yoo-hoo," a voice calls out from behind me.

I swivel around, greeting the petite woman with rich brown skin, eyes that crinkle with laugh lines, and gray, curling hair shuffling over to me from the Spartan Manor parked about thirty yards away. "Hey, neighbor! What are you up to this fine afternoon?"

Ms. Dorothy gives me a sweet smile and indicates the saran-wrapped bundle in her hands. "I made a couple of pound cakes to take to Bingo at the senior center this evening, but I thought you might like a slice or two."

"Oh, Ms. Dorothy, you spoil me." I take the cake, my mouth already watering. Ms. Dorothy is one of the best cooks around, probably the best here in Clayton County. Since the day I moved in, she's made it her personal mission to make sure I never want for baked goods. "Thank you."

"You're welcome, hon." She pats my arm with a wink before plopping down in one of the folding chairs I have set up near the water's edge. Peaches, who loves my neighbor as much as I do, immediately walks over and sticks her head within petting reach. Ms. Dorothy's gnarled fingers begin stroking the fur between her ears.

She eyes my painting. "You started a new one."

"Yeah, I couldn't get the composition right on the other one." I furrow my brow thinking about the canvas I'd given up on this morning. "I figured it was better to just start over than try to make it work."

"You know, I said the exact same thing about my ex-husband," Dorothy quips, which makes me snort.

"Which one was that? Husband two or three?"

Dorothy shrugs. "Probably both."

"But you finally found Mr. Right in the end," I remind her. "Unless all those stories about you and Robert were fiction."

"Oh no, those were the real deal." The dreamy look she always gets when she talks about her late husband appears, lighting up her face. "That one was a love story for the ages."

"From what you told me, it definitely sounds like it," I reply, a little wistfully. "You're lucky in that way. I don't think everyone finds that kind of love in their lifetime."

Dorothy considers this before nodding. "That's true, I suppose. Although it definitely took a few wrong decisions before I finally made the right one."

"Was it hard?" I ask her. "To keep putting yourself out there?"

"Of course," Dorothy presses a palm to her heart, "but I've never regretted being open to it, even if it didn't always work out. Love is scary and there are no guarantees. Sometimes you just have to jump off the cliff first before you know if you'll fly. But if you do . . . " Her face lights up again and her laugh lines deepen. "Well, that makes it all worth it, doesn't it?"

"You sound like a Hallmark card," I tease. "Besides, if my last relationship is any indication, I think I prefer my feet firmly on the ground."

"What about that handsome landlord of ours?"

"What about him?"

Dorothy lifts a brow and gives me a "don't even try to deny it" look.

"There's nothing between me and Jensen. He can barely even look at me without grimacing."

"That's because he doesn't want to admit his feelings. Trust me, I know the signs."

My first instinct is to argue with Dorothy, to tell her that it's not even slightly possible, but then there it is again, the memory of our photoshoot, playing on repeat in my mind. There was *something* there that day, something happened between us out in that field, and as much as I want to forget about it, I can't.

"But you don't want to admit yours either, so there's that."

I snort. "Ms. Dorothy, I don't have feelings for him. He's too . . . grumpy and . . . and . . . "

"And a total dish?" Dorothy helpfully supplies. "I mean, good gravy, that man knows how to wear a pair of blue jeans."

"Ms. Dorothy!" I laugh. I mean, she's not wrong. Not in the slightest.

"What? I'm old, not dead!"

We're both cackling when the sound of truck tires rolling up the lane gets our attention. Peaches perks up, the vibration in the ground waking her from the snooze she'd been taking at Ms. Dorothy's feet.

All at once, the levity drains right out of me.

"Speak of the devil and he shall appear," I murmur under my breath.

The truck slows to a stop and I brace myself, for both the man and the emotions I'm about to experience. But when Jensen steps out of the cab, his expression catches me off guard. He's not smiling, but he's not exactly frowning either, and when his eyes meet mine, the usual stare doesn't pierce through me. No, his expression is more . . . thoughtful. Which is almost just as disarming.

"Callie," he breathes, nodding in my direction. "Ms. Dorothy." He gives her a small smile, and jealousy spikes through me for a split-second. It's been a minute since he smiled at me like that.

"Sorry to bother you both. I just came to get Peaches." He eyes the dog laying at Ms. Dorothy's feet with exactly zero shame.

"Oh, you're not bothering us at all, is he, Callie?"

My cheeks burn as Jensen's eyes move to meet mine again. "Um, not at all." I twist the paintbrush in my hand. "I was just messing around, and Dorothy stopped by with some dessert."

"I've got some for you too, boy. Don't you move now, ya hear?" She hurries to add, hustling for the door of her RV, leaving me and Jensen alone.

Jensen chuckles. "Yes ma'am," he says, though his eyes never leave mine.

We stand like that for several long seconds, and it feels just like those first few minutes before a thunderstorm hits, when the clouds roll in and the sky is rumbling, and you can practically feel the electricity in the air. I half-expect lightning to start streaking across the sky.

"I applied for that job you told me about," I blurt out, needing to fill the silence with *something*. "The one at the elementary school? I actually had an interview with them yesterday, and it went really well. So, uh, thank you for that."

Jensen lifts a shoulder and lets it drop. "Glad I could help." His words are formal, but less clipped than usual.

The conversation between us dies as I quickly scan my brain for something else to mention. Peaches saves me by trotting over to Jensen and flopping down at his feet.

"Oh, so now you're happy to see me," he murmurs, squatting down to give Peaches belly rubs. "You ready to go home?" His hands move as he gives her the sign that I assume means home, and she jumps up, tail-wagging and yipping a little bark.

"Let's go then," he tells her, standing back up. He walks over to the truck and opens the door. "Come on, girl." He gives her another sign, and she happily jumps into the cab.

"Here you go, honey," Ms. Dorothy has returned, another saran-wrapped package in her hands. "There's a regular slice and a chocolate one for you."

"Thank you." Jensen reaches for the cake and offers another small smile. "Well, I'll let you ladies get back to it. Ms. Dorothy," he gives her a little nod and then turns to me, "Callie."

A tiny shiver cascades down my spine at the sound of my name. I manage to lift a hand and give a little wave. "Jensen."

I watch as he backs the truck up and coasts down the lane toward his farmhouse. Ms. Dorothy clears her throat, drawing my attention back to her very amused face.

"What?" I ask, although from the look she's giving me, it's pretty obvious what she's implying.

"What was that you were just saying? Something about no feelings for that boy?"

"I *don't* have feelings for him."

"Mmmhmm." Ms. Dorothy purses her lips, clearly not buying it. "Girl, the only one you're fooling is yourself."

"It's . . . complicated." It's undoubtedly the lamest excuse I can possibly give, but I don't know how else to explain it.

"Matters of the heart usually are," Dorothy replies, sagely.

"Tell me about it," I sigh just as my cell phone rings. I scoop it up and see my cousin's name flash across the screen.

I swipe to answer the call. "Hey, what are you—"

Mabel's excited voice cuts me off.

"Okay, don't move," I tell her when she's finished. "I'll be right there."

—

Mabel pounces the second I cross the threshold, and I barely have time to close the bungalow's front door before she barrels into me. "Oh my God, Callie! You're never going to believe what happened."

"Well, don't keep me in suspense," I say, laughing. I have no idea what's got my cousin acting like she just won front row seats to an NSYNC reunion tour, but whatever it is, I'm here for it.

"A producer from *Good Day, Alabama* called!" The pitch of her voice gets higher with each word. "They saw my post about you and Jensen's photoshoot and they want to interview me! Can you believe it?"

"Wait, seriously?" I reach for her hands and squeeze. "Mabel, that's amazing!"

"I know, right?" she squeals, returning my squeeze with one of her own. "I've already gotten a ton of new inquiries for photoshoots, but I never imagined this kind of publicity."

"It's about time the rest of the world realized how amazing you are." I wink. "You better let the diner know you'll need less shifts in the coming weeks because I predict you'll be very busy."

Mabel's features droop a little, some of her energy waning. "You really think so?"

"I know so. It's *Good Day, Alabama*, Mabs! This is huge!"

"It is," she agrees, though her degree of excitement is still low. "But there's one more thing."

"Oh?"

"They don't just want to interview me. They want to interview you and Jensen as well."

"Oh." Definitely wasn't expecting that.

"Please say you'll do it." Mabel's concerned eyes narrow. "I'm not sure they'll want to talk to just me, and—"

"Of course, I'll do it," I break in, smiling to reassure her. "Anything for you, you know that."

Relief washes over her features, and she throws her arms around my neck. "Thank you, thank you, thank you!"

I laugh, squeezing her back. "You're welcome."

"And you'll ask Jensen, won't you? I would, but I think he'll be more inclined to say yes if you're the one who asks him."

"Um, sure." My voice is calm, but my stomach flips over. Talking to Jensen makes me all kinds of nervous—though I'm not sure whether that's a good or a bad thing. *Just listen to your head,* I remind myself. *Listen to your head and you'll be fine.*

"Thank you, Callie!" Mabel beams. "You're the best cousin ever, do you know that?"

I'm still reeling a little from her request, but I don't want to steal her sunshine, so I pivot. "You know, I think news like this calls for a little something, don't you?" I give her a pointed look.

Mabel instantly brightens. "Are you thinking what I'm thinking?"

"I don't know," I play along. "Are *you* thinking what *I'm* thinking?"

She begins to bounce up and down on her toes, her eyes bright. "We say it on the count of three." She holds up her hand and begins to count. "1 . . . 2 . . . 3!"

"Thirsty Horse!" We shout together and then immediately erupt into laughter.

"I can't think of a better way to celebrate than dollar drinks and two-stepping at our favorite dance hall," I declare, doing a little shimmy.

"Friday?" Mabel beams as she does her own silly dance move.

"Friday," I confirm. "Can't wait."

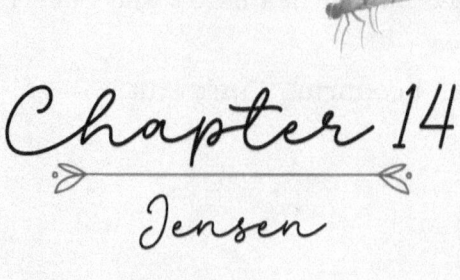

Chapter 14

Jensen

The shop is bustling with people. Even with the door to my office shut, I can still hear the clanging and banging of tools in the bays, chatter coming from the waiting room, and the music we play over the speaker in the lobby. It's not overly loud, more ambient than anything, but I crave quiet. No, I *need* quiet, and this is hardly the place for that.

Most of the time, I find the busyness of the shop soothing. It keeps my mind occupied and my hands busy, keeps me from running straight off the edge I always feel so precariously close to. But on days like today, when every sound is magnified, and when the chaotic energy of the place presses in on me, threatening to snatch the next breath from my lungs, my office offers little solace.

Squeezing my eyes shut and pinching the bridge of my nose, I let out a deep exhale, trying to force some of the pressure from the front of my skull out through my nostrils.

Maybe if I'd gotten a full night's sleep, I would be better equipped to handle today, but the usual shadows had been my unfortunate bedfellows, digging their claws into my mind and robbing me of my peace.

It wasn't my usual nightmare, either. Callie floated in and out of my subconscious, while the shadows held me in their grip, and each time I woke, gasping and clawing at my chest, it was her name on my tongue.

I let out a groan and drop my head into my hands. I just need this day to be over already. Once the last customer leaves, I plan to go home, curl up on the couch with my dog, and pretend that the rest of the world doesn't exist. It's Friday night, which means there are two whole days ahead of me where I don't have to pretend I'm holding it together.

There's a knock on the door, the sound exacerbating the throbbing in my temples.

"Come in," I groan, fully expecting it to be Frank with more supply orders. Business has been booming lately, and we've been running through our usual cache of parts and materials. "Just put them on the corner of my desk."

I wait, but when Frank doesn't respond with his usual, "Roger that, Boss Man," I look up. Callie is standing in front of my desk, holding a crystal dish that's covered in tin foil. The color of her t-shirt matches her eyes and with her long hair twisted back into a ponytail, I can see just how slender her neck is. Her strawberry-pink lips are lifted in a hesitant smile.

"Hi." She gives me a little wave. "I hope you don't mind me just stopping by like this. The guy out there in the service bay told me it was okay to knock."

I stare at her for a moment before my brain decides to supply me with a response. "No, it's fine." I tap the massive stack of papers in front of me. "I needed a break anyway. What can I help you with? Everything okay with the RV?"

"Oh yeah, everything is fine. I just wanted to stop by to bring you this." She holds out the bundle. "I was going to bring it by the farmhouse, but I used Mabel's kitchen, and the bungalow isn't far from here. It's an apple pie. I made it myself." She gently sets the pie down in front of me. "Sutton told Mabel that it was your favorite so . . . "

She trails off, nervously chewing the corner of her lip as she waits to see what my response is going to be. It's then that I realize what a jerk I've been to this woman. She's done absolutely nothing to deserve the way I've been treating her. First, it was ghosting her when she reached out after the photoshoot. Then, it was all of our awkward run-ins around town, and every moment since she became my tenant, I've acted like she was some kind of thorn in my side that needs to be removed. I owe her an apology.

"Callie," I breathe out, anger at myself swelling in my chest. "I—"

"You don't have to eat it if you don't want to," she hurries to cut me off. "It won't hurt my feelings or anything, I just wanted to do something nice, and my mama always said that the best way to show how you feel is with a pie. So," she points to the pie. "Thank you."

I pull the pie a little closer, the warmth of the glass dish seeping into my skin, and the smell? It's heavenly. "This really isn't necessary."

"Yes, it is," she insists. "I got that job at the elementary school." Her face lights up. "They called me this morning."

"That's really great, but you don't owe me thanks for that. You got that job all on your own merit."

"True, but I wouldn't have even known about the job if it weren't for you. Besides, I was thinking," she lets out a low breath, "maybe it could be a thank you pie but also a peace offering?"

There it is. The elephant in the room. And despite my horrible behavior, it's her that's brought it up. God, I really am a jerk.

I stand up and walk around my desk. "I think it's me that owes *you* a peace pie. I've been . . . Well, I haven't been the friendliest. And you didn't deserve that. I'm really sorry."

She shrugs. "It's okay."

"It's not, and I can promise you that I'm not the kind of man who takes out his baggage on other people." I give her a half smile. "Or I try not to."

It's not a great explanation, but there's no way in hell, I'm getting into all that now. It's the best I can offer her.

"You've been nothing but kind to me since the photoshoot, and I hope you can forgive me for my behavior. If you're open to it, I'd like for us to be friends."

The words spill out of me, and I ignore the pang of disappointment settling in my gut at the word. *Friend.*

Callie studies me for a moment, her brow scrunched as if she's waiting for me to change my mind. "You want to be my friend?"

"I do," I tell her as earnestly as I'm able. "Think maybe we can just start over?"

There's a pause and then her cheeks lift. "Sure. I'd like that." She holds out her hand to me. "Hi, I'm Callie."

I wrap my hand around hers, ignoring the sensation it sends shooting down my arm. "It's nice to meet you, Callie. I'm Jensen."

Her smile morphs into a full-blown grin at that, and my god it's such a lovely sight, I nearly stop breathing.

Friend, friend, friend. My brain reminds me, and even though there's a part of me that doesn't want to let her go, I drop her hand.

"Well, I won't keep you, I'm sure you've got a lot of

work to do here." Callie flips her ponytail over her shoulder and reaches for the keys she's placed on the corner of my desk. "Thanks again for giving me the heads up about the job. I owe you one."

I point to the pie. "Nah, I think we're square. Especially if it tastes as good as it smells."

That earns me another smile. "Oh, it does," Callie assures me. "I don't think you'll be disappointed."

"I'm definitely going to have to hide this from the guys." I nod toward the shop. "I'm not sure how you got it past them, but I'll be lucky to get a few crumbs if they find out I've got homemade pie in the office."

"If that happens, just let me know and I'll make you another one."

"Deal."

Callie takes a step toward the door, but then turns back, her eyebrows drawn together. "There's one more thing."

The concerned look on her face has me stepping closer. "Yeah?"

"I need to ask you something."

"Okay," I say, my spine stiffening. I don't like the unexpected. "Shoot."

"*Good Day, Alabama* wants to do a feature about the photoshoot. You know, since the pictures went viral and all. They want to interview us."

She catches me by surprise that's for sure, and when I don't immediately respond, the V between her brows deepens. "If you don't want to, I totally understand, but it would really mean a lot to Mabel if you said yes. It would really mean a lot to me, too."

A live televised interview? Definitely not my kind of thing, but the look on Callie's face hits me square in the chest. Besides, given my behavior, it's the least I can do. "I'll be there."

"Really? You don't mind?"

"I don't mind," I say, offering a smile.

Callie reacts by throwing her arms around me, tugging me into a hug. "Thank you, Jensen. You have no idea how much I appreciate this."

Her body is warm against mine, but the shock of having her this close renders me frozen. She leaps back a second later, her cheeks bright pink. "Sorry, I—" She clears her throat, clearly embarrassed. "Okay, well, I better get going. I promised Mabel I'd come over early so we could get ready together. We're headed out to the dance hall tonight to celebrate the news. But, um, enjoy the pie!"

She gives me a little wave and dashes out of my office before my brain has a chance to catch up, but once it does, I sink back down in my chair, my eyes landing on the warm apple pie sitting atop my stack of papers.

I should have hugged her back, and the disappointment and frustration spiraling in my gut agree with me. I run a hand down my face and let out a breath. *Friends*, I remind myself. That's all. *Just friends.*

My stomach flips over as the door to my office flies open and Frank pops across the threshold like a damn jack-in-the-box. "Do I smell pie?"

—

"Well," I look over at Peaches who is curled up on her dog bed by the fireplace. "She definitely wasn't wrong."

I scrape the remaining tidbits of pie off my plate and lick the fork. I'd managed to bring at least a quarter of Callie's pie home after splitting it with the guys, and after scarfing my dinner, I'd plopped down in my chair with a slice as my reward after a very long day.

Things had gotten better after Callie's visit, though I didn't want to think too hard as to why. So instead, I'd busied myself at work, keeping my mind occupied so it couldn't ask any questions.

Now that I'm home, there are fewer distractions and already thoughts are forming in my brain, what-ifs that I don't want to even consider.

"Nope," I mutter under my breath as I walk to the sink to put away my dishes. "Don't even go there."

Yet, that doesn't stop me from scooping up my phone from the counter and pulling up the photos I shouldn't have saved but did. I slowly swipe through, taking in every detail. Sure, the photos are lovely and Mabel's talent behind the camera is clear, but I'm more drawn to the shape of Callie's mouth and the way her hair shines in the golden sunlight. She's stunning in these photos which only makes my brain conjure up images of her in real life. I think of today, of how beautiful she looked, standing there in front of my desk, and my pulse quickens.

And now you're friends, my brain reminds me—to which my heart gives a pathetic little flop. *It's for the best,* that same voice reasons, and I don't bother arguing. Because it *is* for the best. Although, that doesn't stop me from wanting to be around her.

Even if I can never act on it, being around Callie makes me feel . . . lighter. Even now, with the shadows lingering, waiting to pounce, I crave that feeling.

There's just something about her, something about the way she makes me feel. It's a mercurial high that I know is only going to wreck me in the end, but maybe just maybe if I can keep it together and keep things in perspective—*Just friends, Shepherd. Just friends*—then maybe it's okay to take another hit. Right?

Callie's words from earlier come back to me then: *I promised Mabel I'd come over early so we could get ready together. We're headed out to the dance hall tonight to celebrate.*

The mental image of her at the dance hall, dancing with other men has me squirming in my seat. I don't like it at all. Yet, it's not my place to feel this way. I shouldn't care who she dances with. It shouldn't matter to me.

But dammit, it does.

Just friends or not, it matters.

I don't give myself time to dwell. I tap the screen, dialing Sutton's number. "Hey, you busy tonight?" I say in the way of a greeting when she answers.

"Not really. Ethan is at a sleepover down the street, so I was thinking of drinking an entire bottle of wine and watching reruns of *The Office.*"

I'm already pulling on my boots. "Well, don't pop that cork just yet. Get ready, we're going out tonight. Pick you up in fifteen."

Chapter 15
Callie

"Over here!" I call out, waving to Mabel, who's weaving her way through the mass of people crowding the Thirsty Horse Saloon. Friday nights are usually pretty busy, but once a month they do dollar drafts, so it's even more packed than usual tonight and nearly impossible to find a table.

Thanks to my excellent powers of persistence, I've managed to snag the last remaining high top in the place, while Mabel worked her magic at the bar. She expertly dodges a pair of drunken frat boys and a bachelorette party all in matching glittery tank tops and sets our drinks on the tabletop. "Whew," she says, pretending to swipe at her brow. "I thought they might have to revoke my waitressing card tonight. These drinks almost didn't make it."

I laugh, reaching for mine. "Well, it's a good thing you're a badass photographer then." I lift my cup. Already, my toe is tapping to the beat, my body thrumming with energy. "To my incredible cousin and her amazing talent."

Mabel taps her drink against mine. "I'll drink to that." She takes a big swig. "This place is wild tonight."

"Yeah, but that's why we love it." The Thirsty Horse isn't a fancy establishment. The pine floors are scuffed and stained, and the walls are covered with neon signs and old posters from performances over the years. Knox Wilder & The Reckless flyers from the live show a few months back are the current wallpaper. None of the tables or the chairs match, and the bathrooms are always questionable at best. But this is our spot and has been ever since we were old enough to walk through the doors.

Every big moment in our lives has been celebrated here, and we've never cared that it's a dive. Good beer, even better music, and cute guys looking to dance. It's the perfect place to celebrate Mabel's success and my new job.

It's been a long time since I was here. Too long actually, and I can feel my smile drooping when the last time pops up in my memory. It was a few years back, and Adam begrudgingly came to Dayton Springs with me for a visit. I'd brought him here wanting to show him a good time, give him the opportunity to loosen up and have a bit of fun. I'd wanted him to see a side of me I hadn't yet had the opportunity to share with him yet, but the entire time, all he'd done was complain. The beer was too flat, the floors were too sticky, and there were way too many people crowding the dance floor. We'd spent the entire night bickering, and I hadn't been back since.

"Hey," Mabel's voice calls me back to the present. "You okay?"

I nod. "Yeah, I'm good. I was just thinking about the last time we were here."

Mabel's face immediately turns into a scowl. "I swear if I ever see Adam the A-hole again, he's getting a junk punch from me."

Laughter bubbles in my throat. "I would actually pay good money to see that."

"I may be small, but I'm scrappy." Mabel straightens her shoulders trying to look taller than her barely 5'1 frame, which only makes me laugh more.

"Very true."

Beside us on the table, Mabel's phone lights up.

"It's been over two weeks now, and my notifications are still going crazy," she says, flipping the phone around so I can see. Her post about the photoshoot keeps gaining traction—which is probably how the news station caught wind of it.

"You know, everyone in the comments keeps asking for an update. They want to know if anything happened between you and Jensen." She gives me a coy look, but

I know her well enough to know that she's fishing, and not just for social media purposes. My amazing but nosy cousin wants the deets.

"You already know the answer to that."

"So, he's still being all prickly porcupine, huh?"

"Not quite. I mean, he's been better lately. When I brought him that pie today, he was actually nice. He told me he wanted to be friends."

Mabel holds up both hands, her eyebrows lifted. "Wait, you didn't tell me the pie you made today was for Jensen."

"You didn't ask." I roll my eyes at the look on her face. "But, yeah, as a thank you. I wouldn't have gotten the job if he hadn't told me about it in the first place."

"A simple 'thank you' wouldn't have sufficed?"

"I don't know, I just wanted to do something nice. He's letting me live in his RV, he helped me get a job." I shrug. "I just figured I owed him a small gesture of my appreciation."

"And that's it? Just your appreciation?"

"That's it."

"You sure about that?" Mabel taps at her phone screen, does a few quick swipes, and then flips the phone back around. "Are you seriously going to look at this photo and tell me that you're not attracted to this man."

I let out a sigh. "You know I am but we're just going to be friends. It's better that way. After Adam, I think I could use a break, don't you? I'm done with love."

Mabel considers this. "Being with the wrong person doesn't mean you should stop looking for the right one, Cal."

"I know, but I want to make sure that I don't find my-self in that same position again. The last thing I need right now is any kind of complication, and honestly, I'm not convinced relationships are even worth it at this point." *Even if every time I look at him, the magnetic pull I feel is so strong it steals the breath right out of my lungs.*

"All I'm saying is that whatever this is," Mabel points to the screen, "it's not something you usually see be-tween two people who are just friends. And the entire internet agrees with me. In fact, they're already asking for another photoshoot with you two."

"Well, the internet is just going to have to slow its roll. Jensen and I are friends. And that's that."

Thankfully, I'm saved from Mabel's rebuttal when a guy in a white cowboy hat and equally white smile strolls up to our table. "Hey there, ladies. Either of you interested in a dance?"

I seize the opportunity. "That would be great. Be back in a sec, Mabs!" We have an unspoken rule to only dance one at a time so that a) we can keep our table, and b) that someone is there to watch our drinks. Small town or no, you can never be too careful.

I let the stranger lead me out onto the dance floor. He tells me his name is Dan as the opening strains of a new song begin, and then there's no time left for con-versation because we're too busy spinning around the floor. There's just something about two-steppin' across a wooden floor, the clack and stomp of cowboy boots, the twirl of my hair as my partner spins me out of his arms and then back in. Dan's pretty good as far as dance partners go, very respectful and fun, and he makes me laugh which is an added bonus. When the song ends, I thank him for the dance and return to my table, out of breath.

"Your turn," I tell Mabel, noticing that a tall stranger with dark hair is already making his way over to us. Once they're on the dance floor, I sink down into my chair and take a sip of my drink. My skin is flushed, but I don't mind. This place makes me feel free, and it doesn't matter if I'm a little sweaty or my hair is flat. All that matters is the beat of the music and the way I feel when I'm dancing.

I smile, watching as Mabel and her partner complete a series of complicated twists and turns. It's always nice when the good dancers show up to the bar, though I've never minded showing a newbie a step or two.

Mabel returns, cheeks pink and laughing, and for the next hour or so, we do our usual rotation of holding on to our table while taking turns with various part-ners. I dance with Dan a few more times and with Steve, the dark haired guy Mabel danced with first. I've also danced with Gregory, the nearly seventy-year-old cowboy whose wife recently passed away. He's, by far, my favorite partner.

But even with all the fun I'm having, my mind keeps wandering to a certain blue-eyed, grumpy mechanic.

"What's that look about?" Mabel asks, refilling her cup from the water pitcher we requested from the bar. "Your face is all weird."

"Nothing," I tell her, trying to play it off, but when she gives me that "are you seriously going to lie to me, I've known you your whole life" look, I sigh and admit the truth. "I was thinking about Jensen."

"Oh, you were, huh?" Mabel smirks.

"Stop." I shove her shoulder, though I'm laughing when I do it. "It's not like that."

"Then what's it like?"

I shake my head because I don't have an answer. I know it's better for me to keep my distance, to just keep things friendly, but even when I try, I can't stop him from invading my thoughts. I find myself thinking about him and wondering what he's doing, and even though I'm having an absolute blast with my cousin in one of my favorite places in the world, I can't help but wish he was here.

Mabel starts to say something, probably to completely call me out, but a tall, sandy-haired man saunters over, reeking of whiskey. "Hey there, ladies," he slurs, his eyes glassy. "One of you pretty ladies want to take a spin on the floor with me?"

Mabel and I share a look. While we love dancing, we make a serious effort not to do so with sleazy or drunken partners. "No thanks, we're taking a break right now," Mabel tells him.

"Come on, don't be like that." The man leans closer, his breath hot on my face. "I just want one little dance."

My heartbeat spikes at his words. There's an undercurrent in his tone, and although he's smiling now, I have a feeling if we continue to brush him off, he won't be as friendly, especially given how much he's had to drink.

I know there are people in the bar that will back us up if this guy starts making a scene, but the last thing I want is something like that ruining our night. Besides, I figure after he gets the attention he's after, he'll slink back off to the bar and leave us be. One dance I can handle. "Okay," I tell him, "Just one."

Mabel grabs my forearm. "Are you sure?"

"It's fine," I assure her. "I'll be right back."

The drunk guy smirks as he leads me away from our table. "I don't think your friend back there likes me."

I don't bother responding, instead I focus on the beat of the music. The drunk's hands are sweaty when he reaches for mine, and I can't help but grimace as he grips my fingers. He's a little uneasy on his feet and his movements are sloppy at best, but it's not the worst dance I've ever had.

Thankfully, after a few laps around the dance floor,

the song ends. I step back, putting some space between us. "Thanks for the dance," I tell him, eager to return to my table.

"Now wait a second," he calls after me. "Where you going?"

I don't bother stopping to respond, and he grabs my bicep, jerking me back a step.

"I'm going back to my friend," I tell the guy. "Our dance is over."

"Well, I think I'd like another one." His fingers dig into my skin. "Come on, girly, you know you want to dance with me again."

"I don't think so."

"Now come on, don't be like that."

My heartbeat races as I think about my options. So much for trying to avoid a scene. I should've known better than to engage with this creep in the first place, but usually the drunk ones slither off after they get their dance. I assumed this guy would be the same.

Clearly not.

"Thank you for the dance," I try again, all the politeness gone from my voice. "I'm going to go back to my table now." I rip my arm out of the guy's grasp.

His face instantly changes. "Listen here, I said I wanted another dance and you're not going anywhere."

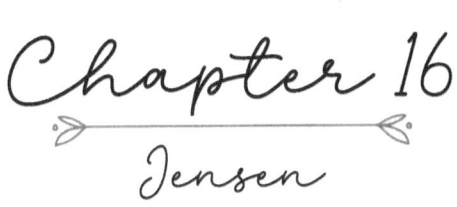

Chapter 16
Jensen

The dimly lit dance hall is packed with people, and as Sutton and I move through the crowd, tension tightens my shoulders. "Maybe this was a bad idea," I grumble, dodging a waitress carrying a tray full of Jell-O shots.

Sutton smacks me in the stomach with the back of her hand. "You're only saying that because big groups of people make you cranky."

She's not wrong. Crowds have never been my thing, and the chaotic energy in here isn't helping my nerves.

"Besides, once you find Callie you'll feel a lot better, I'm sure," Sutton teases, yanking on my arm and leading me through the sea of bodies.

A groan rumbles in my chest, but I let her pull me along. When I'd fessed up in the car about my reason for wanting to come here tonight, Sutton had been ecstatic and declared herself my official wing woman. A job she was clearly taking very seriously.

"Look!" she shouts above the music a few minutes later, pointing at one of the high tops in the corner.

Mabel's short stature is easily recognizable, even in the low lighting, but there's definitely something off about her expression. Sutton must see it too, her eyebrows scrunching before she makes a beeline for the table.

When Mabel spots us, her face lifts, not in surprise at seeing us here, but in relief. "Sutton! Jensen!" She waves us closer.

Sutton hurries to her side. "Hey, you okay?"

"Yeah, I'm fine, but I'm worried about Callie."

The single sentence triggers something inside me, putting every instinct I have on high alert. "Where is she? What's wrong?"

"This guy came up to us and asked for a dance. He was clearly drunk, and we tried to brush him off, but he was pretty insistent." Mabel leans around me and points in the direction of the dance floor. "Callie's out there with him now, and I don't know, there was just something about him that rubbed me the wrong way."

I'm already walking toward the dance floor, my eyes scanning the couples moving in time with the music. At first, I don't see her, but as I move closer, I spot her.

A golden spotlight overhead illuminates her beautiful face. It's a relief to see her, but her lips are pressed into a line and she looks like she's counting the seconds until the song ends. Thankfully it does, right as my boots hit the polished hardwood floor.

I keep my eyes on her as I maneuver around the couples exiting the floor, and that's when I see the guy she was dancing with grab her by the arm and yank her closer.

Seeing his hands on her ignites a fire inside of me, and I rush over to Callie, my blood roaring in my veins. I reach her right as the guy growls in her face, "You're not going anywhere."

It takes every ounce of strength I have not to rip his arm from his body, but I try to stay calm.

"Actually, she is." The words come out low and gravelly, but loud enough that the lowlife's eyes snap to mine. They're bloodshot and glassy, but they must see clearly enough because they widen for half a second and then he releases his grip on her.

Callie looks up at me, but I keep my eyes on him, making sure that my expression clearly communicates what will happen if he doesn't walk away.

"Sorry," the drunk guy mutters, stumbling back a step or two. "I didn't know she belonged to anyone."

I bristle at his choice of words, which only make me want to punch him even more, but I just give him a terse nod. "Well, she does."

The words come out like a warning, meant to keep this loser from getting any more ideas. Still, I can't deny the way they make me feel. There's a deep undercurrent of satisfaction that runs hot underneath my anger, a tiny thrill over that claim.

I run a hand down Callie's arm, and she steps close enough that my chest brushes against her back. She melts into me, and I move my hand to her waist to support her.

The drunk guy's nostrils flare, but he's at least smart enough not to push things further. He brushes past me, knocking into my shoulder as he staggers back to the bar, muttering under his breath.

I wait until I'm sure he's not coming back and then I gently turn Callie in my arms, needing to see her face. "Are you okay?"

Callie nods, though her eyes fill with tears. "I'm fine."

The sight of those tears nearly cracks my chest wide open, and the need to touch her, to somehow make her feel better and safe again wipes everything else from my brain. I reach for her, cupping her head and tilting it back gently so I can see her better. I can't stop my thumbs from swiping across her smooth cheekbones. "Hey, it's okay. He won't bother you again."

"Thanks," she says, pulling away so that she can swipe at her nose. "I'm fine, really. It's just that my waterworks have always been linked to my emotions. When I get mad, well, I cry. The fact that he had the audacity to put his hands on me like that makes me want to punch him the face."

I admit I'm having the exact same thought, especially since he made her cry. The sight of Callie crying makes me want to burn the entire world to the ground. I throw a hand over my shoulder. "It's not too late, we can track him down. I'll hold, you punch."

"That's okay," she says with a laugh, as a new song begins to play over the loud speaker. "This is too good a song to waste on a guy like that."

Hearing her laugh eases some of the adrenaline still coursing through me, though the instinct to wrap my arms around her and pull her close is as strong as ever. I don't want to think about what it means, don't want to answer the question I've been asking myself since I decided to come here tonight. All I want is to be near her, to hold her.

So, when the overhead lights dim to match the slower pace of the song, I take a deep breath and say, "Well then, how about we dance instead?"

Chapter 17
Callie

Jensen holds out his hand, those stormy eyes churning with intensity. The look he's giving me is one that makes it very hard to breathe.

My head is swimming and the urge to cry again swells up in my chest. I can't tell if it's still anger at that jerk for putting his hands on me or the fact that Jensen is standing in front of me. Either way, it's overwhelming.

It's all I can do to nod, to let the smooth, sweet strains of the music make my decision for me.

Just friends, I remind myself, but when I put my hand in his, every cell in my body ignites. Electricity zips through me when he wraps the other arm around my waist, pulling me close as he leads me to the center of the dance floor, where couples are already swaying and spinning in time with the music.

With his hand pressed into the small of my back and his other clasped warmly around mine, Jensen guides us through the steps, moving expertly to the music. I'm already near breathless, but this realization that Jensen Shepherd can dance robs me of the last bit of oxygen in my lungs.

"Are you sure you're okay?" Jensen dips his head, so I can hear his low murmuring voice over the music.

I suck in a ragged breath and nod. The words I want to say sit heavy on my tongue. *I'm even better now that you're here.* Instead, I stick to something safer. "You know, I never would've taken you for the two-steppin' type."

Jensen's eyebrows lift. "No?"

"I figured you were more the 'sit at a table and brood with a beer' type."

A deep laugh rumbles in his chest. "I do enjoy the occasional brood and beer, but right now, I'm exactly where I want to be."

Heat rushes into my cheeks at his words, but I don't know if he means here with me or just here on the dance floor. *It's probably the latter,* the voice of reason whispers in my ear. A sinking feeling makes my stomach flip over.

This is what you want, I remind myself. *No complications.* The words only make the churning in my stomach worse. As much as I've been avoiding it, I can't ignore how this man makes me feel. I'm undeniably attracted to him, and I have been from the moment the blindfold came off at the photoshoot.

And I don't want to be friends with him. Or at least not *just*.

The realization has me tripping over my own feet.

Jensen tightens his grip, keeping me from smacking the shiny floor.

"Sorry," I mutter, embarrassment and frustration swirling in my chest.

"I won't let you fall." The certainty in his tone, the sweet reassuring way he's holding me only makes the tightness in my chest worse. If he keeps touching me like this, I'm going to completely lose any sense of self composure I have. I tear my eyes away from his and glance down at the floor, staring at my boots as a means of distraction.

My heart pounds as I focus on the pattern of our steps, anything to keep my mind off how much I like the feel of his hands on my skin and how I desperately want him to pull me even closer. Instead, my brain chooses this exact moment to supply me with the memory of our kiss from the photoshoot. Only it doesn't feel like a memory. Sweet Magnolias, I can practically taste him on my tongue, can feel the desperate press of his fingers into my skin as he held me, the warmth of our bodies pressed together.

"Stop it," I growl, furious at my own consciousness for being so cruel.

Jensen stops abruptly, halting our slow circle around the dance floor, and I realize, to my absolute horror, that I've said the words out loud.

"Callie?" His face is lined with concern.

"I didn't mean you," I blurt out. "I just meant . . . " I have no idea how to explain. "I just . . . " My eyes drop back to my boots, and I step out of the circle of his arms. "Sorry, I wasn't meaning you." I'm two seconds away from bolting when Jensen reaches out a hand and gently lifts my chin with a finger.

"Callie." There's no question in the word this time, and a warm shiver skips down my back. God, I will never get tired of listening to this man say my name.

"Jensen."

He studies me for a moment before the corner of his mouth lifts in a half smile that makes my knees wobble. And when he opens his arms, I don't hesitate to step into them.

He pulls me close, much closer than before, and any lingering bits of embarrassment melt from the radiating warmth of his skin. With one hand pressed into the small of my back and the other holding our entwined fingers against his chest, Jensen moves with the slow, sweet refrain of the music.

My blood sings in my veins as we glide across the smooth polished floor, in and around the other couples.

Quick, quick, slow, slow. Quick, quick, slow, slow.

Jensen finishes the sequence by sliding his hand to

my shoulder blade and pushing me gently under his other arm, spinning me. The move is effortless, and my cheeks lift, the colors of the dance hall melting into a glowing kaleidoscope as I spin.

Jensen must see my smile because he immediately spins me again, this one more complicated than the last which only delights me more. Then it's just me and him, twirling and spinning beneath the lights, our bodies moving in perfect rhythm, as the music swells. He dips me low, swinging me back up against his chest, and I feel the steady thrum of his heartbeat beneath my palm.

Face to face now, Jensen's thumbs move back and forth across my back in a sweet caress that makes my entire body flush. When he dips his head, his lips just skim the shell of my ear as he hums along to the music, holding me tightly against him.

The nearness of him is intoxicating and my chin lifts, my own mouth ghosting across the smooth skin just beneath his jaw.

Jensen lets out a low moan, pulling back just a little so he can look at me, his eyes wild with what I can only describe as the exact same thing that's pinballing back and forth in my chest.

There's a single moment that hangs between us, as if time itself has slowed just enough for us to decide, for us to make this choice.

No complications, the voice in my head whispers

weakly.

But my heart, my wild chaotic heart, is saying something else entirely.

We move toward one another, slowly, achingly slow, until there's no more space left between us.

Jensen's lips brush mine in a sweet, soft touch that feels like both a promise and a question. The feather-light touch makes my knees feel like they're going to give out on me, and I wobble in his arms.

He tightens his hold on me, as I push upward on my tiptoes, my lips finding his in a tender graze of their own. A reply, a confirmation that I want this to happen, that I want him to kiss me.

He smiles then, only a small, slight curving of his mouth, and there's nothing but sublime silence in my head as I wait for him to fully claim my lips with his.

But in half a heartbeat, the darkness wrapped around us shifts as colorful bright lights illuminate over our heads. We pull back, blinking and confused, only to realize the song has ended. Couples exit the dance floor as new ones hurry onto the floor, already moving to the faster, more upbeat tune.

Jensen steps backward, putting space between us, though he doesn't let go of my hand. "Um, should we . . . " he trails off, throwing a thumb over his shoulder to indicate the table.

Disappointment swims through me, but I manage a smile and nod.

He leads me through the crowd, his hand still tightly wrapped around mine, and it's the lifeline I need. Now, that the moment has passed, I'm not sure what to make of what just happened out there. Already I feel the claws of insecurity threatening to sink into me, but Jensen doesn't let go of my hand, and I don't want him to.

Mabel waits by our table, and I'm not surprised at all to see Sutton standing next to her. It isn't hard to read the expressions on their faces, having witnessed what just passed between Jensen and me on the dance floor, but thankfully, no one comments on it.

"Your turn," I say as cheerfully as I can to my cousin while giving Sutton a little wave. I gesture to the dance floor. "It's getting a little crowded out there though."

"That's okay," Mabel replies, swirling her straw around in her cup. "I'm in need of a refill, so I think I'll sit this one out. You can go again if you want." She looks from me to Jensen, her expression a little less subtle this time, and I roll my eyes.

Jensen hasn't said a word. His stiff shoulders match the stern set of his jaw. I have no idea what he's thinking but he still hasn't dropped my hand, and for the life of me, all I want is to rewind the clock, to go back to those few seconds before the song ended.

Heat rushes up the back of my neck travelling into my cheeks, and I fan them with my free hand. The dance hall suddenly feels way too small. "Actually, I was thinking of getting some fresh air. It's a little warm in here."

Jensen turns to me, his eyes burning with the same wildfire I observed on the dance floor. "Want some company?"

My answer is immediate. "That'd be nice."

I see it then, that same small curve of his mouth, the tiniest smile that turns my insides into mush.

"If you're ready, I could give you a lift home, if you want."

"Okay," I tell him and then look to Mabel, who I realize I'm totally abandoning if I leave here with him.

"Oh that's a great idea," Mabel quips, giving me a bright smile and pointed look that clearly says, *I'll be totally fine! You should go.* "Sutton and I were just talking about getting another round. I can give her a ride home."

"Yeah," Sutton pipes up, her smile that of a co-conspirator. She gives Jensen the same look Mabel gave me. "You two go on ahead."

I reluctantly pull my hand from Jensen's to hug my cousin. "You sure?" I whisper in her ear.

"Yes, go!" She hisses, giving me an extra squeeze.

Jensen hugs Sutton and gives Mabel a little nod before turning back to me.

"Ready?" he asks, and I nod.

The Thirsty Horse has gotten significantly more crowded, and while Jensen doesn't take my hand again, he stays close as we weave our way through the crowd, his palm pressed against my lower back as we walk. It's a small thing, but it feels bigger somehow.

Outside the dance hall, the night air is cool against my flushed skin, and I let out a little sigh as we walk toward Jensen's truck. We aren't saying anything, but the air between us is charged, crackling with the same electric energy I know we both felt out on the dance floor.

Jensen pulls the keys from his pocket and opens the passenger door for me. Once I'm safe and secure inside, he walks around and gets behind the wheel, turning the keys to make the truck roar to life.

We pull out of the parking lot and onto the main road while I try for the life of me to think of something to say. Now that we're no longer touching, the silence of the cab is nearly as loud as the question zipping through my mind. *What now?*

I sneak a peek at Jensen. He keeps his eyes on the road, but there's a furrow in his brow as if he's thinking hard about something. I can't help but wonder if he's asking himself the same question.

What now?

What now?

What now?

My knee bounces up and down as heat prickles along my skin. In the cab, the scent of him—clean and with a hint of something citrusy—floods my senses, dizzying and addictive. There's only a few feet between us, and it feels like there's a crackling current pulling me toward Jensen, daring me to close the gap.

My mind spirals in all directions, replaying the sound of his low, husky voice in my ear—*I've got you*—the fierce almost possessive glare he'd given the drunk guy, and the way his blue eyes turned to liquid fire as we danced, burning underneath the lights as his fingers tugged at my waist, pulling me closer. And oh sweet magnolias, the brush of his lips against mine and the way he—

Jensen yanks the wheel, snapping me back to reality as he pulls the truck over and onto the shoulder of the road. He's gripping the wheel so tightly, his knuckles are white.

"Is everything okay?" I ask, looking behind us to see if there was some hazard in the road I missed.

"Yeah." Jensen eyes find mine in the darkness. "There's just something I need to do before I take you home."

My brain barely has time to process the words before he leans into me, his fingers spearing through my hair as he pulls me to him, his lips capturing mine.

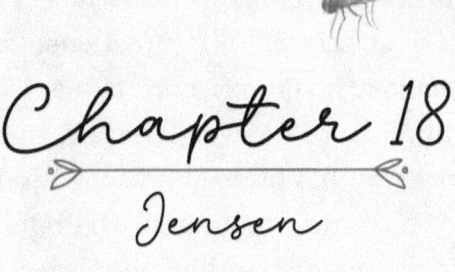

Chapter 18

Jensen

No matter how hard I gripped the steering wheel, I couldn't fight the overwhelming desire to be closer to Callie, to touch her again. I'd thrown the truck in park and reached for her, desperate to feel again what I felt out on the dance floor.

Kissing her now feels like I've been thirsty my whole life and finally, *finally* I've found a source of water. Cradling the back of her head with my hands, I slant my mouth over hers, claiming it without hesitation. Callie's lips match the near wild rhythm of mine, and her fingertips dig into my biceps as she clings to me.

Perfume, light and floral, floods my nostrils, and I can't stop the sound that rumbles in my throat. The smell of her combined with the taste of her kiss and the feel of her soft skin underneath my hands—it's almost too much, this feeling of needing someone, needing *her.*

Callie's mouth opens and I sweep my tongue inside, deepening our kiss. It's everything I've been desperate for these past few weeks despite trying to fight it and everything I know I shouldn't want but do.

Heat surges through my entire body. The shadows that keep me numb are as cold as the darkness that creeps in from my nightmares, but with Callie in my arms, I feel so blissfully *warm.*

I never want it to end, but when a semi-truck flies by, the sound shakes the cab of the truck and startles us apart. We jump back, both wide-eyed and breathless. Callie's rosy pink lips are slightly swollen and her hair is mussed, but her eyes are bright. She's never looked more amazing than she does right now.

"You're beautiful." The words come out as a whisper, surprising us both.

"Thank you." She brushes a few loose strands of hair out of her face, tucking them behind her ear like she needs something to do with her hands.

"You're welcome."

Silence—just a few seconds too long—fills the cab. It's the kind of silence that you want to break but don't know how.

My mind spins in a dozen directions as I watch Callie settle back into her seat, annoyance flaring up in my chest. There's entirely too much distance between us now thanks to the spacious cab. I could push the center console up and have her ride in the middle seat right next to me, but I'm not brave enough to ask. So, I focus on easing the truck back on the road, keeping my eyes trained on the white lines.

I didn't plan for this to happen when I decided to show up at the dance hall. I mean, I was definitely motivated by the thought of other men being on the receiving end of one of her smiles, but I didn't expect to leave with her. I certainly didn't expect to kiss her like that.

Back at the Thirsty Horse, holding Callie, laughing with her, and spinning her around to the music had felt like the most natural thing in the world. Kissing her just now felt like coming home—and I have no idea what to do with that.

I'd meant what I said back at the auto shop. I want us to start over, to be friends. But how in the world am I going to be just friends with this woman when being near her, when kissing her makes me come alive?

Maybe you should stop being a chicken shit and just go for it. It's Kase's easy drawl that I hear, the memory of his infamous smirk that comes to mind. I almost roll my eyes, but then a pang of sadness catches me in the chest. Because it's not really Kasey's voice, and he's not here to give me advice, much as I might need it.

"Hey, Jensen? Can I ask you a question?" There's a catch in Callie's voice that pulls me from my thoughts.

We're almost home now, so I nod as I turn down the

dirt road that leads to the farmhouse. "Of course."

I wait for her to ask whatever is on her mind, but there's only silence in the cab. When I look over, she's chewing on the corner of her lip, her brows drawn tight, and she's got a small piece of thread that she keeps twisting and untwisting around her finger. She looks as unsettled as I feel.

"Callie?" I gently prompt as we pass the farmhouse and head down the lane that leads to the RVs. She doesn't answer, and once I've parked the truck in front of the Airstream, I turn off the ignition and face her, giving her my full attention.

She lets out a sigh. "You don't have to answer if you don't want to."

"Whatever it is, just ask."

"How come you came to the dance hall tonight?" The words tumble out of her mouth in a rush. "I mean, don't get me wrong, I'm glad that you did. I'm just a little con-fused." She pauses, swallowing before lifting her chin. "I know we said earlier that we were going to be friends, but what happened back there doesn't feel like friend-ship. I don't know, maybe it's just me but—"

"It's not," I assure her, needing her to understand even though I'm not sure how to put it into words. "It's not just you." I let out a low breath. "I probably shouldn't have, but I came to the dance hall tonight because I knew you were going to be there. I was sitting at home thinking about you, and before I knew it, I was putting my shoes on and getting in the truck."

Callie studies me, her eyes searching mine. "But what does that mean?"

I rub at the back of my neck as I look away for a second and then back at her. She deserves the truth, even if it guts me to say it.

"It means that I want you," I admit, voice low. "More than I should. But I can't—" I shake my head, the words catching. "I can't let this be any more than that."

Part of me wants to stop there, but I know I have to tell her the whole story. "And you deserve to know why." I take another deep breath and let it out slowly. "Four years ago, my life as I knew it ended."

"Kasey?" Her voice is gentle, almost hesitant, like she's worried she'll hurt me by bringing him up.

I nod. "That's part of it, of course. Losing my best friend was . . . *is* . . . one of the hardest things I've ever gone through, but it's more than just that." I take another deep breath, already feeling the familiar ache in my chest begin to grow, sprouting claws. "Four years ago, just a few weeks after Kasey died, my wife left me."

Callie stills beside me, and I hear her sharp intake of breath.

"Her name is Anna, and I foolishly believed we'd be together forever. But loving her like I did wasn't enough to make her happy, to make her stay. When she left, it felt like a bomb had exploded in my life, shattering my entire world into pieces. It's taken me a very long time to put things back together again, and if I'm being honest, even now, there are still pieces missing."

It's not the whole story, but it's more than I've admitted to anyone in a long time, and I begin to tremble, my body reacting viscerally to the words. I've spent so long trying to cleanse the poison of that pain, but there are still times when I feel my systems shutting down, when my body can't fight the poison, when it threatens to choke the life right out of me.

Callie reaches for my hand, her fingers tightening around mine. "Oh God, Jensen. I can't even imagine. I'm so sorry."

"Thank you." I give her hand a squeeze. "It is what it is, I guess. The point I'm trying to make is that I'm not whole, Callie. I don't know if I ever will be again. But from the moment I met you on the day of the photoshoot, I haven't been able to stop thinking about you. I've tried to keep my distance, tried to convince myself that whatever it was I felt around you would pass, but it never did. Which frustrated me to no end." I give her a pointed look. "I'm truly sorry again for my behavior these last few weeks. It wasn't anything you did. I just didn't understand why I couldn't get you out of my head."

"You already apologized for that."

"I know, but I *am* sorry. I think you're an amazing woman. All I've wanted since we met is to be near you, but I'm not in a position to be close to anyone—I don't even know if I can. All I know is that when I was sitting at home tonight, imagining you out there on the dance floor, I realized the only man's hands I wanted on you were mine. So, I got in my truck."

I sink back against the seat, my eyes on Callie as she processes everything that I've thrown at her. I can see understanding on her face, but there's something else too, something I don't know how to decipher.

"I get it," she says, her voice steady. "I can't stop thinking about you either. I wanted to believe that it was a fluke, some weird side effect of the photoshoot or something, but I feel a connection to you that I haven't felt in a long time, maybe ever. But . . . " she trails off, straightening her shoulders. "I don't need complications in my life right now. Not after Adam."

"So, we're on the same page then?"

"Yeah, I guess so, but what exactly does that mean? We just go on pretending that we aren't attracted to each other?"

My pulse spikes at the admission that she's as drawn to me as I am to her, but I keep my face neutral. "No, I don't think we have to take it that far, we just keep it casual." The words come out sounding steady and confident, like I've got this whole thing figured out, but there's a part of me that recoils at the word. *Casual.* How is that even possible when just a smile from this woman completely unravels me? *This is the way it has to be,* I tell myself, ignoring the sharp twist of my stomach.

Kasey snorts in my head. *You sure about that, Shep?* I ignore him.

"Casual," Callie repeats, more to herself than to me. "I think I can do casual. Just two friends who enjoy each other's company. Easy and uncomplicated."

"Exactly." I should be relieved that we've laid it out on the table, but I feel far from settled. *This is the way it has to be,* I repeat.

Callie opens her mouth to say something, but then shuts it quickly, offering me a smile as she reaches for the door handle. "Well, I think I'm going to head inside. Thanks for bringing me home."

"Anytime," I tell her, though there are a dozen other things I want to say on the tip of my tongue.

I watch her walk to the door of the RV, the golden light from the porch catching in her hair for a moment before she gives me a small wave and disappears inside.

I don't drive away immediately. I just sit there, my hands on the steering wheel, eyes glued to the front door, like I expect it to open again. It doesn't.

Which is probably a good thing because I don't know what I'd do if it did.

"Just friends," I murmur, as I crank the truck and point it toward home. "We just keep it casual."

You know this is a bad idea, right? Kasey's voice is loud enough that I wince.

I don't answer him.

Chapter 19
Callie

The Clayton County flea market isn't much to look at on weekdays, but on the first and the third Saturday of the month, the old livestock grounds come alive. Vendors from all over Alabama transform the open-air barns and feed houses into a bustling marketplace.

Rows of tables and booths line the walkways, each covered with everything from locally sourced honey and soy candles to vintage road signs, antique picture frames, mason jars full of jams and jellies, and rusted farm tools that tell the stories of another life. There's even a table full of decades old McDonald's happy meal toys still in their original packaging for sale.

I chuckle as a little boy with blue-stained teeth and a snow cone nearly as big as he is skips past me, his mother chasing after him. Next to me, two older women are haggling with a vendor over the price of a handmade porcelain pig wearing a chef's hat, and an older gentleman in a faded and worn *Crimson Tide* hat calls out greetings in a booming voice.

"Mornin' to you! Y'all looking for something special today?"

Nineties country music crackles over a loudspeaker and the sweet scent of kettle corn drifts by on a breeze, mingling with the curling smoke plumes from the BBQ pits near the back.

I walk slowly, appreciating the cozy chaos. The flea market is one of my favorite spots in all of Dayton Springs.

It's also the perfect distraction from my thoughts of Jensen.

It shouldn't be an issue, especially since we decided to keep things casual, but sweet magnolias, that man has been running through my mind ever since we left the Thirsty Horse together. I don't want to spend every free moment I have thinking about him, but I can't help it. He's the first thing I think of when I wake up in the mornings and the last thing I think about before I fall asleep.

My artist brain isn't helping, either. Every time I sit down to paint, it's the deep blue of his eyes that I'm mixing on my palette or it's the curve of his lips I'm sketching in a notebook.

It's been over a week, but I can't stop replaying our conversation in the truck, still can't stop seeing the look on Jensen's face when he told me he wanted me, only to use his next breath to tell me that he couldn't pursue anything further.

It was exhilarating and crushing all in one which confuses the ever-loving hell out of me.

Easy. Simple. Uncomplicated—that's what we decided, what we both said we wanted. But the feelings I've been wrestling with the last few days feel anything but easy.

It hasn't helped that every time we run into each other now, I have this overwhelming urge to run my hands up his toned forearms, to trace the colored lines of the tattoos I'm dying to see more of, to kiss the mouth I can't stop sketching.

Yesterday, Peaches had wandered into my yard and spent the evening with me while I painted after work. Once it got dark, I'd walked her back home, and Jensen had greeted me on the porch with a smile that nearly knocked the wind right out of me. And then he hugged me. I could've stayed on that porch with his arms around me until the cows came home and it still wouldn't have been enough time.

Which doesn't exactly scream casual does it?

I let out a low, frustrated sigh as I stop by a local artist's table, thumbing through the prints she has for sale. The collection of watercolor flowers is lovely, but not even the beautiful lines and pastel hues can distract me—mainly because they aren't the vibrant spectrum of colors that decorate Jensen's body.

Heat rushes up my cheeks, and I move past the vendor's table in a hurry. I spy a table covered in vintage Coca Cola memorabilia and head in that direction. Seems safe enough.

But just as I'm admiring the collection—"Callie?"

I close my eyes and breathe out through my nose. I'd know that deep, gravelly voice anywhere, and apparently, so does my body. If the layer of goosebumps erupting all along my skin is any indication.

I spin slowly. Jensen's blue-eyed gaze slams into mine, and my heart skitters and nearly stops.

"Hi," I manage, the word breathy.

"This is a nice surprise." Jensen runs a hand down my arm in greeting, which only makes the goosebumps worse. "I wasn't expecting to see you here today."

"You either." I step back, needing a little air, and point to the canvas bag slung over his shoulder. "Doing a little shopping?"

"Yeah, I try to get out here at least once a month to pick up a few things for the RVs."

I picture the Airstream and all the little details that make it feel so homey. From the moment I first saw it in the listing photos and then again when I stepped inside it for the first time, it had felt like me, it had felt like *home*. It hadn't occurred to me to consider how much thought and care goes into creating a space like that, and the realization that this is who Jensen is—someone who spends his weekends at flea markets and antique fairs to find the perfect pieces makes me want to know him more, to understand more of his quiet, intentional ways.

"Is this where you got all the decorations for my Airstream?"

"A lot of them, yeah. I go to a few local auctions when I can, estate sales are great too. But I always find the best stuff here."

"It's the best," I agree. "I used to come here a lot with my mom before she died. She always said that with a little bit of luck and patience, you could find just about anything here." My fingers brush against my locket, a habit of mine when I talk about my parents.

"She died when you were young?"

"When I was fourteen. Both my parents, actually. Car accident." The old, familiar twinge of sadness tugs at me. It's been years now, but I still miss them. "They were on their way to pick me up from a sleepover. It took me a long time to realize that it wasn't my fault, but I still think about what would've been, ya know?"

"God, Callie. I'm sorry." The understanding and sincerity in his voice make my throat ache and I have to blink back the tears I feel forming.

"The hardest part is time," I admit. "It's so fleeting. My dad had a really wonderful laugh, the kind that came from his whole body, ya know? I worry sometimes that I'll forget the sound of it. And my mom? She gave the best hugs. She'd wrap her arms around me and squeeze me so tightly that I never wanted her to let go. I don't ever want there to be a time that I don't remember her hugs." I sigh, smiling a little as the memory of Mom and me skipping around the aisles fills my thoughts. "Places like this help though."

Jensen nods, though his eyes are far away. I know he must be thinking about Kasey, so I step closer, laying a hand on his forearm. His palm lands on top of mine and we stand there for a few seconds in silence until Jensen clears his throat and gives me a soft smile. "Would you want to walk around with me?"

The look on his face has me nodding before I can talk myself out of it and I'm rewarded with an even bigger smile.

This is fine, I tell myself as we head over to the next rows of tables. Jensen releases my hand, but he stays close as we stroll, his arm brushing against mine. Tingles skip up and down my skin whenever he touches me. *Just keeping it casual.* I almost snort at the thought.

Jensen takes his time browsing, pausing to flip through a stack of old vinyls or to inspect a tarnished pocket-watch. He's quiet too, his focus on the hunt. Every time he finds an item of interest, his brows scrunch together as he inspects it, turning it over carefully in his hands. I'm supposed to be shopping for knick-knacks, but my eyes keep drifting back to him.

"What?" he asks when he catches me staring, an old wooden washboard in his hand.

"Oh nothing, I'm just wondering if you were some kind of pirate in another life."

His brows lift. "A pirate?"

"Yeah. You seem to have a knack for finding treasure." I indicate the washboard. "It's beautiful. When do you think it was made?"

"1930s, 1940s maybe," he tells me, running a hand along the side of the wood, inspecting the craftsmanship. "See this?" He points to a spot of discoloration. "The wood oxidizes over time. You won't find that type of coloring in a reproduction. And the grooves here? They were made from use."

I trail my finger down the grooves in the wood. "Do you think the people who made this ever thought it would end up in a place like this?"

"Probably not." Jensen lifts a shoulder and drops it. "I think that's why I've always liked vintage pieces. They come with a story."

"Did you always know you wanted to restore RVs?"

"It was something my grandpa used to do, and when I was younger, I would go with him to junkyards to look for scrap parts and then he'd spend all weekend teaching me about how things worked and what to do when they didn't. It was my grandmother's job to decorate the RVs once PaPaw was finished with the restoration.

She'd travel around to antique fairs and garage sales and find just the right pieces to make the place shine."

He shifts the washboard under his arm. "It's some of the fondest memories I have growing up. It really wasn't till about ten years ago though that I started doing it myself. I was stationed out in Virginia and missing home. Then I was out driving around one night and I saw an old Winnebago sitting on the side of the road with a *For Sale* sign on it. That was my first one. It took me a long time to fully restore it, and I made a lot of mistakes, but once I started working on it, all of PaPaw's lessons started coming back." He smiles, his eyes clearly seeing another time.

"Well, as someone who is very much benefiting from your work, I'd personally like to thank your PaPaw," I joke, giving a little salute.

"So . . . you like the place, then?"

"More than like," I confirm. "If I could hug the RV I would."

"I'm glad." Jensen smiles, almost shyly, and steps closer to me. "I like knowing you're happy there," he says, reaching up to tuck an errant strand of hair behind my ear.

The din of the flea market has all but faded away around us and even though I probably shouldn't, I lean into his touch. I can't help it, and when he gives me that half smile of his and says things like that? Well, I'm as good as gone.

"And having you so close by, well, that's a bonus."

The words wrap around me like a blanket, warming me from the inside out. Jensen's gaze is piercing now and just when I think he's going to pull away, he leans down to brush his lips softly against mine. It's not a long kiss or a deep one, but the effect it has on me is instantaneous. My pulse quickens and warm tingles dance across my skin.

Ever since our conversation in the truck, it feels like a wall between us has been knocked down. I'd known from the moment I met him that he carried around a lot of weight on those broad shoulders of his. I just hadn't known how much.

The look on his face when he told me about his exwife had broken my heart, and I still couldn't understand how anybody could do such a thing. I'd been trying to remind myself that there are two sides to every story and that I didn't know Anna from Adam, but to leave your husband while he's grieving the devastating loss of his best friend seems unforgivably cruel. It wasn't my place to judge, but looking into Jensen's deep blue eyes, eyes that are as deep and as soulful as the ocean, I can't fathom such a thing.

Because you're falling for him.

The thought pops up, clear and matter of fact in my mind, as if I'd asked a question about the weather.

There's no point in denying it, but there's no point in admitting it either. A piece of me is really upset by this realization, and I have no idea how to make heads or tails of it. So, I just shove the thought as far back into my mind as I can. *Casual. Keep it casual, Callie.*

We move on to the next set of tables, the conversation light and easy as we browse. When my stomach growls loudly enough for him to hear, Jensen chuckles and steers us toward the back part of the market where all the food vendors are set up.

There's a big white tent to the right of the food trucks where a dozen or so picnic tables have been set up, but it looks like most of them are occupied. So, when our number is called and we grab our food, Jensen leads me to a shaded, grassy area near the edge of the grounds. There's an old wooden fence that has seen better days and a broken-down water pump that's rusted and peeling from the elements. Beyond the fence, though, is a wide-open field, covered in wildflowers. It's a perfect panoramic view of the Alabama countryside I love so much.

We plop down in the grass and dig into our food. We don't talk much at first, both of us too focused on chewing to be much use in the way of conversation, but eventually, we slow down and I catch Jensen eyeing me.

"Do I have barbecue sauce on my face?" I ask, swiping at my chin with a paper napkin.

"No," he chuckles, "You're just really cute when you eat."

"Is that a nice way of saying I eat like a cow chewing

cud or something?" I ask, feeling a little self-conscious.

"You most definitely do not look like a cow," he assures me. "You just looked like you were really enjoying that sandwich." He purses his lips to keep from laughing. "I was afraid to say anything because I didn't want to ruin the moment you two were having." He pantomimes me eating my sandwich, a dopey grin on his face as he fake chews.

I ball up my napkin and toss it at his face with a laugh. "Well, it *is* the best barbecue I've had in a while. You're just jealous because your street tacos aren't nearly as yummy."

Jensen catches the napkin and tosses it back at me. "We both know street tacos trump barbecue any day."

"You can't be serious."

"As a heart attack." Jensen lifts a brow in challenge.

It's so cute, I can't even think of a good comeback. "Fine." I pretend to wave a white flag. "If you say so."

"I say so." Jensen grins.

His easy smile is my undoing, I swear. Even though my brain keeps repeating three words over and over— Simple. Easy. Uncomplicated—I know for a fact that it's too late.

—

I'm almost finished with an entire pint of Ben & Jerry's by the time Mabel walks through the door.

"Hey!" She beams when she sees me sitting on her couch. "I didn't know you were stopping by to—" She stops walking when she sees my face and then her eyes drift to the nearly empty carton in my hand. "What's wrong?"

I swallow the mouthful of ice cream I just shoveled in and let out a sigh. "I think I'm falling in love with him."

"Okay." Mabel plops down next to me, reaching for my spoon. "You make that sound like a bad thing."

"It is. This is exactly what I didn't want to happen. I mean, what will the cats think?" I'm attempting to use humor to deflect how upset I really am, but I can tell from the way Mabel scoots closer that she doesn't buy it.

"Callie, would it really be so bad if you had feelings for him? Jensen's a really great guy."

"He is," I agree. "He's funny and kind and—"

"Hot?" Mabel interjects, which makes me laugh.

"Well, yeah, obviously. But . . . but I'm not sure I'm ready. I went into this determined not to let him get into my head. No complications, that's what I said. But the more I try not to think about him, the more he invades every thought I have."

"Maybe there's a reason for that."

"But this isn't what was supposed to happen," I wail. "We were supposed to do the photoshoot and that was it. I was going to go on my merry way, swearing off stupid love and never getting hurt again. Now, I've gone and fallen for him and what exactly am I supposed to do with that?"

"For starters, you might want to tell Jensen how you're feeling."

"Why? It won't change anything. I already know how Jensen feels. He's attracted to me, but he doesn't want anything past that. Just *casual*." I spit the word.

"But *you'll* feel better," Mabel argues, her smile turning sad. "Trust me, you don't want to spend a single second with the ghost of what you wished you'd said."

I can tell from the faraway look in her eyes that she's thinking of her ex. I snuggle in closer. "Can I ask you an honest question?"

"Yeah, of course."

"After everything that happened," I give her a knowing look, "do you still think it was worth it? Love, I mean." I try not to ever bring him up, I don't want to put salt in wounds that I know still ache for her, but in this case, I can't help it.

Mabel presses her lips together, thinking it over. "Yeah, I do," she says a minute later. "Even knowing how it ended, I wouldn't change a thing. Sullivan and I . . . " She gives me a sad smile. "For better or for worse, it was worth it."

"But Jensen lives in this town. If it ends badly, where will I go?" Dayton Springs has always been my home, my safe place when the rest of the world becomes too much. I can't risk that. Can I?

"Psssh." Mabel waves a hand. "Girl, you know all we have to do is sic the quilting circle on him. Those old biddies are scary enough to run anyone out of town."

It's a joke, of course, but it does make some of the tightness in my chest ease.

"This is your home, Callie," Mabel continues, more serious this time. "And it always will be. Will it be awkward if you break up? Yes, but it's not a reason to change your zip code. It's a risk, sure, but nothing worth having comes easy."

"What if I get hurt again?" The fear I feel when I consider this is enough to rob me of breath. With Adam, I'd been stung and my confidence came out a little bruised, but I wasn't as utterly devastated by the end of our relationship as I thought I should've been. But Jensen? Somehow, I know deep inside me that if I let myself love him, I'll never recover from it if it ends.

"Well, then you pick up the pieces and you keep going. Feelings like the ones you have for Jensen aren't going to go away. Trust me, I would know. Scared or not, if you've fallen for him, there's really only one thing you can do."

"Eat my weight in Ben & Jerry's?"

Mabel snorts. "Well, that is *one* option."

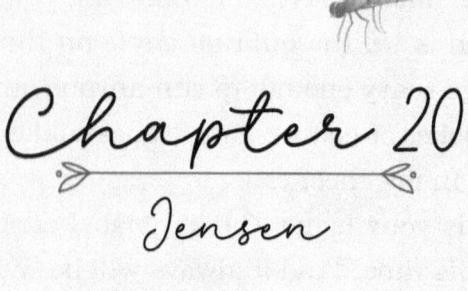

Chapter 20

Jensen

Leaving the truck running, I jog up the short path and rap on the RV's door with my knuckles. I wait, rocking back and forth on my heels until the door swings open.

"My, my, my." Ms. Dorothy looks me up and down, pressing a hand to her heart. "You've come to ask me to run away with you, haven't you, boy?"

I play along, dipping my head. "If I thought you'd agree, I'd have asked a long time ago."

"You're kind to indulge an old woman." Ms. Dorothy pats my cheek. "But you do clean up nice. It's not every day my handsome landlord shows up looking so dapper."

The fabric of my suit jacket pulls a little between the shoulders, and I'm missing my Levi's right about now, but I figured the occasion called for more than the usual jeans and t-shirt.

"We've got that television interview today. I'm actually headed to the station now, and I told Callie I'd give her a ride. I figured I'd stop by and bring you this first." I hold up a lightbulb in my hand. "You mentioned yesterday that the light in your refrigerator had gone out."

"Oh, you sweet thing. That could've waited a day or two. My condiments are just fine in the dark."

"Anything for you, Ms. Dorothy. You know that."

"Well, I appreciate it." She takes the lightbulb and drops it in the front pocket of her flowered apron. "You better not keep my pretty neighbor waiting."

I'm not sure what my face looks like when she mentions Callie, but my heart definitely reacts, and from the knowing look Ms. Dorothy gives me, it's almost as if she can hear it racing.

"And Jensen?"

"Yes ma'am?"

"You let yourself love her, okay?"

My eyebrows shoot up. Dorothy and I talk a lot, but not about anything too deep. I've never told her much about my personal life, and she's never really asked. I haven't breathed a word to her about Callie and how I feel about her.

"Don't be so surprised. Your face gives you away every time you look at that girl. It ain't hard to read." She takes a step closer and lays a hand on my arm. "It also ain't hard to tell that you've been carrying a lot of hurt around for quite some time. And that kind of hurt isn't all that easy to let go of. But listen, I've been paying attention, and I know that whatever is simmering between you two is the real thing. Don't let what's been dragging you down keep you there."

Surprised by the turn of our conversation and the way it makes a lump rise in my throat, all I can do is nod. "Yes, ma'am."

"Good. Now, go get our girl."

"Yes, ma'am," I say again because even though my mind is spinning, rolling Dorothy's words around like a marble in my head, I am anxious to see Callie. It's been like this ever since the Thirsty Horse. When I'm not with her, I'm practically counting down the minutes until I see her again. Whether it's running into her at the flea market or watching her paint through my kitchen window, I can't seem to get enough of her. Even Peaches is enamored—I swear, my dog spends more time with Callie than she does with me. Not that I mind. Every time Callie brings her back, it's another minute I get to spend with her.

You know what you look like? One of those cartoon characters with hearts in its eyes, Kasey laughs, his voice loud in my ears.

"It's not like that," I argue, stepping up to the landing to knock on the door. "We're keeping things simple between us."

Keep telling yourself that.

I must be scowling when the door opens because Callie's smile droops. "Hey," she says tentatively.

"Morning." I shake my head, wiping away the image of Kasey's teasing grin and give Callie one of my own. "You ready?"

"Yeah, let me just go grab my bag."

When she steps out onto the landing, the air in my lungs damn near evaporates making me cough. She's wearing a rose-colored sundress that hugs every curve like my truck on a backroad. There's a gloss coating her lips that matches the color of her dress and her hair is curled, hanging across her back in waves. She looks absolutely stunning standing in the morning light, the sun making the crown of her head glow like a halo.

"Are you okay?"

"Yeah," I wheeze. "Sorry about that. I think I swallowed a fly or something."

Kase snorts. *Real smooth, Shep.*

Callie lets out a laugh that distracts me from my desire to lift a certain finger up in the air and gives me a playful shove. "Well, maybe you should learn to breathe through your nose."

I roll my eyes, but don't bother with a comeback. I opt for a compliment instead. "You look amazing."

"You think so?" She smoothes the front of her dress. "This is my first time ever doing a live interview like this, and I wasn't sure what to wear."

My fingers itch to touch her, so I satisfy them by

placing a palm on the small of her back to lead her to my truck. "You're perfect." I'm not just talking about the dress, either.

"Thank you. You clean up pretty nice, too."

"I have exactly one suit," I confess. "There's usually not too many occasions to wear one around here."

"Well, we should definitely change that."

I hold the door open for Callie as she hops up into the cab, warmth creeping up the back of my neck. I'm not used to a woman complimenting me, and I like it way more than I should.

The ride to the station only takes us about forty-five minutes, and we keep things pretty light, singing along to the radio and swapping stories from our week. Having her next to me in the truck is like scratching an itch I haven't been able to reach. When I'm with her, everything just feels *right.*

"Have you ever been here before?" I ask, as we pull up to the television station.

"No, but I grew up with *Good Day Alabama* playing in the background of my childhood. It's a little surreal that we're here. And kind of intimidating."

"It's not too late to put her in reverse," I offer, only half-joking. "We could go for coffee instead."

"Coffee with you sounds amazing, but . . . " Callie sighs.

"But you love your cousin way too much to bail on her last minute?"

"Yeah, and I'm kinda hoping to get a glimpse of Jim Bann."

"The weather guy?" This makes me snort.

"He's not just a weather guy," Callie fires back, her nostrils flaring in a way that makes me chuckle even more. "He's the best meteorologist of all time. There's not a soul in Alabama that would disagree with me on that. I'll take pity on you because you're a transplant, but you should know he's a legend around here."

"It's cute seeing you get all riled up over the weatherman," I tease, knowing I'm pushing her buttons.

"Listen here, Shepherd."

"Oooh, using my last name. I like that."

"Stop distracting me." Callie smacks my shoulder and continues. "Jim Bann is the reason we all survive tornado season around these parts. In fact, you know how serious the situation is just by what he's wearing. He's got his suit jacket on, things are still okay. But you see that man's suspenders? Well, you better hunker down. It's gonna be a long night."

"You're a little starstruck."

"It's *Jim Bann*," Callie says it like it's the most obvious thing in the world.

Once we make it through security, we're ushered up to the main floor where we're taken to a green room. Mabel is waiting for us there, looking bright-eyed and nervous as a woman with light brown skin and voluminous curls wearing a headset fits her with a microphone.

"Hi!" She waves us over. "My name is Lenora but most people just call me Lennie. I'm one of the producers on the show. You must be Callie and Jensen. We're so excited to have you with us today."

Lennie makes quick work getting both Callie and I set up with microphones and then gives us a short rundown of what to expect. "Charlotte Cannon, our host, will do a little introduction and then she'll invite you to join her on the set."

She directs us over to a small sitting area where a bunch of refreshments have been set out. I help myself to a lemonade, while Callie and Mabel chat excitedly. I leave them to their girl talk and focus on taking small sips of my drink. Now that we're here, minutes away from being on live television, my stomach is twisting and turning.

"You okay?" Callie comes over, her fingers trailing along my forearm. "You're looking a little pale."

"I don't like the spotlight much."

"I don't either. I say we let Mabel do most of the talking."

Mabel pops up over Callie's shoulder, a grin worthy of the Cheshire Cat on her face. "I'm good with that! I never met a camera I didn't like."

Callie rolls her eyes. "I can confirm this."

"Well, it's up to you then, Mabel. Make us look good."

We don't have to wait long before Lennie is back,

double-checking the battery packs on our microphones before leading us into the studio where filming takes place.

The set is made up of an oversized, bulbous armchair and a matching couch. There's a coffee table with flowers in the center and a massive screen projecting the *Good Day Alabama* logo. The sight doesn't help the tidal wave rolling around in my stomach, but Callie, sensing my distress, moves a little closer, pressing her body against mine. "We got this," she whispers just as a cameraman signals us to get into position.

A woman wearing a deep maroon suit steps onto the set, her tan skin glowing under the stage lights. Her long black hair hangs straight past her shoulders, and her bright smile must have some kind of extra wattage in it—it almost hurts to look at.

A cameraman counts her down as she positions herself in the armchair.

"Good morning, everyone. My name is Charlotte Cannon, and this is *Good Day, Alabama!*" She beams into the camera while a short jingle plays. "First up on today's show, we've got the scoop on a romantic photoshoot that's become a viral internet sensation. You've seen the photos and now we're going to meet the couple everyone is talking about. Join me as I welcome the photographer, Mabel Callahan, and her swoony subjects, Callie Dawson and Jensen Shepherd!"

Charlotte holds out her arms, greeting each of us

with a hug as we join her on set. Mabel sits closest to her, while Callie and I take the other end of the couch. The lights overhead are overwhelmingly warm, but Callie's hand brushes over mine, reassuring and grounding.

"So, Mabel," Charlotte begins. "Why don't you start off by telling us a little bit about you and how you got the idea for this photoshoot?"

Callie was right about Mabel. She shows absolutely zero nerves as she chats with Charlotte, talking about her business, how it's been her dream to do photography full-time, and her inspiration for the shoot.

"It's called a chemistry or stranger session, and the idea is to take two people who have never met and photograph them in a romantic way to see if there's any chemistry. It's like a blind date. I'd been wanting to do one for a while, and all the pieces sort of fell into place."

"Did you have any idea it would turn out as well as it did?"

Mabel shakes her head. "Not at all. I mean, I hoped that it would, but you never know how people are going to interact with one another. Even couples who have been together for years can look a little stiff when you turn the camera on them. I knew it was a gamble, but,"—she turns to grin at Callie and me—"these two had chemistry for days! So, nothing to worry about there."

Charlotte chuckles, reaching for a tablet on the coffee table. "I'll say." She taps the screen and a montage of photos from the shoot replace the *Good Day Alabama* logo behind us.

"Callie, Jensen, what was it like? Most people find blind dates a little awkward, and you two had a pretty unconventional one. No pressure, am I right?"

"At first it was a little . . . " Callie looks over at me, searching for the right word.

"Weird?" I supply with a half-smile.

She laughs. "Yeah. It was definitely a little weird at first, but I don't know, we just started talking and after a while, we sort of forgot the camera was there. It was comfortable by the end, like we'd known each other for forever."

"But that's not the end of the story." Charlotte leans forward. "Mabel, you posted the pictures on social media and since then, they've gone viral." A screenshot of Mabel's post comes up on the screen behind us, a red circle around the number of views. "Over three million people have seen your work. How does that make you feel?"

Mabel speaks into the camera, her cheeks pink. "I'm still in shock. I wasn't expecting that kind of response, and I definitely didn't expect the photos to go viral, but here we are. It's overwhelming in the best way. Every artist hopes that people will take notice of their work, but this was beyond my wildest expectations. It's been an amazing experience."

Callie reaches over to squeeze Mabel's hand. "No one

deserves it more than Mabel."

"The artistry is clear." Charlotte taps the tablet in her hand and the screen behind us changes to a different selection of photos. "These are stunning, Mabel. Truly, beautiful."

Mabel looks like she's about to combust from happiness as she beams at Charlotte. "Thank you so much. I really appreciate it."

Charlotte turns that 100-watt smile on Callie and me. "The internet isn't just obsessed with Mabel's photos. They're obsessed with the two of you." Another tap of her finger and the screen behind us fills with comments.

Charlotte reads off a handful.

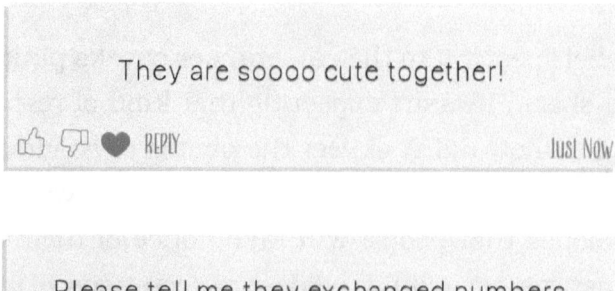

She looks up from her tablet. "Everyone thinks you make a pretty great couple. So I have to ask, where do things stand between you two?"

"Oh!" Callie's cheeks pinken. "Well, Jensen and I are . . . friends."

"Just friends?" Charlotte cocks her head. "Come on now, don't be shy. Surely with that kind of chemistry there's a little something extra cooking, no?"

"Well, um, I mean . . . we're . . . "

Another tap of Charlotte's finger and the screen behind us fills with the image of Callie and I kissing. The intimacy of the moment, our connection—it's impossible to deny, especially with it being magnified on the screen like that.

I can tell from how rigid Callie has gone next to me that she's not sure how to answer the question. Sure, we've talked about how we're both attracted to each other, but is that something we really need to discuss with the entire state of Alabama?

"Well, if you're not sure, then perhaps a second date is in order?" Charlotte coos, turning to Mabel. "What do you think about that Mabel? Are you up for another round with these two?"

Mabel's eyes widen a little and immediately dart over to Callie. Charlotte has definitely caught us all off guard with her suggestion.

Charlotte reaches up and holds two fingers to the small earpiece in her ear. "Annnnd," she trills, "my producer just informed me that there are thousands of comments coming into our livestream as we sit here! Your public is demanding an encore. What do you guys say?"

I bristle at her game show host-esque tone, and Callie's smile has slipped slightly. Even Mabel's demeanor has shifted, which makes me want to do something to fix it. I can sense Callie's discomfort at being put on the spot, even though she's trying to keep it together for the camera's sake.

"I think we'd be up for that," I say, the words rushing out of me in a hurry. I don't give myself time to think too much about them.

Charlotte claps her hands together in victory and Callie sags a little. I'm worried I've overstepped, but she smiles when I catch her eye.

"Well, there you have it, folks. Looks like we're on for another chemistry photoshoot! Mabel, I think I speak for all our viewers when I say we can't wait to see more of your work." She winks at us before turning to the camera. "And with that, we'll be right back."

A producer gives the signal that the broadcast has gone to a commercial break, and in a flutter of "nice to meet you" and "thanks for coming by" we say goodbye to Charlotte Cannon and are whisked off set and back to the green room area.

Lennie meets us there and helps us remove our mics. "Great segment," she tells us. "You're welcome to watch the rest of the show if you like." She gives a little wave and disappears, leaving us alone and gaping at one another.

"Sorry about that." I rub a hand down my face. "I didn't mean to answer for everyone, but I just—"

"No, no, it's fine." Mabel presses a hand to her chest. "She caught me so off guard, I didn't know what to say."

"She kinda ambushed us," Callie adds, pursing her lips. "That definitely wasn't how I thought the interview would go."

Mabel chews the corner of her lip for a second before blurting out, "I don't hate the idea of a second photoshoot though."

Callie laughs. "Of course, you don't. Another chance to go viral, huh?"

"No," Mabel argues. "Another chance to photograph my favorite subjects."

"Uh huh." Callie lets out a sigh. "I guess it couldn't hurt. Jensen?"

I should probably say no. We're supposed to be keeping things casual between us, and if I'm given a chance to act . . . well, *less* casual with her then I'm not sure I'll be able to stop.

But one look into Callie's deep green eyes makes up my mind for me. Even if deep down, I know it will only ruin me in the end. "Like I said, I'm up for it."

Mabel's face lights up like she's just won the lottery, which makes Callie laugh. She looks so damn cute, I almost stop breathing.

Is doing a second photoshoot a good idea? Probably not.

Am I gonna strike a match and toss it onto that pile of gasoline anyway?

Yup. Looks like it.

Chapter 21

Callie

One Week Later

"So where exactly is she taking us?" Jensen asks, carefully maneuvering his truck around a massive pothole. We've been bumping along a dirt road for more than half an hour now with no real idea of where we're headed.

I hold up the crumpled pink post-it note Mabel handed me yesterday. "Your guess is as good as mine," I tell him. "All she gave me was this."

The location for the photoshoot isn't on Google Maps, so she'd jotted down a few vague directions and landmarks for us to follow. "You can't miss it!" she'd told me confidently. But now, I wasn't so sure. Dayton Springs is a small town and fairly rural, but I've never been to this particular area. Uninhabited and wild, there's not a soul in sight.

"You know, it kinda looks like a place

someone might bury a body," Jensen deadpans, his voice low and deep. When I look over at him, the right side of his mouth is quirked upward, which makes me laugh.

"Let's hope not," I joke. "Otherwise this is going to be a very different type of photoshoot."

Jensen chuckles and then casually reaches across the seat to take my hand. My heart trips and stutters and nearly stops when his thumb begins gliding across my skin in soothing circles.

Ever since the dance hall, things between us have felt different, and even more so in the last few days since our *Good Day, Alabama* interview. Charlotte Cannon's suggestion to do a second photoshoot went nearly as viral as our original one, and all our social media accounts have been blowing up with notifications and mentions ever since. It's nuts how invested everyone is in this whole thing—a little unnerving, too. I'm still trying to figure out what to do about my not so-uncomplicated feelings for Jensen and having what feels like the entire world focused on us doesn't help.

The one thing I do know is that when I'm with Jensen, everything else just fades away. I want to be near him, to spend my time making him laugh—even if there is a small part of me that still worries, still wants to run screaming the other way in the name of self-preservation. The rest of me, though, wants to take Ms. Dorothy's advice and jump right off the cliff to see if I can fly. Hell, I think I already have. And god, I want Jensen to fly with me.

I steal a glimpse of him. He's keeping his focus on the road ahead, but he's still holding my hand firmly in his and his expression is content, his features relaxed. Is it because he's feeling the same thing I am?

Will you fly with me, Jensen? My heartbeat is pounding so hard, I wonder if he can hear it.

Thankfully, a much-needed distraction appears around the next curve. My cousin is standing on the side of the road, waving at us from beside her car, which is parked at the edge of a dilapidated barn.

Jensen lets go of my hand so he can maneuver the truck behind Mabel's car, and the loss of contact makes my stomach flip over.

Sighing, I unbuckle my seatbelt and get out.

"You found it!" Mabel beams, hurrying over to wrap her arms around me.

"Barely," I tell her, returning her hug. "Where on earth are we?"

"You'll see," she tells me with a wink. "Come on, we have a bit of a hike ahead of us, and I want to get there before we lose the light."

"A hike?" I look over at Jensen who lifts his brows. "We're not doing the shoot here?" I point to the barn.

"Definitely not." Mabel scrunches her nose like I've just suggested we do the photoshoot in a trash heap. "It's just the landmark that marks the beginning of the trailhead." She slings her camera bag over her head. "Follow me."

I look down at my maxi dress and sandals. "Um, Mabel. I didn't exactly dress for a hike."

"There's a path," she assures me. "It's a little over-grown, but you'll be fine. I promise."

Without waiting for any kind of response, she forges ahead, slipping between two tall trees and into the woods. "Uh . . . " I start to protest, but Mabel pops her head back out of the tree line and waves me forward. "You coming?"

Jensen moves before I do, heading toward where Mabel is waiting, but as he passes me, he holds his hand out behind him. It's a simple thing, a small gesture that might not mean much to someone else, but to me it's an acknowledgment of my feelings. It's not the first time, either. In his own quiet way, Jensen makes me feel seen.

Adam had an uncanny knack for always making me feel like I was too much. Too loud, too needy, too everything. And I spent so long trying to make myself be smaller.

But with Jensen, I don't have to be small. Even if it's something as silly as being hesitant about traipsing through the woods in a dress, he somehow gives me the quiet assurance that my feelings have value.

I take his hand, as gratitude swells in my chest, and let him lead me down the path. Mabel is already several feet ahead, bounding along like the uneven terrain isn't at all an issue for her. The path is more than a little overgrown, and we have to slow down several times to go around or directly over fallen logs and limbs.

We come across a particularly large tree laying directly in our path. Jensen hops up and helps me up onto the tree's trunk. "She really is trying to kill us," I grumble, as Jensen jumps down and then reaches for me to help me to the ground.

"Don't worry," he tells me, his hands lingering at my waist. "I've got you."

The words soothe my irritation, and I step a little closer. "Thank you," I murmur, peering up into his face. His grip tightens, and when his hand lifts to cup my neck, every cell in my body seems to ignite. When he touches me, I don't want him to stop.

"Hey you two!" Mabel's voice cuts through the air. "Save it for the photoshoot, will you?"

I step back automatically with a groan. "So, remember that whole burying a body thing?" I ask Jensen and then cut my eyes over to my cousin. He lets out a laugh, and the sound is so wonderful, it makes me want to say something else to make him laugh again. It's literally the best sound in the world.

"Come on," he tells me, re-claiming my hand in his.

We walk for another fifteen minutes or so before Mabel spins around, her eyes bright. "It's just beyond here," she tells us.

"What's . . . " I start to ask but trail off as a sound

registers in my ear. "Is that a . . . "

"You'll see," she singsongs gleefully, holding out her arm to indicate that we should go on ahead.

Whatever sarcastic retort was forming in my head completely evaporates the moment Jensen and I step through the trees. The clearing isn't very big, but just ahead is a towering rock formation and one of the most beautiful waterfalls I've ever seen. Silver-white water spills over the edge of the stones like a silken curtain, sending tiny droplets of mist into the air. The pool below looks cool and inviting with mossy rocks outlining its edges. Overhead, golden sunlight filters in through the canopy of trees and catches the spray from the falls making it shimmer. It's breath-taking.

"Whoa," Jensen murmurs.

"Yeah, what you said," I agree, my eyes still focused on the falls.

"Well?" Mabel bounds up beside me. "What do you think?"

"It's beautiful. How did you even find this place?"

Mabel gives me a coy smile. "A good photographer never reveals her secrets." She winks and then taps her camera bag. "You guys ready to get started?"

I look to Jensen who nods. "Yeah, we're good to go. Where do you want us?"

"Why don't you start right over there?" Mabel points to a spot by the water's edge. "I'm gonna need a second to adjust the setting and check the lighting, but then we'll get this show on the road."

While Mabel fiddles with her equipment, Jensen and I head over to the spot she indicated.

I don't know why, but I'm feeling super nervous all of a sudden. I want the photoshoot to go well, for Mabel's sake if nothing else, but it also feels like this is some kind of tipping point for Jensen and I. I'm not sure what to make of the tangled ball of emotions sitting in the pit of my stomach.

"You ready for this?" I ask, keeping my voice light and cheery.

"I think so." If Jensen is feeling any of the nervousness I am, he doesn't show it. He reaches for me, his fingers trailing down my bare arm. "I'm here with you."

I almost groan out loud. How am I going to pretend I'm not falling for this man when he says stuff like that?

Or maybe you don't pretend. Maybe you tell him?

I press my lips together to keep from yelling, "Mind your business!'" at the logical side of my brain.

"Okay! I think I'm ready." Mabel bounds over, a thick, red camera strap around her neck and her Nikon in her hand. "Let's start with some movement photos. But don't look at the camera, look at each other."

Jensen holds out his hand, and I loop my fingers through his. I use my other hand to grasp the edge of my long skirt, lifting it up just slightly so I can walk more easily over the rocky ground.

When Mabel gives us the signal, we walk in her direction, smiling at each other. It feels a little awkward at first, especially with Mabel yelling directions over her camera, but then Jensen makes a funny face at me and it makes me laugh, the sound bursting out of me. He laughs too, and Mabel squeals, "Yes! That's perfect!"

We walk a few more paces while Mabel snaps more shots. "Okay, I want you right here." She directs us to a spot with the waterfall just off to the right behind us. "Jensen, I want you behind Callie, with your arms around her."

Jensen moves behind me as she directed, wrapping his arms around me and pulling me flush, my back to his chest. In the name of keeping things simple, we've barely touched these last few weeks. We've hugged a time or two, held hands, and even briefly brushed our lips together, but we've been holding back—and I think we both know it. But here, now, we don't have to do that.

It feels so incredibly good being this close to him, and I place my arms on top of his and lean into him. He dips his head, almost as if on instinct, his nose skimming the shell of my ear and the soft skin of my neck.

I'm vaguely aware of the clicking of Mabel's camera, but the pounding of my heart is much louder. Even though the air is thick with humidity, goosebumps break out along my skin.

It's not the same as before, though. This isn't the sweet nerves of a first meeting. This is magnetic. Voltaic. It's a geyser of boiling water about to erupt.

Without waiting for instruction from Mabel, I flip around, wanting, no, needing to see his face. His arms tighten around me as I wrap my arms around his neck, the movement so natural it feels like I've done it a thousand times before.

Jensen's eyes are on mine, all wild and stormy like usual, but there's a softness there, too, a vulnerability that I've only ever seen a handful of times before.

I step on my tiptoes, wanting to be even closer, and I squeal a little when Jensen lifts me off my feet. Our faces are level now, and I smile as I press my forehead against his. "Hi," I whisper, grinning at him.

"Hey, pretty girl," he murmurs, and I swear every nerve-ending inside me ignites, sending a wave of heat over my entire body. The desire to kiss him overwhelms me, but Mabel pops up next to us, talking animatedly about the shots she's already captured.

"These are amazing," she gushes, flipping the camera around so we can see a few previews. "And we're only just getting started." Her eyes are wide and bright, and it makes me smile to see how happy this is making her. But admittedly, there's a part of me that wishes she weren't here. That it was just Jensen and I in this place, with nothing but the waterfall.

Mabel directs us through several more shots on the bank. Jensen and I aren't saying much to each other, but there's something crackling between us. It's electrifying and wild, and every time he touches me, I feel it zipping through me.

"Okay, so I have an idea, but it would require you to get a little wet." Mabel looks at me and then Jensen for approval. "What do you say?"

"I'm fine with it," Jensen replies, his eyes sliding over to mine. "I mean, if Callie is."

I nod quickly, forcing myself to tear my eyes away so I can make eye contact with Mabel. "You're the boss, Boss!"

"Great!" Mabel squeals with excitement and then leads us over to the water's edge and points just beyond it. "The water is shallow right here, and I think it's pretty sandy at the bottom. Can you both walk out into the water?"

Kicking off my sandals, I lift my skirt with one hand and put my other one in Jensen's outstretched palm. We carefully maneuver ourselves out into the pool, using each other for balance and laughing when we both slip once or twice.

"Easy now," Jensen murmurs, tightening his grip on me when I lose my footing and almost fall. "I've got you."

I know he means he won't let me fall in the water, but it's the second time he's said it, and somehow the words feel like they mean more. My heart pounds in response.

Will you fly with me, Jensen?

We walk out until Mabel tells us to stop. The fabric of my skirt is floating on top of the water, pooling around my thighs, where the water is hitting me. The spray from the waterfall floats on the breeze, coating our skin and hair.

"Okay, Jensen, I want you to dip Callie backwards, and Callie arch your back just a little."

One of Jensen's hands grips my waist and the other lifts to hold me securely across the shoulder blades, dipping me low enough that the tips of my hair skim the surface of the water. I lean my head back, enjoying how incredible it feels being held like this, so secure and safe, and freeing.

Mabel squeaks her approval, but it isn't her praise that has me lifting my leg. Jensen's hand moves automatically to cup me just below the knee before he deepens the backward arch of the dip.

We stay like that for just a moment, and then he slowly begins to lift me back up, keeping me steady. He releases my leg, and then we're standing pressed against each other, chest to chest.

"If you want to kiss her, that's totally okay with me!" Mabel calls out, and it makes us both laugh.

But then Jensen gives me one of those rare smiles as he reaches up to the side of my neck, lifting my chin. "You don't have to tell me twice. I've been wanting to do this all day."

Then his lips are on mine, and everything around me fades to nothing. There is only the feel of his mouth, the heat of his body warming mine, and the sweet swirl of his tongue. He kisses me like it may be the last time he ever does it, every touch, every caress reverent, yet wild.

And then he dips me again, his lips never leaving mine. Mabel's camera clicks and she shouts something, but my brain is much too busy to decipher her words.

Jensen lifts me into an upright position and slowly pulls back, leaving us both breathless. His eyes lock on mine and there's so much swimming in them, that's it hard for me to understand what that look means. If it's anything close to the thoughts in my head, then we're on the same page.

Fly with me, Jensen. Fly with me.

Mabel wastes no time. "Okay, walk back over here." She indicates a sandy bank just a few inches away from the shore, where the water laps the ground. Her tone has shifted a little, she's more focused now. "Jensen, I want you to sit in the water there. Callie, I want you in his lap."

Chapter 22

Jensen

The water is cool against my back, drenching the bottom of my shirt, as I sit down in the pool. Silt at the bottom stirs around as I stretch my legs out in front of me.

"Okay, Callie, go ahead and sit on his lap."

Mabel gives the instruction and damn it if my heart doesn't immediately begin to pound, as if to say, *yes, yes, yes.* I want Callie close, want to feel her body pressed against mine again. It's like this every time I'm around her. Every smile, every touch, even if it's just the brush of her fingers, soothes something deep inside me. It's as if I'm nothing but raw edges and jagged pieces, but when I'm around her, when she's near me, I don't feel so much of the ache.

Callie moves toward me, the damp

skirt of her dress, clinging to her legs in a way that makes my mouth water. She's so incredibly beautiful I almost can't stand it. I know it's probably going to ruin me in the end, but I just want my hands on her. Even if it can never go farther than this, even if it's just the photoshoot that's making this possible, I want every second of this. I want *her.*

"Face him, Callie," Mabel directs, and Callie sucks in the corner of her lower lip, as if nervous. I offer her a smile, one that I hope is reassuring and her cheeks lift. She straddles me then, her legs wrapping around my waist. My arms automatically wind around her, pulling her even closer. "Sorry," she whispers. "I hope I'm not crushing you."

There's uncertainty in her voice, worry that I know her stupid ex put there when he consistently told her she wasn't enough. A flash of white-hot anger spikes in my chest.

"Callie," I lean in, my lips right at her ear. "You're perfect. Everything about you is so incredibly perfect. And I've never wanted anything like I want you right now."

The words come out on their own, entirely uncensored and as real as the water around us. I think we're both a little surprised by them, but I'm glad I said them.

I hear Callie's sharp intake of breath, and just to make sure she knows I mean it, I lean down and press my lips to the soft skin of her neck.

There's a pause, as if Callie is trying to decide if she believes me or not, but then I grin against her neck when she leans her head back, exposing more of her beautiful skin to me. I kiss her again, taking my time to move my lips across the smooth plane, my teeth giving her a playful nip.

As if I've unlocked something inside her, Callie tips forward, claiming my mouth as she slides her fingers into my hair. Her fingernails graze my scalp and a warm shiver cascades down my back. God, kissing her feels like it should be a crime, and I moan as she deepens the kiss, her mouth opening for me. I swirl my tongue around hers and lift my hand to cradle the back of her head.

She feels so good underneath my hands, against my lips, in my mouth. Everything about her is beyond what I ever imagined or thought I was even capable of experiencing.

There's a moment when I feel the claws of grief and pain dig into my chest, as if reminding me that I am damaged beyond repair, that all of this is fleeting. Just a temporary high that will only crack open the barely stitched-over wounds in my chest and leave me bleeding.

But it's worth it. So damn worth it.

The shadows may swirl, but they can't claim me, not now with this amazing woman in my arms, her kiss breathing life back into the depths of my soul. I don't want to think too hard about this and what it means. I just want to keep kissing her.

So I do.

I'm not sure if it's a few minutes that pass or an hour, but eventually we come up for air. Callie's chest heaves slightly and her cheeks are tinged pink. "Wow," she whispers, and it's so damn cute I want to kiss her all over again.

I probably would have, but at that moment I think we both remember Mabel and turn to look at her. She's sitting cross-legged on the bank with her camera in her hand and the biggest grin on her face.

"Oh, sorry," Callie lets out a breathy laugh. "I think we um . . . got a little carried away there for a second. Where do you want us now, Mabs?"

Her awkwardness is adorable. I don't care one bit that her cousin just witnessed that kiss. I poke her in the ribs which makes her laugh, squealing as she scrambles off my lap.

It's tempting to reach for her, to pull her back down into my arms, but instead, I follow suit and stand up.

"Actually, I think you guys do better when I'm not giving so much direction." Mabel waves a hand at the waterfall. "Go play," she gives us both a wink. "And just pretend I'm not here."

"Come on," I tell Callie. "Let's take a closer look at the falls."

"Okay, how—" The rest of her sentence gets cut off

when I scoop her up in my arms and start wading back into the water.

Callie is laughing, her head tipped back as she kicks her feet playfully. I walk till the water hits me just below the chest, still cradling Callie in my arms. "It's so beautiful here," she murmurs, her eyes on the falls.

My eyes are only on her. "You sure are," I whisper, but I know she heard me because her eyes snap to mine.

"You can't keep saying stuff like that."

"Why not?"

She swallows, and I can see she's wrestling with herself to say the words. But then she straightens her shoulders. "Because I'm falling for you, Jensen."

The words slam into me, but it's not pain that I'm feeling reverberating throughout my entire body. It's possibility. And hope. And for the first time in a long time, I want what's possible.

"Would it be bad if I said I'm falling for you, too?"

Callie's eyes widen at my words. "What? Are you sure? I thought we agreed to just keep things casual between us."

I surprise even myself when I reply, "I don't think I can do casual with you, Callie." And it's the truth. Even though there is something inside me that's roaring its head off, screaming at me that this is all a mistake, that I don't deserve this, all I can focus on is that feeling of possibility.

I think about what Sutton said. *Then breathe, Shep.*

And I realize in this moment that I want to. Even though I'm terrified, even if I can only take this so far, whatever it is that exists in this moment, I don't want to let it go.

"I want to try," I tell her. "I don't know what this mangled heart of mine is capable of, Callie, I really don't, but when I'm with you, all I know is that it doesn't hurt as much. I can breathe again, and I can laugh again and whatever that means, I want to hold onto it. I want to hold on to you."

The words are spilling out of me and that thing inside me roars even louder as if to warn me, to urge me to stop this before it's too late, but I can't. I don't want to ignore how Callie makes me feel.

Callie's beautiful face transforms, all her worry and doubt vanishing into a smile that nearly knocks me over. "Okay," she tells me, her eyes bright.

"Okay?"

"Yeah," she giggles, pressing a quick peck to my mouth.

The heat of her kiss, there for an instant and then gone the next second, nearly has me groaning, but the sweetness of her words wraps around me like a warm blanket.

Laughter rumbles in my chest. "Okay, huh? Well, how angry do you think Mabel will be if we get a little more wet than we are right now?"

"What do you—"

I grip Callie tighter and let myself fall backward into

the deeper end of the pool, pulling us both underneath the crystal water.

I let go of Callie as soon as we're under and we kick toward the surface. She comes up sputtering, shock lining her features, but then she's laughing, which was the exact reaction I was going for. I've heard millions of sounds in my lifetime, but her laugh? Yeah, that's one of my favorites.

"Hey!" she shouts, swiping her palm across the water to splash me. It hits me square in the face, which only makes her cackle more.

"Oh, it's on," I tell her, and then we're dunking each other and splashing around like two teenagers.

"I surrender," Callie says, wrapping her arms around my neck.

I reach down and grip her legs, pulling her to my waist, where she automatically winds her legs around me. "Do you now?"

"Yeah," she tells me, and I kiss her.

I keep kissing her until a rumble overhead has us both pulling apart to look up at the sky. It's then that I realize just how little light is coming in through the trees. It had been sunny when we arrived, but now the sky is an ominous gray.

"Um, guys?" Mabel calls from her position on the bank. "I think there's a storm moving in. We better head back."

Disappointment washes over me, but the trees are

already swaying in the breeze from the front moving in. We make our way to the shore.

"Hey, before we go, do you think we could do one more thing?" Mabel asks after she's done packing up her camera equipment. She pulls her cell phone from her back pocket. "Can we make a quick video? Everyone is dying for more of you both, but it might take me a day or two until I can get a preview up."

Callie looks to me for approval and I nod. "Gotta give the people what they want, right?"

Mabel grins, tapping on her phone to open her favorite video platform. "Hey y'all," she speaks into the camera. "I just finished up a very special photoshoot with . . . " She steps to the side and holds out the phone so that Callie and I are in view. I throw my arm over Callie's shoulders and we both wave.

"If you thought the first photoshoot was amazing, wait till you see the shots from this one!" Mabel pans the camera around, giving the audience a brief look at the waterfall, and then refocuses the camera back on her face. "Stay tuned, more soon!" She blows the camera a kiss and ends the video. "Oh my gosh, everyone is going to go nuts! I can't wait to post this." Another peal of thunder rumbles overhead. "Which better be sooner rather than later!"

We all hurry along the trail back to our cars, the first droplets of rain starting to fall.

The goodbyes are short, Mabel hugging each of us

before scurrying to her car. "Be careful heading back," she calls out to us, opening her passenger side door to dump her gear. "Callie, call me later, okay?"

The rain is really starting to come down now, and Callie lets out a little squeal as I grab her hand and pull her toward my truck.

We make it into the cab just as the heavens open up, rain pouring down in thick sheets. Loud peals of thunder clap overhead and off in the distance, lightning streaks across the sky.

"Gotta love this time of year," I murmur.

"What is it they always say though?" Callie says, peering out the window and up at the sky. "April showers bring May flowers." She smiles and then shivers, as if a chill just crept down her back.

"You're cold." I immediately reach for the temperature nob on the console, cutting the air and switching over to heat. "Sorry, I should've thought about that before I dunked us."

"Don't worry about it." Callie swipes at the smudges of mascara underneath her eyes. "I don't think either one of us expected we'd need a towel for this photoshoot, and I'm glad you did it. I'm sure the photos turned out amazing."

"Here," I pull a hoodie from the back seat and hand it to her. "At least take this, I can't stand the thought of you sitting over there shivering because of me."

"Thanks." She smiles, and pulls it over her head.

It's way too big for her, but seeing her in my clothes does something to me, and the need to kiss her hits me square in the chest.

"Come here," I tell her, reaching for her across the seat. It feels so easy, so natural to do this. To want to kiss someone and then do it. But not just someone. Callie. God, I could kiss her for hours and never get tired of the way her lips feel against mine, of the way she tastes.

Can I really have this? Can she really be mine? Questions flood my thoughts but I shove them away, pulling my lips from Callie's only when a loud peal of thunder shakes the cab.

"Come on, let's get you home."

Chapter 23
Callie

Jensen fires up the truck and begins the bumpy trek back into town. Every time he takes his eyes off the road to look over at me, warmth sinks deep into my bones.

Maybe it's the actual heat blowing through the vents. It might be the hoodie he gave me, which smells so much like him that it takes everything I have in me not to press my nose into the fabric and inhale deeply.

Or . . . maybe it's just Jensen.

Maybe it's just the way he touches me, the way he holds me like I'm something precious, the way he kisses me, always as if it's the last time he'll do it.

Oh god, this is it, isn't it? I've absolutely flung myself right off the cliff for him . . . and I think he has, too. A smile lifts my cheeks at the realization.

Buzzzz . . . buzzzz . . . buzzzz . . .

My phone starts to vibrate. When I pull it out of my bag, I notice the home screen is lit up with notifications. "Whoa," I murmur, swiping my finger across the screen. "Looks like Mabel just uploaded the video she took of us at the falls."

In the cupholder between us, Jensen's phone is also vibrating like crazy.

"She works fast."

"She must have posted it as soon as she got in the car," I say, scrolling through the comments. "Everyone is absolutely losing it over us." I flip the phone around so he can see how fast the comments are popping up. "It's kinda . . . " I trail off, not quite sure how to describe it.

"Intense?" Jensen supplies, apparently on the same wavelength as me.

"Yeah. I mean, I'm really happy for Mabel. She's already booked a dozen jobs from the first photoshoot and the publicity from the *Good Day, Alabama* interview, and if this is already going viral, I can't imagine what it's going to do for her business. But these people seem *really* invested in you and me. And they don't know anything about us. I mean, we could be axe murderers for all they know."

"Are you?" Jensen lifts his eyebrows in mock terror. "An axe murderer, I mean?"

I smile sweetly and bat my eyelashes at him. "I guess

you'll find out soon."

We both laugh, and I go back to scanning the comments. "They're calling us the perfect couple, which is nice and all, but no pressure, right?"

"I think people just want something to invest in."

"I get that. I mean, everyone loves a good story, right?" I shrug. "I don't know, I guess it's just a little weird when *you're* the story, you know?"

I can't help it, but my brain automatically hits rewind, images from the last six years flashing through my thoughts. All the times I stood in the background so that Adam could be the center of attention, all the ways I made my light dimmer so that he could be the brightest and best thing in the room. "Or maybe it's just me."

Jensen reaches across the console and takes my hand. "It's not you. It is a little strange seeing all these folks on the internet shipping us like we're some celebrity couple instead of two country kids trying to figure it out in rural Alabama. But that doesn't mean we're not worthy of being rooted for."

It's an unexpected response, especially from Jensen, but I like the way the words settle and soothe me. "I like the way you put that. Takes the pressure off a little bit."

"We could always just toss our phones out the window," Jensen suggests, pressing the button that makes both of our windows start to roll down.

I shriek out a laugh as a gust of wind and rain splatter hit me in the face. "Nope, no thank you!" I yell over the storm outside.

Jensen winks and rolls the windows back up. "Okay, well if you're sure."

"I guess it's entertaining if nothing else. I mean, listen to some of these," I point to the screen.

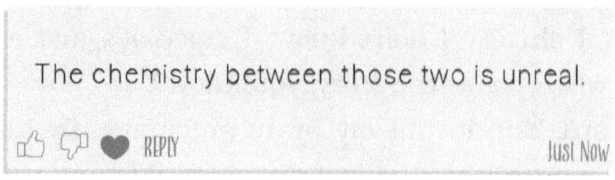

The chemistry between those two is unreal.

"*The chemistry between those two is unreal*," I read. "And the next comment after that is nothing but like fifty fire emojis."

"And all of this just on the video?"

"Mmhmm," I keep scanning. "There's a bunch of comments directed at Mabel. She teased that she'd have the photos up soon, and everyone is begging her to get them up as soon as possible. And then there's stuff like this . . . " I clear my throat and begin to read off a handful of the comments:

OMG LOOK AT THEM!
They are just the cutest!

Holy swoon, Batman! They are totally endgame.

If they don't fall in love, I will stage a protest!
Seriously, they're adorable!

👍 👎 ❤️ REPLY   Just Now

Omg, are they officially together yet?
Because my heart needs to know!

👍 👎 ❤️ REPLY   Just Now

BRB, tearing up. Gah, can we get an
update already?

👍 👎 ❤️ REPLY   Just Now

I'm calling it now. Those two get married and
have the prettiest babies anyone has ever seen.

👍 👎 ❤️ REPLY   Just Now

I shake my head and look up from my phone. "I'm not sure they're going to be able to handle the photos once Mabel posts them." I blush when I think about some of the poses from today's shoot. They're definitely more intimate and personal than our first session. It's a little weird to think about strangers seeing them. I let out a little laugh and look over at Jensen.

He's gripping the steering wheel with both of his hands, and his eyes are firmly fixed on the road ahead, but there's a rigidness in his posture that wasn't there before.

"Jensen?"

He doesn't look at me, but a muscle ticks in his jaw. His brow is furrowed and there's a thunderous look on his face that darkens his features and rivals the storm outside.

All the warmth leeches from my body as if a bucket of ice-cold water has been tipped over my head. Something is wrong, very, very wrong.

"Is everything okay?" I ask timidly.

"Yeah," he responds, though his tone is clipped. "Just trying to focus on the road."

The rain is coming down pretty hard now, and I'm sure it's not the easiest to drive in, but there's something about his answer, the cold timbre of his words, that makes my stomach drop.

I start to ask another question, to say something, anything that will get him to talk to me or explain what just happened, but everything about his demeanor and body language has me shrinking inside myself instead.

"Sorry, I'll stop talking so much so you can focus." My own voice comes out softly, barely above a whisper, though I know he hears me. I keep waiting for him to reassure me that it's fine, that he likes hearing me talk. But he doesn't. He keeps his gaze straight ahead, almost as if he refuses to look at me.

It's just the rain. It's dark outside, and he's trying to keep the truck on the road. The voice of reason comes to my aid. *The roads are slick.*

But as much as I want the explanation to make sense, it just doesn't. We were fine a few minutes ago, joking and laughing, and before that?

Jensen's words from before come back: "*I want to try. I don't know what this mangled heart of mine is capable of, Callie, I really don't, but when I'm with you, all I know is that it doesn't hurt as much. I can breathe again and I can laugh again and whatever that means, I want to hold onto it. I want to hold on to you.*"

How in the world did we go from that to this?

I want to ask him, but he's gripping the steering wheel so tightly he reminds me of a coil that's wrapped so snuggly that the slightest pressure will make it snap.

I must have said something wrong. Must have pushed some kind of button. I go back over our conversation in my head a few times, but I can't find the blunder. I can't seem to figure out what line I crossed.

By the time we pull onto the gravel driveway that leads to the farmhouse, I'm near tears, with my arms wrapped tightly around me.

What happened? What went wrong?

Jensen drives slowly past his place and brings the truck to a stop just outside my RV. "Thanks for the ride," I tell him, forcing an upbeat and chipper tone.

He nods but doesn't look at me.

"Do you want to come inside? I can make us some tea or something?" I don't even have any tea bags inside, but it's a desperate attempt to remedy this weirdness.

"I gotta get home and check on Peaches," Jensen tells me, still refusing to look my way.

"Okay, no problem." I unbuckle my seatbelt and pull the hoodie over my head. "Um . . . here you go. Thanks for letting me borrow it." I leave the hoodie on the center console and throw open the door. I get out in a hurry, and I've only just barely shut the door before Jensen is off again. He might as well have peeled out given how much of a rush he's in to get away from me.

The rain is pouring now, and I know I should go inside and get dried off, but I can't make myself move. It's like I'm stuck in quicksand, and the longer I stand out here, watching Jensen drive away, the more sure I am that the ground is never going to release me, that I'm going to be stuck out here forever wondering what the hell just happened.

"Move," I grumble, willing my body to do something. "*Move.*"

But I can't. I can't take a single step until I figure it out. I run over our conversation again and again in my mind, but I can't find the misstep, can't determine what it was I said or did that set him off. But something happened.

It's Adam's voice I hear in my head then, all the times he berated me for things that were "my" fault, all the ways I fell short in his eyes. Tears fill mine as the memories slam into me like a battering ram, all the words he'd hurled at me like weapons, all the times he broke me and never bothered to put me back together again.

More memories flood to the surface, but these are of Jensen. Like a movie reel, every moment we've spent together flashes before my eyes. The moments when he was so tender and kind mix with the ones where he was standoffish and distant. But this last one, this ride home from the photoshoot, is unlike the others. Jensen has gruffed at me before, but nothing like this.

A dozen different rationales spring up as my mind tries to justify it, tries to justify his behavior, and even though some of them make sense, I still can't land on one that explains this feeling in my chest. Hot and all-consuming, it licks through every cell in my body.

Maybe it's a sign. Maybe Ms. Dorothy was wrong after all. Maybe jumping off the cliff is simply that. Not flying. Falling.

Falling.

Falling.

Falling.

"No!" I shout the word, forcing that horrible thought as far away from me as I can. I realize then that it's anger, hot and unruly, filling my chest and spreading through my entire body. The heat of it like a wildfire that completely consumes everything else, including my ability to excuse what just happened or accept that I've flung myself into nothing but pain and rejection . . . again.

Not this time. Whatever happened in that truck, it doesn't negate every other moment between us. Every touch, every caress, every kiss. I know it wasn't just me that felt it. It wasn't just me that came alive under the lights of the dance hall or at the flea market. It wasn't just me that admitted things I never thought I'd admit beside that waterfall.

Falling or flying. Falling or flying. Falling or flying.

My heart pounds with an answer, and I know what I have to do.

My feet lift. I'm no longer stuck in quicksand.

Chapter 24

Jensen

I park my truck in its usual spot and kill the ignition. The rumble of the dual exhaust fades, leaving only the pounding of the rain reverberating through the cab. But it's not enough to silence the screaming in my head.

Every muscle in my body is tense, adrenaline pumping through me as if I've just run a marathon. My lungs are tight, and I know I'm not getting enough air. I need to move, to breathe, to do something other than just sit here, but all I can think about is the look on Callie's face when I dropped her off. The utter devastation and confusion that outlined every feature. The hurt in her eyes that she was trying not to show.

I press the heels of my palms into my eyes trying to rub away the image, but it's like its burned into my retinas, forever branding me with a reminder of what an absolute coward I am.

I should have just told her. I should have said something to explain it, but there were no words for the violent, unyielding war that had ignited inside of me. Her words had punched through me like a dozen bullets, absolutely eviscerating me, and she'd had absolutely no idea. I should've told her right then, but I couldn't say more than a few clipped words as I bled out. It was all I could do to just keep the truck moving in a straight line.

The shadows have been lingering for a while, just waiting for an opportunity. Now, as they sink their claws into my chest, tearing at my old, ever-bleeding wounds, I relish the agony that slices through me. I deserve every bit of it after what I just did to her.

It's a reminder, no, an absolute declaration that I do not deserve her. Do not deserve what I so carelessly offered her back at the waterfalls. *But you already knew that,* my own voice whispers. I sag against the seat and hang my head as a powerful rumble of thunder overhead shakes the cab of my truck.

The hoodie Callie had on sits in a crumpled heap on the center console. I reach for it, and it still holds the heat of her skin. I bring it closer, sinking my nose into the fabric and god, it smells like her. Sweet honey and vanilla flood my nostrils and it brings tears to my eyes. Unable to take it anymore, I pull the keys out of the ignition and toss the hoodie in the backseat.

Outside, the storm is wild, with wind whipping through the trees, making them sway and bend in ways that only those in this area can understand. Rain falls in sheets around me, and even though my clothes were already damp from the photoshoot, I'm soaked thoroughly to the bone in seconds. The darkened sky ignites with streaks of lightning and resounding booms of thunder that echo around the valley and back. Spring in Alabama can be dangerous, indeed.

Even that acknowledgement doesn't make me quicken my steps. I move slowly, each footstep heavier than the last until I make it to the porch. The screen door creaks when I open it, shoving my key into the lock. The living room is dimly lit with a single lamp in the corner, but Peaches leaps up from her bed to come greet me. Her tail whips back and forth so quickly, her happiness that I'm home making the lump that's formed in my throat grow even larger.

I kneel down and she immediately hops into my lap, her tongue lapping at any exposed skin she can find. "Hey girl," I murmur, wrapping my arms around her. She's squirming, trying to get at my face, but I bury it in her soft fur.

I take the comfort she offers me, even though I don't deserve it, and run my hands along her back until I find the strength to stand again. "Come on," I give her the sign for *eat*. "Let's go get you some—"

Thunder erupts over the farmhouse, the sound making the windows rattle, but that isn't what steals the words from my mouth. It's the sound of my name.

My head whips back to the screen door, to see Callie marching across the grass.

I shove through the door, letting it slam behind me. "Callie?" I call out. "What are you doing?"

She's soaked, her hair plastered to her face, the fabric of her dress clinging to every curve, but she doesn't seem to notice or care. I wince as a streak of lightning cracks the sky open right above her, but she doesn't even flinch. Her eyes are locked on me, blazing with fire, as she stomps toward the farmhouse.

I leap from the porch and rush toward her. "What the hell are you doing?" I demand. "Are you trying to get yourself killed?" I reach for her, but she steps away from me, avoiding the contact.

"What am *I* doing?" She lets out a bitter laugh. "I think a better question is what are *you* doing?" Her hands clench into fists at her side. "Cause I've been trying to figure it out, to figure *you* out, and I can't make it make sense."

Overhead a bolt of lightning, streaks across the sky, electricity crackling through the air. "We need to get out of the storm." I motion to my house. "We can talk in—"

"I'm not going anywhere with you," Callie spits the words. "I just came here to tell you that I'm done. Done with whatever *this* is," She motions between the two of us. "I'm done, Jensen."

She doesn't say it, but I hear the double meaning of her words: I'm done with *you*, Jensen.

The ache in my chest swells to the point of physical pain, but I breathe through it, keeping my face neutral. This is what has to happen, even if it kills me in the process. "Okay," I huff out.

"Okay?" She repeats the word. "That's it, just okay?" The look she gives me is searing, full of anger and disappointment and it eviscerates a layer of my self-control.

"What do you want me to say?" I growl, heat surging through my body. "You said you're done with me. Fine, you're done."

Callie stomps closer, her chest heaving. "Just like that, huh?"

I lift a shoulder and let it drop.

"No." she shakes her head. "No, you don't get to just shrug it off like that. You don't get to pretend that it doesn't matter, that you don't care." She's shaking now, and I can't tell if it's from the chill of the rain or her anger. I want so badly to pull her close, to wrap my arms around her, but I cross them over my chest instead and level her with a stare.

"I'm sorry, okay? I thought we could be friends, maybe more, but it was all just a mistake." I fling the words like a dagger and when they find their mark, the flash of pain in Callie's eyes nearly sends me to my knees. But I keep going. It's the only way. "You should go, Callie."

I school my features as the shadows swirl around me. I just want her to leave so I can fully surrender to them. They can sense it, practically crowing with victory as I feel myself sinking deeper and deeper into their depths.

Callie's cheeks are leeched of color and from the droop of her shoulders, I can tell she's still reeling from my careless words. My breath hitches, and I tear my eyes away, unable to look at her anymore. "If that's it then . . . " I turn on my heel, fully intending to stalk inside my farmhouse and slam the door behind me.

But another bolt of lightning crackles across the sky, this one much closer than the last. The clap of thunder that follows is almost immediate. The storm is now right over our heads.

Callie jumps at the sound and lets out a little squeak of surprise. I should walk away like I planned, but it's that little sound, that simple little vulnerability that cracks open my chest. I stalk closer, grabbing her hand and pulling her toward the farmhouse. "Come on," I yell over the wind, trying to ignore the heat of her hand searing into my palm.

Under the covered porch, we're a bit more protected from the elements, but the storm isn't letting up. I drop Callie's hand. "Let me go get my keys. I'll drive you back up to the RV."

"No thanks," Callie argues, rubbing her hands up and down her arms, trying to ward off the layer of goosebumps that covers her skin. "I'll wait until it calms down a bit. Then I'll walk."

"Well, come inside at least. Get dried off and—"

"No, thank you." She cuts me off. "I'd rather wait out here." She refuses to look at me, keeping her face trained on the storm just beyond the stairs.

"Are you always this stubborn?" I demand, unable to stop myself.

"Are you always this much of an ass?" She fires back, and the look of disgust she gives me nearly cleaves me in half.

"Yes," I answer because what other answer is there? I may have forgotten myself, may have gotten too wrapped up in a reprieve that was only supposed to be temporary, but reality, cold and harsh, has shaken loose the hold she had on me.

"Why can't you just talk to me?"

"I don't know what you want me to say?"

"Seriously?" The fire returns to Callie eyes. "Well, how about for starters you explain to me how you can touch me and hold me like you did today, how you can say you want to try this for real with me, and then practically throw me out of your truck five seconds later as if I don't matter? You can stand there and pretend like it was some kind of mistake or misunderstanding or whatever, but you forget that I was there." She digs her phone out of the pocket of her skirt, taps twice, and waves it at me. "You can't tell me this is a mistake."

A picture of us from the first photoshoot is displayed on the screen. In the picture, we're kissing, but it's mostly my features that are prominent, and the enraptured look on my face is one that I'm not sure I can explain away.

"It was just for show," I try, the excuse falling flat and we both know it. "I was trying to help out a friend."

"Okay, what about today?" She presses. "Every touch, every caress, every time your lips touched mine. Was it just for the camera? Or what about when you told me that you wanted to hold on to me? Was that all for show, too?"

Yes, my brain urges me to say. But my heart, my stupid, stupid heart is screaming the opposite, and I can't think over the noise.

"It was . . . um . . . "

Callie's cheeks lift in a small smile. She noticed my fumble. "See? It's not just me that felt the connection. You can lie all you want and say that it was just some trick of the camera lens, but I know you felt it. Look me in the face right now and tell me that you didn't."

Deny, deny, deny, the shadows hiss in my ears, but it feels like all my strength has evaporated. I don't want to lie to her.

"I felt it," I admit, my voice barely audible above the storm, but from the way her nostrils flare, I know she hears me.

"Then tell me what happened? One minute we were

laughing and the next minute it was like I stabbed you or something. Was it me? Did I say something? You have to tell me what I did wrong."

Her voice cracks on the last syllable.

"It's not you," I rush to tell her, needing her to understand as messed up as this is, it has nothing to do with her. "It wasn't anything you did, Callie. It's me that's the problem."

"Oh, the old classic, it's not you, it's me." Callie looks like she wants to punch me, and god, I wish she would.

"You owe me a better explanation than that. After my ex dumped me, I didn't want to find someone else. I was ready to swear off love for good. But then you came along and everything changed. Even after what I've been through, you let me believe that it was okay for me to open my heart to someone again. You made me feel like no one has ever made me feel, like I mattered, like I was worth something. And then just like that, you build a wall between us and I want to know why."

She's absolutely right, she deserves an explanation. But I can't give her one, not without ripping myself open. Not without revealing truths about myself that I don't want to face.

"You need to go home, Callie." I say, forcing the words out. I don't mean for them to come out harshly. I flinch at the gruffness of my tone.

"No." She stares me down, unphased. "I'm not going anywhere until you tell me why."

"Go home," I try again. "I don't want you here." It's a lie and my damn heart almost shatters when her face crumples, but I have no alternative.

It takes her a second to collect herself, but when she does, she lifts her chin and huffs out a laugh. "You don't mean that. I can see it in your expression. You're lying."

Am I that transparent? If she can see that, what else can she see? "I'm not."

"Fine." She steps into my space, swiping the wet strands from her eyes so she can peer up at me. "Touch me."

"What?" Shock ripples through me.

"I want you to touch me," she says again, reaching for my hand. "If you really want me to go, then you're going to have to say it again. But first . . . " She yanks me closer, pulling my arm and placing my palm on her cheek. "Say it again."

Her skin is soft underneath my fingertips, and I can't stop myself from swiping my thumb across her cheekbone. "I . . . Callie, I . . . ." I can't think when all I want to do is drop to my knees in front of her and beg her not to go.

But I can't do this. I *can't* have this.

I don't deserve it, don't deserve *her*. And even if I did, it wouldn't matter. The only thing I can offer her is broken pieces, damaged goods.

I yank my hand away and step backward, putting space between us. I can't be close to her, can't touch her or I won't have the strength to do what needs to be done. "Just go, Callie. Please, you need to go home."

"I won't." She moves closer, eyes blazing, cutting across the space I just created between us. "Not until you tell me why. I spent too many years of my life letting someone steal my voice and make me feel like I wasn't worth anything more than the scraps he threw my way. I'm not doing that with you. If you really want me to go, then you have to tell me why. Don't you think I deserve that?"

"Just go."

"I'm not going."

"You need to leave."

"And you need to tell me what's really going on."

"Callie, you need—"

She cuts me off again. "I'm not going anywhere. So just tell me. Why are you—"

"Because I'm not good for you," I finally explode, the words spilling out with such force it makes me ache.

Callie scoffs. "You don't get to decide that for me."

"I can't do this." I try to find the words to make her understand. "I thought I could keep things casual, that I could stop myself from letting things go too far, but today at the falls, I let my walls down for a split second. I realize now that it was a mistake. I can't let you fall in love with me, Callie, I can't."

"Well, too bad!" she yells, throwing her arms out. "Because I already did, you big, stupid, stubborn jerk.

It's too late."

Her confession knocks the wind out of me. "Don't say that."

"Why? Because it scares you? Well, get over it, Jensen. You don't get to tell me how to feel. I want you, Jensen, and if I want to throw myself off a cliff for you, then that's my choice to make."

No, no, no, this can't be happening. I can't let this happen. "You can't love me."

"Why not?"

And there it is, the sharp edge of the guillotine that's been hanging over my head from the moment she pulled off that blindfold, from the second I realized that I could breathe around her. It presses against my skin, drawing blood.

"Because I already know how this story ends."

Callie sucks in a breath, clearly a little surprised by my answer. "This is about Anna."

"No, it's about you and me. You say you want me, that you've fallen for me, but it won't last. Not when you realize what you'd have to give up to be with me."

"What are you talking about?" She takes a step back, her eyes searching mine.

"I know I'm making a lot of assumptions here, Callie, but you have to trust me. Everyone thinks that love can conquer anything, but that's a lie. There are some things love can't save you from. And when you have to face that reality, it damn near cleaves your soul in half.

It's like a bomb that explodes, filling your body with shrapnel. No, it's worse than that. It's like someone died, the grief of it, and you almost wish they had because it would be easier than the truth."

Tears fill Callie's eyes, even though I know she doesn't understand what I'm saying. But it's like a dam has broken inside me and the words pour out. "When you think about your future, you want it all, right? A nice house, a beautiful wedding, and . . . kids one day, right?"

Callie's eyes are wide, and I know I've more than shocked her with the turn of this conversation, the seriousness of it. She just stares at me.

"Answer the question."

"Yeah, I do. One day but—"

"No," I shake my head, "That's it. If you want that, I can't be the one to give it to you. As much as I want you, and god, Callie. I do. I want you more than I've wanted anything in this life. But I can't be unfair to you." Everything hurts, and the words are like razor blades slicing through me.

"Unfair to me? What does that even mean?"

"It means you need to go," I choke on the words. "I'm broken and damaged and there's nothing anybody can do about it."

"I still don't understand." She glances down at the puddle of water pooling around her feet, like the answer might be there, then back up at me, blinking against the confusion. "What are you saying?"

"I'm saying that I . . . " I swallow. "I can't have children, Callie. There's no future with me. And if I let this continue, you'll figure that out just like Anna did. So why delay the inevitable?"

Chapter 25
Callie

It takes a second for the words to sink in, but once they do, all I can do is gape. I'd been so furious when I marched over, heat surging through my body as I imagined a dozen different ways I could tell Jensen to go kick rocks. But now—now, all I can feel is the icy chill of the rain on my skin and a deep ache in my chest for the man standing in front of me.

Jensen's face is all hard lines, but it's his eyes that betray him, dark and as wild as the storm that rages around us, and swimming in agony so profound it extinguishes the fiery anger burning in my gut.

"Is that what happened?" I ask. "Is that why she left?" I'm not sure I have the right to ask, but I need to know. I need to understand. The wind steals my words almost as soon as they leave my lips, but I know he hears them from the way he flinches.

At first, I don't think he's going to answer, but then he lets out a ragged breath and nods. "She said there was no reason to stay, not when I couldn't give her what she wanted."

The words settle between us, heavy and unyielding. Jensen lets out a low sigh, so full of resignation and pain it nearly breaks my heart in two. I don't know the whole story, but I can see it all over his face—the soul-crushing rejection. It cloaks every feature and hangs over his head like a shadow.

I've known rejection, but not like this. This is agonizing loss. It's earth-shattering betrayal. It's utter devastation, the kind some people never come back from.

My brain, trying to process everything, spins and whirs and then clicks with a realization. One of the comments from earlier, the ones I was reading out loud in the truck, mentioned something about us getting married and making pretty babies. It hadn't even registered with me then, but now it makes sense. Right after reading all the comments, that was when Jensen's behavior had changed.

"In the truck," I whisper. "The comment about us getting married and having . . . " I trail off, not even wanting to say the words so I don't trigger him more. The tortured look on his face is all the confirmation I need.

"I'm so sorry. I had no idea, and if I'd known, I'd—"

"It's me that should be sorry."

I start to shake my head, but he holds up a hand. "No, please. Let me apologize. I was a jerk today, and there isn't an excuse for my behavior. You deserve so much more than that. Which is exactly why we're having this conversation right now. I'm so sorry I let it go this far. I knew better, I really did, but I told myself that it was okay to let myself have a reprieve, even if it couldn't last. I wanted that, the peace that you gave me, even if it was only temporary. It was selfish of me. I know that now. I just got so swept up in . . . in you, Callie. You made me feel whole. You made me *forget*. And if you've thrown yourself off a cliff, then I'm free-falling right beside you, but we both know it's not enough."

I realize then what he's really saying. It's the same thing I've been telling myself for years. The same, horrible mantra that feels like it's tattooed on my skull.

I am less. I am unworthy. I am nothing. I am undeserving.

I am not enough.

A sob rises in my throat for the brokenness in front of me. For the same brokenness that I carried around for six years. Until recently, when a grumpy mechanic made me believe differently.

A feeling far more powerful than sadness or empathy surges through me. I take a careful step closer to Jensen and another. He tracks my movements, but he doesn't pull away when I'm close enough to touch him. I search for the words to tell him that he's wrong, but I know he won't believe me. I need him to understand. So, I tell him the four words tattooed on my *heart*. "Fly with me, Jenson."

His eyes widen at the words and he shakes his head. "You don't know what you're saying."

"Yes, I do. I know exactly what I'm saying, and you need to hear it. It's enough, Jensen. *You're* enough." I step up on my tiptoes, pressing my palms into his chest and trail my mouth along his jaw. "Fly with me," I whisper.

Jensen's body tenses and his breathing is ragged, but slowly, he wraps his arms around me, pulling me closer. I lean back a little to peer into his face. He looks absolutely terrified, and the war raging in his eyes makes me ache.

"You know what Mrs. Dorothy told me? She said that sometimes you just have to jump. There's no way to know whether you'll fall or you'll fly, you just have to have the courage to try. But I'm starting to think it's more than that. I think it's a choice. We get to choose. Flying or falling. Falling or flying. It's up to us to decide." I lift a hand to his cheek. "So, what do you say? Will you fly—"

Jensen crashes his lips to mine, stealing the rest of my sentence and my breath. This isn't just a kiss. It's an answer, fierce and unrelenting, as his hands tangle in my hair.

A thrill, sharp and electrifying, shoots through me as his mouth moves over mine, desperate and claiming. My fingers twist in the fabric of his shirt as I pull him closer, matching his urgency with my answering kiss. Just as hungry, just as untamed.

As his tongue sweeps over mine, I swear it's as if the world tilts and the only thing keeping me anchored is the feel of his hands moving across my skin, sliding down my back to hold me against his chest. I step up on my tiptoes, deepening our kiss and chasing the taste of him in my mouth.

Heat surges through me as Jensen slowly walks us backward until my spine presses into the wall. My body molds to his, my hands sliding up over his broad shoulders as I wrap my arms around his neck, giving as much as I'm taking.

I thought I understood fire, thought I knew what it meant to burn for someone else, but the inferno inside my chest is searing. It's feverish and incendiary.

Jensen pulls his mouth away from mine, leaving me gasping, as he trails his lips along my jaw and down the column of my throat, each press of his lips into my skin like a scorching brand.

It feels so unbelievably good, I don't want him to stop. He presses a kiss to my bare shoulder, his fingers toying with the thin straps of my dress as he moves the fabric aside to kiss more of the skin there. I shiver when he puts the strap back in place, his thumb moving back and forth in a soothing circle.

My fingers find his face and trail along his jaw. He leans into my touch, his eyes finding mine. "Callie," he murmurs, his voice low and rough. It's a plea and an apology, and I can feel the way he's holding himself together, holding himself back as if he's afraid I'll regret all of this later. But I won't. There's not a single touch that I would trade, not an ounce of me that wants this moment to end. For the first time in so long, I feel like that girl who used to paint with reckless abandon, who used to do what she wanted without a care in the world. I feel like the girl I used to be.

I feel alive in a way that I'll never be able to paint because there are no hues in existence that can match the vibrancy of his touch. No shade or tint that can mirror the way my body responds to him. No spectrum of color that can truly capture the depth of what it feels like to be in his arms. I don't want him to hold back from me. I don't want careful. I don't want restraint. I want *him*.

I lean in, brushing my lips against his, slowly and deliberately. He shivers beneath my touch, and I kiss him again. I'm still burning, but I don't want to rush, don't want him to mistake the feverish flurry for something else.

Jensen's hands slide down my sides and over the curve of my waist down to my thighs. His fingers grip me tightly and then he lifts me into his arms, my legs wrapping around him and eliminating any remaining space between our bodies. "Tell me to stop, Callie," he pulls away to whisper roughly in my ear. His lips skate across the skin of my jaw and down the crook of my neck, as he trails kisses across the curve of my shoulder, over my collarbones. "You have to tell me to stop," he murmurs between breaths.

"I can't," I breathe, the smell of pine and mint from his aftershave mixing with the dampened earth and the rain from the storm. "I don't want you to."

One of Jensen's hands goes around me, gripping my waist while the other trails up my spine to cup the back of my neck, supporting me as he pulls us away from the wall. His mouth captures mine again and sweet magnolias, the way he kisses me should be criminal.

He doesn't pull away as he carries me to the door, his lips never leaving mine as he pulls the screen open and brings us inside. In the living room, he gently puts me down, his hands holding on to me as I slide down the length of his body.

Jensen swears low in his throat, and I pull back to see him glancing down to where Peaches is standing up on her hind legs, her front paws pressed into his side. Her tail wags and her tongue darts out of her mouth trying to lick whichever of us she can get to first. A snort bubbles up in my throat as he gives her a gentle shove. "Down," he growls, giving her a sign. "Go lay down." He gives her another sign and points to the dog bed by the fireplace. She gives us both a look that reminds me of an eye-roll, but she does what he says, trotting over to her bed and flopping down with a huff.

I laugh again and when Jensen looks at me, his mouth is quirked up in a grin so beautiful it feels like I might cry.

"I love hearing you laugh," he tells me, leaning in to nip at my bottom lip. A whimper escapes me, every nerve cell in my body igniting. "And that," he whispers against the skin of my neck. "I love the sounds you make when I touch you like this." His fingers trail down my arms and I shiver.

"Please," I murmur, my hands gripping his waist. "Don't stop." Everything inside me is electric, my body humming with the current as it courses through every inch of me.

Jensen's eyes darken as he lifts me again, scooping my legs out from under me and holding me with one arm around my back and the other under my knees. His stormy gaze makes my pulse race, and I kiss him with an urgency that scorches, his lips meeting mine step for step. When we come up for air, he lifts his brows at me, as if to ask the question, "Are you sure?"

I stare into those wild eyes of his and nod, just once, but with all of the certainty of my soul.

He leads us into the hallway, the booming of my heart matching his footfalls against the smooth hardwood floor. The bedroom is dark, save for the dim light filtering through the window. Rain batters the roof, the rhythmic sound filling the small space as wind howls through the trees. I'm usually afraid of storms, but not here, not when I'm wrapped in Jensen's arms.

His hands are everywhere now, his fingertips roaming every inch of me, as if he can't get enough. My own hands lift, and I'm shaking as I reach for the hem of his shirt, pulling the wet fabric away from his body to slide my palms up against the hard plane of his stomach. The heat of his skin beneath my fingertips is overwhelming and not enough.

As if he reads my mind, Jensen pulls the shirt up and over his head. The soaked material clings to his body, but he rips it away, tossing it on the floor at our feet.

His fingers find the zipper of my dress, his touch light as he tugs it down, the fabric slipping from my shoulders to pool at my feet. His eyes roam across my body as he tugs me closer.

My hands slide upward, tracing the lines of ink that swirl across his chest. He's so beautiful, I can hardly stand it, and I step up on my toes to press a kiss to his chest, right over his heart.

His lips find mine again, and there's nothing but the feel of his skin against mine, the sweet whisper of breath between us.

We're on fire, he and I, but this isn't the blazing inferno from before.

It's slow ribbons of magma carving lines into stone, molten and transformative. Consuming. Re-shaping.

And together, we burn.

Chapter 26

Jensen

If it were possible to capture a moment and live in it forever, I would choose this one. The rain has slowed outside, casting the room in a peaceful stillness. Callie is dozing next to me, her legs entwined with mine, and one of her hands rests on the arm I have slung over her, holding her to my chest.

She's so beautiful it hurts, and there's definitely a small part of me that's convinced that this entire thing is a dream. Or a nightmare designed to torture me. I trail a finger down her arm, watching as her skin pebbles beneath my touch. I love that I have that effect over her, the goosebumps on her flesh a sign that she's as affected by my touch as I am by hers.

Fly with me, Jensen. My cheeks lift

when I think of her whispered request, of the way her hands had pulled me closer, the way her mouth had opened for me. I close my eyes, letting the memories flood my senses. The sweet honey of her skin, the gentle brush of her fingertips across my body, the look in her beautiful eyes, so full of desire and certainty.

I could live in the memory of it all until the end of time and die a happy man, but I know I won't get that lucky. Already I can feel the shadows creeping in on me. They're lingering in the corners, waiting and biding their time until they can claim me again. I've stopped trying to wish them away—wishing is pointless. It changes nothing. These shadows are my punishment, my cross to bear. Not even time with Callie can keep them at bay, at least not for long. They own me, now and forever.

I lean down and press a kiss to Callie's temple. I don't mean to wake her, but she stirs, her eyelids blinking slowly as they adjust to the low lighting of my bedroom. Her cheeks lift in a lazy, contented smile. "Hey, you," she says, rolling over to face me.

"Hey, pretty girl."

All I can think about is how much I want to kiss her, so I dip my head to capture her lips with mine. She lets out a sound of approval, like the purring of a cat, wrapping an arm around my neck to pull me even closer. I let myself get lost in the kiss, savoring the feel of her underneath my hands and the way her body fits so perfectly with mine. If kissing her could somehow make things right, I'd spend the rest of my life just like this.

But absolution isn't in the cards for me, and the old realization has me pulling back while the shadows cackle gleefully.

Callie studies my face, and I'm not sure exactly what she sees there, but her brows furrow. "Are you okay?"

"I'm better than I've been in a long time," I tell her and mean it, though the truth is far more complicated. "How are you?" I'm a little nervous to hear her answer, and I brace myself.

She puts a hand to my face, tracing the outline of my nose, my lips, my jaw and then up to soothe the worry away from my forehead. "I'm perfect."

I let out a breath, relief flooding through me. I've gotten so used to hearing the worst that it always surprises me when something good happens. My time with Callie has been nothing short of life-changing, and I hope she understands what today means to me, what *she* means to me. But there's a torrent of emotions swirling inside my chest that I'm struggling to process. I swore to myself that I would never be in this place again, that I would never let anyone get this close. It was the only way I could survive.

But what do you do when the one thing you should stay away from is the very breath in your lungs?

I'm in love with this woman. Utterly and entirely, and as much as I want to deny it, as much as I want to protect us both from it, I can't. There's nowhere far enough that I can run, nothing that I can say that will make this work. It's too late . . . and that absolutely terrifies me.

The panic swirling in my gut must show on my face because Callie's expression changes, her brows knitting closer together. "Jensen?"

I hear her call my name, but the sound is distorted, like we're underwater. Black shapes dart across my field of vision, and it feels like there's a 300-pound weight sitting on my chest. The pressure builds, threatening to crush me. My hands reach for Callie, gripping her as if she can anchor me, but I'm slipping. My lungs sputter with breaths coming too fast, too shallow.

"Jensen?" Callie sits up and pulls me upright. "Are you okay?"

I want to answer her, but I can't. Gasping, my eyes find hers, swimming with worry. I've had attacks like this before, but I've never mentioned them to anyone. Not even Sutton.

"It's okay," she says, her voice soothing, though a little shaky. "I think you're having a panic attack, but I'm here and you're going to be alright." She's a beacon in the darkness that's crowding in on me, like a lighthouse on the shore in a storm. She covers my hands with hers and squeezes. "Just breathe."

But that's the problem. As much as my lungs are screaming for oxygen, my throat won't open.

"You can do this, low and slow," Callie's voice is calm,

steady. She picks up one of my hands and places it on her chest, right above her heart. She takes my other hand and puts it on my own chest. "We'll do it together, okay?"

She inhales deeply, and beneath my palm, her chest rises. I'm not sure if it's instinct or muscle memory or what, but the next time she does it, air rushes in through my nose.

"That's it. Just breathe with me. In," Callie inhales deeply, "And out." She blows the breath slowly from her lips, and I replicate the movement, even as my body fights against it.

"Again. Just like that." She leans in, pressing her forehead against mine. "Just breathe."

Her touch grounds me, and the crushing weight lifts a little, just enough so I can draw in a decent, full breath. Callie keeps my hands in place, her thumb rubbing soothing circles against my skin. "I'm here," she whispers tenderly. "It's okay. Just keep breathing."

Slowly, I come back to myself, and the world steadies. I drop my face to her shoulder, burying it in the soft skin of her neck. "I'm sorry," I rasp, my voice a little hoarse.

"Hey." She lifts my head, cupping my face between her palms so she's peering into my eyes. "You have nothing to be sorry for, okay?"

I nod, only because I don't know what else to say.

"Have you ever had one before?"

"Yeah, but not for a while," I admit. "They were pretty

bad for the first year or two after everything happened, but not so much lately. It's just . . . "

I hate the words I have to say next. I want to reject them, to fling them as far away from us as I can, but Callie still doesn't know the whole story. If she knew the truth, knew what I've done, she wouldn't be so accepting of me.

"I can't keep you, Callie, and knowing I'm going to have to let you walk out this room absolutely guts me."

"I'm not leaving, Jensen."

"But you should." I swallow. "What happened between us was the most incredible thing that's ever happened to me, but as much as I want this, *you*, I already know how this story ends. You should walk away now."

Callie searches my face. "I know there's things we need to discuss but—"

"Please, Callie. There's so much you don't know, and if you did . . . " I scrub a hand down my face. "Trust me, you don't want to be with me. I don't deserve you."

"You keep saying that, but you don't really believe that do you? Everyone deserves to be happy."

It's nothing I haven't heard before. But it doesn't apply. Not to me.

"I don't." The words come out a whisper.

Callie's eyes widen. "Jensen, you can't really—"

"Like I said, you just have to trust me on this," I interrupt her, feeling some of the tightness return to my chest. I rub at the spot, trying to alleviate the ache.

"I do trust you, but you can't just beg me to leave. Talk to me. Help me understand."

Her gentle pleading makes the ache in my chest worse, and I drop my hand and swallow hard. There's no easy way to say it, no preamble I can give to explain it. So, I rush the words out, ignoring the way they sink their teeth into my skin, like vipers.

"It's true that Anna left me because I can't have kids. That would be bad enough if it were the whole story, but it's not."

Don't, Kase growls in my ear. *Don't say it.*

The sound of his voice in my ear has me gasping, but I have to do this. I have to tell her the truth.

"I killed him, Callie," I whisper, bearing my soul. "I killed Kasey."

She stares at me for a moment, her wide eyes searching mine. "It was a helicopter crash that killed Kasey."

"Yeah," I confirm bitterly. "But he wasn't supposed to be on that helo. If I hadn't . . . If I just . . . " The tightness in my chest makes it near impossible to go on. "It's my fault he's dead."

I half expect her to jump up and try to get away from me or at least glare at me in revulsion or horror, but she doesn't flinch or freak out or look at me with anything other than gentleness.

"I don't understand," she admits quietly. "But I'd like to." She runs a hand down my arm and gives a little squeeze. "If you want me to."

She's not forcing me to talk about it, not demanding answers as others might. She's giving me the choice, and I honestly think she'd be okay with it if I couldn't tell her what happened. She'd understand, and that is even more proof that I don't deserve her, and all the more reason to tell her.

"If I'm going to tell you, I have to start at the beginning." I reach for Callie's hand and entwine my fingers with hers. I need something to hold on to, something that will anchor me.

She squeezes my hand tightly and nods.

I stare at our joined hands, breath rattling in my chest as my body braces for what's coming. The warmth of her palm seeps into mine, a steady reassurance, but still a tremor works its way into my limbs. For a moment, I reconsider telling her, but then she swipes her thumb across my knuckle in a silent gesture of comfort that says, *it's okay. I'm right here next to you.*

So, I exhale slowly and welcome the weight of the memories as they press in on me, sharp and unrelenting. "It starts with Anna. We knew each other as kids and grew up in the same small town in Texas. We always ran in the same circles, but it wasn't until 7th grade that we even paid much attention to each other. She was this determined, outspoken brainiac, and I was a shy, country boy who had no idea what he wanted. We met in gym class that first week when she demanded I be her partner for badminton. Didn't ask, just told me that's what was going to happen. And I didn't argue. Every day after that, she'd boss me around, and I would do whatever she said, mainly because I liked the smile she gave me when she got her way.

We stayed friends through high school, but I finally got the courage to ask her out our senior year. She just grinned and said, 'Well, it's about time you asked me that.' And from then on, it was her and me against the world. By the time we graduated, I knew I wanted to marry her, but I also knew there was no way she'd say yes until she finished college. So, I joined the army, and she went off to work on her degree. Long distance wasn't easy, but we made it work, and whenever I got leave, I did everything I could to make up for lost time. All I wanted was to make her happy.

We got married a month after she graduated and moved to North Carolina. I was stationed at Ft. Bragg and she got a job working for a city councilman. For a while, everything was perfect. We were really happy."

I pause, letting the echo of that happiness linger for just a moment. "But it didn't last . . . After a few years, we decided we were ready to start a family. Anna was one of six kids, and her dream was to have a large family of her own. I never had any brothers or sisters, so I was all for it. One, two, twelve, it didn't matter to me as long as I had her."

The breath hitches in my throat, and I stumble over my words. Callie squeezes my hand, the reassurance in her gesture enough to help me continue.

"At first, we didn't think anything about it. These things take time, right? But after months and months of negative tests, we knew something wasn't right. Anna made an appointment with her doctor who tried to assure us that everything was normal. We were young and healthy, and it would happen eventually.

Only it didn't happen. Months passed, each one without the good news we so desperately wanted. Anna started to worry that something was wrong with her. A few of the women in her family had some trouble getting pregnant, and she was concerned that she might have some of the same issues. She made an appointment to get tested.

When her tests came back, everything seemed normal, though her iron levels were a little low. The doc prescribed a supplement, and Anna was optimistic it would fix our issues. But a few more months passed, and we didn't get pregnant. So, it was my turn to get tested.

I was confident that my results would come back normal like Anna's, so when the nurse called to give us the results, we weren't expecting to hear that the initial sperm analysis came back abnormal. We barely had time to process the results before we were referred to a reproductive endocrinologist. But still, we were hopeful.

The fertility doc ran more tests and determined that I have OAT Syndrome, which basically means I have a really low sperm count, and what I do have isn't great quality."

I clear my throat, a little bit self-conscious to be sharing something so personal. But Callie doesn't seem uncomfortable. She just listens, holding my gaze as I keep going.

"The doctor warned us that our odds were low. Not completely impossible, but the outlook wasn't great. Still, there were treatments we could try. Anna was optimistic. We both were.

We tried everything: medication, IUIs, and three rounds of IVF, but nothing worked. Anna did acupuncture and we both changed our diet hoping it would help us conceive, but it all failed.

Anna began to grow distant. She was angry over the fact that she couldn't get pregnant. I tried to make her feel better, to do whatever I could to make things right, but it only made things worse. She started spending all her free time researching alternative fertility treatments and homeopathic methods.

The night Kase died I was . . . " I pinch the bridge of my nose. "I was supposed to be on duty that night. It was my shift, and I was the one who was supposed to be up in the chopper. But Anna had found a holistic fertility clinic that she was sure was the answer to our problems. By then, we'd spent thousands of dollars on treatments, and I was beginning to lose hope.

When I voiced my fears, she got so angry at me. Angrier than I've ever seen her. She demanded that I go with her to the clinic. I knew then that she had started to resent me. It was my fault we weren't able to get pregnant, and I felt like I owed it to her to try. So, I agreed to go.

Of course, the only day we could get an appointment was a day I had the training mission. I didn't think there was any way around it, but Kase talked me into taking the matter up the Chain of Command. Once I explained my situation, leadership was willing to work with me. I didn't know until later that Kase offered to take my spot on the mission."

I take a breath, needing a minute before I tell the rest. I've gone over it a thousand times in my head, trying to figure out a way for the story to end differently, but it never does.

"Everything about that night was routine. The preflight checks were performed with no issue and everything was as it should be. The training exercise was running like clockwork, but then . . . then it all went to hell."

Tears clog my throat, and I can feel the walls I've built start to crumble. "It was supposed to be me up there that night, Callie. It was my shift. I was supposed to be the one who died, not Kase."

A sob erupts from my throat. "I should've put my foot down, should've told Anna no, but I was so desperate to make her happy, to do something that would make her love me again. I thought I was doing the right thing, but if I had known . . . " Another sob. "I killed my best friend and then I had to go to his house and tell his wife and son that he was gone all because of me."

Tears drip down Callie's cheeks. "You can't blame yourself for what happened. It was an accident. A horrible, awful accident, but it's not your fault."

"It is though," I argue. "And you know what's sad? I thought that nothing else could hurt as much as losing my best friend, but I was wrong about that, too. About three weeks after the funeral, I came home and the house was quiet. I knew right away something was wrong. I looked for Anna, but couldn't find her. She wasn't in the kitchen or in the garden out back. I thought maybe she was upstairs taking a bath, but when I walked in, the closet door was wide open and the light was still on.

My side was completely untouched, but her side was emptied. There was nothing left but a few hangers on the rack. I found the note she'd written on the bed. It was short, only a few lines, but she explained that she was leaving me. She said she couldn't stick around much longer knowing that we weren't going to work. She wanted children and I couldn't give them to her, so she just couldn't see a future with me any longer."

A wave of exhaustion washes over me, and the damn shadows swoop in at last, relishing in my pain, laughing as they wrap me up in their clutches and squeeze the life from me.

"So now you know," I whisper, with the last of my strength. "I'm the reason Ethan has to grow up without a father. I don't deserve to be happy when Sutton has to spend her days raising her son alone. And Anna leaving? That was my punishment. The universe's way of restoring balance. I took a life, and so it took mine."

I pull my hand gently out of Callie's grip. "You deserve someone whole, someone worthy, but I'm not that man. It's why I keep pushing you away," I add quietly, the truth finally out between us. "I don't know how to be with you without it ruining us both."

Chapter 27

Callie

The words break my heart, but it's the resigned look on Jensen's face that makes the tears well up in my eyes. "Falling or flying, remember? We get to choose. We get to decide what breaks us and what doesn't." I take his face in my hands, hoping he can feel the truth of my words through the warmth of my palms. "And it won't be this."

"You can't know that for sure."

"No, but I'm choosing to believe it. I'm choosing *you*, Jensen."

He starts to shake his head, to tell me that I'm making a mistake, but I keep my hands firmly in place, so he has nowhere to look but into my eyes. "I'm not expecting it to be easy, you know. There's a lot we have to talk about, things that might make us both uncomfortable, but I'm not afraid of difficult conversations or life's uncertainties because if I'm sure of anything, it's how I feel about you. I tried to fight it, tried to tell myself that I was better off without complications or trouble, but I was wrong. I know what I'm walking into. I know what I'm getting and I'm still choosing it, choosing you."

"But I don't deserve that. Not after what I've done."

"You can't keep blaming yourself for what happened to Kasey. It was an accident, a horrible, awful accident—but that's not on you. And Kasey wouldn't want you to spend the rest of your life blaming yourself for it."

"But if it weren't for me, he'd still be here." His whispered words are laced with guilt, and there's a piece of me that recoils at the raw depth of them. That piece, though healed now, unequivocally understands what it feels like to drown in the sea of what might have been, what *should* have been. That piece is where the bones of my own guilt over my parents' death are buried. Not forgotten, but put to rest, and all I want is for Jensen to be able to do the same.

"It's not your fault," I argue. "And what happened with Anna isn't your fault either." I wipe away the tear trailing down his cheek. "She made her own choices, and it breaks my heart to know that those choices broke yours. But this pain, this grief, it's not some divine punishment. It's not a life sentence—not unless you allow it to be one. You have to forgive yourself for not being able to change the ending."

I let go of Jensen's face and reach for the locket around my neck, twisting open the clasp. The pictures of my mom and dad are faded, but their smiling faces beam at us from inside.

"I don't know why terrible things happen, only that they do. But I see a strength in you that a lot of people don't have. It's the type of strength that a river has when it's carving its way through a mountainside. This burden of yours is big, I won't say that it's not, but you can find a way through it— just like a river. If you can take that first step and then the one right after it, and the one after that, I know you'll find it again."

For the first time since I met him, I see something akin to hope flicker in Jensen's eyes. "Find what?"

"Life," I tell him and wrap my arms around him, pulling him close. I nearly burst into tears when his arms come around to crush me to his chest. And when he begins to cry, I hold him tightly, wanting to bring him as much comfort as I can. "It's okay," I murmur, over and over. "I'm here. I've got you."

We stay like that for a long time, and when Jensen finally pulls back, his eyes are red and puffy. But they seem a bit clearer. "I've spent the last four years of my life in absolute hell," he tells me. "Every day, I wake up with these shadows that I can't shake. Guilt. Regret. Agony. I have nightmares almost every night. When I'm not with Sutton and Ethan or working at the shop, I spend every second replaying every detail, reliving every painful memory in high definition . . . at least I used to. When I met you, you made the noises in my head go quiet. It was like for the first time in a long time, I saw a scrap of light at the end of a very dark tunnel. But I'm afraid." He wipes a hand down his face. "God, Callie. I'm so terrified by what I feel for you. I want to fly with you, but there's still a part of me that wonders if that's fair to you? I don't know."

"The only thing that isn't fair to me is not trusting that I can make my own decisions," I say it gently, but firmly. Leaning in, I press a kiss to his cheek and whisper, "Fly with me."

From the depths of my soul, I mean it. I don't care that the future isn't guaranteed or that things will come up later that will be difficult to navigate. All I know is that we deserve this chance. Both of us do.

"I want to, more than anything," he says, stroking the hair away from my face.

"Pain isn't something you can protect me from. It isn't something you can protect yourself from either. Pain is an inevitable part of life. But so is healing."

Jensen's lips find the hollow at the base of my neck and ghost upwards to my ear, his warm breath making me shiver. "Is this real? Can I really have this?"

His earnest question makes tears spring up in my eyes. "Yes," I whisper, as he kisses the corner of my mouth. "Together."

He kisses the other side and lightly touches his forehead against mine. "Together."

The word lingers between us, steady and certain. Jensen isn't whole yet—there are still pieces of him that need time, wounds that haven't fully mended. But he's here, choosing to fly with me. And that's enough.

A low whine comes from the hallway, followed by a soft scratch at the door. I pull back, my brows furrowing. "Was that . . . "

"Peaches," Jensen confirms. "She knows we're in here, and she's not too happy she wasn't invited to the party."

"Oh, that poor baby!" I jump up, wrapping the throw blanket from the end of the bed around my torso, and hurry over to open the door. Peaches bounds in, a flurry of white, and makes a beeline for the bed. She jumps up and worms her way into Jensen's lap, licking him as if she hasn't seen him in a year. "Okay, okay," he tells her, scratching her behind the ears. "You found me."

I laugh as Peaches gives him a face full of kisses and flop down next to them on the bed. Peaches seizes the opportunity and wiggles over to lay across my legs.

"You sweet little thing," I croon, rubbing her belly. "Did we leave you out there all alone? I'm so sorry, girl."

Jensen reaches over and pats Peaches' head. "I think she's a little keyed up from the weather. She's never been a huge fan of storms."

"Even though she can't hear it?"

He nods. "Animals are pretty perceptive, and her

other senses are heightened. She can't hear the thunder, but she can feel the vibrations from the ground, in the air. She can smell the rain, feel the change in air pressure. It makes her a little anxious. I try to make sure I don't leave her alone if I know the weather is going to be bad. I didn't realize today's storm was going to be quite so intense."

"There's a front moving through. Jim Bann was talking about it on the news this morning. He said there was a possibility of severe weather over the next couple of days."

"Jim Bann, huh?" Jensen quirks an eyebrow at me. "Are we at suspender level threat yet?"

"No," I roll my eyes. "And you better be glad we're not. It's definitely that time of year." I shove Jensen's shoulder making him chuckle and turn my attention back to Peaches. "I don't love storms either. We'll just have to ride them out together. What do you say, girl?" Peaches doesn't respond to my question, but she leans her head back, tongue lolling to the side of her mouth as I give her more belly rubs. "I'll take that as a yes."

Jensen gets up from the bed, giving me a glorious look at his backside, and goes over to the dresser to pull on a pair of loose-fitting sweatpants. "Are you hungry?"

My stomach chooses that exact moment to grumble loudly. Jensen chuckles. "Guess that answers my question." He tosses another pair of sweats on the bed, followed by a t-shirt. "Here. If you want, we can throw your dress in the dryer."

I pull the clothes on—they smell exactly like Jensen, pine and mint and clean laundry—and follow him down the hallway.

The kitchen and the living room are next to each other, creating an inviting and open space, and I make myself at home by walking around and taking in all the little details. Thick, exposed beams frame the ceiling, and a gorgeous stone fireplace marks the focal point of the room. It's framed by sturdy built-in bookshelves stacked with dog-eared paperbacks and vintage hardcover books. The furniture is mostly leather, but soft and worn, and there are colorful quilts and throws slung across the back of the sofa and the loveseat. Every detail—from the mason jars of dried oranges and cinnamon to the heavy antique lanterns on the end tables—seems to coordinate with the rich brown, cream, and burnt orange threads in the area rug where Peaches has curled herself into a tight ball, tail thumping softly.

It's so authentically Jensen, and it's clear that he's put the same care into his own home that he's put into the RVs. It's charming and homey and feels exactly the way it does when I'm wrapped in his arms.

Jensen comes up behind me, his arms looping around my waist to pull me back against his chest. "You like it?"

"It's beautiful."

"Well, if you like this, you should see the omelet I'm about to whip up for you."

"Ooh, he cooks too?"

His lips press against my neck, sending a shiver down my back. "He cooks too."

Half an hour later, the omelet he serves me is topped with freshly shredded cheese and a sprig of parsley, with orange slices garnishing the plate.

"This is almost too pretty to eat," I say, turning the plate around so I can admire it from every angle.

"Tell that to your stomach." Jensen sets his plate next to me. "I'm pretty sure they heard it growling in the next county over."

I elbow him in the ribs, my cheeks turning pink. "Don't make fun of me."

"Never," he grins, pulling me in for a kiss. The moment our lips touch, hunger overwhelms me—but not the kind that has my stomach rumbling. No, this is the kind that you can never fully satisfy, it's that deep all-consuming desire for another person. That moment when your souls connect and nothing else in the world matters.

I'm in love with you, my heart whispers, and I deepen our kiss, pressing myself even closer. After all the wrong turns and heartbreak, I've somehow managed to end up here with this amazing man that I never want to stop kissing. I thought I wanted simple and easy. Uncomplicated. But sweet magnolias, I just want Jensen.

Knowing he wants me too is better than anything else I could have imagined for myself.

And it all happened because of a photoshoot.

Laughter bubbles in my throat, and Jensen pulls back. His cheek lifts in a half smile. "What's so funny?"

"I was just thinking about Mabel."

"You were thinking about your cousin while I was kissing you?"

The look on his face makes me snort. "No, not like that. I was just thinking about you. How amazing you are, how happy I am that we're here together like this, and how it all happened because of the photoshoot. I guess I was just thinking that I owe Mabel at least a dozen pints of Ben & Jerry's."

Jensen leans in and nips my bottom lip, making me gasp. "Make it two dozen."

Then he's kissing me again, and every other thought evaporates from my head. Just Jensen.

That is until my stupid stomach interrupts, growling like it's never tasted food a day in its life.

"Well, that's embarrassing," I say with a sigh.

"Nah," Jensen kisses my forehead and slides the plate closer. "It's cute."

We dig in, and sharing a meal together feels like the most natural thing in the world. I can't help but study him as we eat, searching his face for any trace of panic or doubt, but there isn't any. He's more relaxed than I've ever seen him and though I know it's still there, his burden seems less.

"What?" he asks, when he catches me staring.

"I'm just really glad that we're here."

"Me too."

"And you're still feeling okay about all of this? I mean, a lot has happened today, and I just want to make sure—"

Jensen answers by cupping my neck and crashing his lips against mine.

We don't end up finishing our omelets.

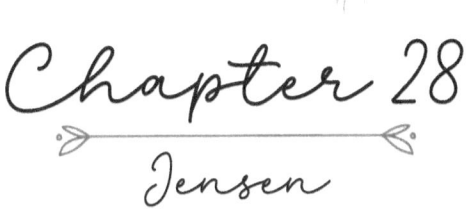

Chapter 28
Jensen

"Hey, Boss Man? That Chevy Silverado is all finished up. Want me to get Sarah to ready the paperwork?"

"Go for it," I yell back, not bothering to look up from the cracked serpentine belt I'm replacing on an old Tahoe. "Make sure she gives the client a discount for having to wait so long."

"Roger that."

I swipe at the sweat beading across my forehead and grimace at the grease on my hands that I've likely just smeared on my face. Saturdays are always pretty busy at the auto shop, but two of my mechanics called out this morning leaving us short-staffed with a full schedule just a few days before spring break. We're already behind on appointments and our clients are having to wait longer than usual, which frustrates me to no end. Kasey worked hard to create a strong reputation of quality customer service for the shop, and I've made it my mission to maintain that. But damn, days like today make it difficult.

It's not quite noon, but the day is already turning out to be uncomfortably warm. We've got all the bay doors open and the windows too, but the humidity is thick and unyielding. Gray clouds have started rolling in and there's thunder rumbling in the west. A good rain might cut the heat, but if these clouds get any darker, we'll be getting more than a spring shower. There's no operating electrical equipment during a lightning storm, so we need to get our clients out the door before the weather hits.

Classic rock pumps out over the loudspeaker, and I use the rhythm of the drumbeats to pace myself, humming along as I work as fast as I can. I'm on the second chorus of Tom Petty's *Free Fallin'* when I spot Callie walking toward me, the keys to her 4Runner dangling from one hand.

The sight of her sun-kissed shoulders in a green tank top that matches her eyes, golden hair cascading down her back, and strawberry lips that I'm already aching to taste nearly sends me to my knees.

It doesn't matter that we've spent nearly every second of the last few days together, I can't seem to get enough of her. Of her laughter, the softness of her skin, and the way she wraps her arms around me and holds me in the quiet stillness of night. If I thought she filled my head before, now it's like she owns every thought in my brain. And god, just being around her makes me feel so alive. It's like I've been living underground for years and now that I've emerged, I can't soak up enough of her sunlight.

The old shadows still lurk in corners, but I haven't felt as much of their pull these last few days. For the first time in four years, I'm starting to believe there might just be a time when I won't feel them at all.

"Hey, pretty girl," I wipe my hands on a rag then wrap them around her waist, pulling her closer. "What are you doing here?"

She presses her lips against mine in a kiss that's over entirely too quickly. "I wanted to see you. I hope that's okay?"

"Of course, you can come by anytime you want." I tuck an errant strand of hair behind her ear. "How are you?"

"I'm good. I just came from the diner. Mabel asked me to stop by so she could tell me the news in person." She pulls her phone out of her pocket. "Looks like we broke the internet again."

Callie shows me Mabel's post about the second photoshoot, and there are so many people reacting to it, it's almost impossible to get to the bottom of the comment section.

"And how's Mabel handling it?"

"Oh, she's as happy as a lark, and already planning to offer more blind date sessions in the future. She's gotten a couple of calls about it already. She even told Joe at the diner that she needed to work less hours, so she can give the photography business more of her attention."

"Good for her, that's really great."

"It is," Callie smiles. "It's what she's always wanted. I'm just really happy for her, you know? She deserves this."

"And what do you think our adoring public would do if they discovered that we're officially together?" I tug her even closer.

"Oh, I think they would go absolutely nuts over us."

"Want to make a post or something? To help Mabel?"

"I think we've done enough for Mabel. And besides, now that I have you, I want to keep you all to myself." She gives me a soft, lingering kiss that nearly makes me moan. I cup her cheeks and kiss her back.

I don't want to let her go, but the business-minded side of my brain reminds me that making out with Callie in the middle of the shop probably isn't exactly professional behavior. Especially when you're the boss. I pull back with a sigh. "Best not to give the customers a show."

"Yeah, you know how quickly rumors tend to fly around these parts. Wouldn't want to give anyone the wrong idea about us," Callie says with a teasing smile.

"The wrong idea, huh?"

"If we're not careful, people are going to think you like me. That you *like, like* me."

I almost open my mouth to argue with her—*Like, like you? No, Callie. I'm in love with you.* Instead, I play along.

"Is that so? Well then, I guess I better not do this anymore." I lean in and press a kiss to the sensitive spot just below her ear.

"Or this," I whisper, my mouth ghosting across the hollow of her throat.

Callie's fingers curl into the fabric of my shirt. "You definitely shouldn't do that." Her voice is breathy.

I lift my head, grinning.

I'm in love with you. I'm in love with you. I'm in love with you.

The words echo in my head in time with my heartbeat. I want to tell her, want to whisper the words against her mouth, but not here in the middle of the auto shop. So, I lean in, settling for a kiss instead.

Our lips have barely brushed when Frank comes barreling around the corner.

"The Bronco Sport in bay two—whoa, sorry about that, Boss!" He whirls around covering his eyes, which makes Callie giggle.

"It's fine, Frank," I groan. "Callie just stopped by to say hello."

Frank gives her a smile and a salute. "Right, well, whenever you get a second, I need your opinion on the Bronco." He turns on his heel and hurries away without waiting for a reply.

"We're short-staffed today," I explain, "and way behind schedule."

"I should go then. I'm distracting you."

Callie starts to pull away, but I tighten my hold on her, not quite ready to let her go yet. "Don't go, not yet."

"I don't want to keep you from work."

"Give me one more minute. There's something in my office for you." I interlock my fingers with hers and lead her down the hallway. I pass the door to my office and turn down another hallway, stopping at a door near the end. I push it open and step into the dark room, pulling Callie in behind me.

"Um, this doesn't look like your office."

I fumble for the light switch on the wall, flipping it on to reveal the supply closet. "There are windows in there," I explain, pulling her flush against me. "And before you go, I just have to do this."

I capture her lips with mine, walking us backward until her back is up against the metal shelving.

This kiss isn't like the one out in the bay, slow and unhurried. It's like wildfire—all-consuming. Blazing heat.

Callie's fingers tunnel into my hair as her tongue caresses mine and I yank her even closer as she lets me claim her mouth, one hand cradling the back of her head, the other gripping her hip.

God, she feels so good pressed up against me, and the vanilla scent coming off her skin floods my senses. She's everywhere—underneath my hands, in my every thought.

"Jensen," Callie breathes as my mouth moves to the sensitive spot just below her jaw. The sound of my name of her lips makes me shiver, and I scrape my teeth gently against her collarbone.

Her hands land on my shoulders, fingertips digging in as she lets out a soft sigh. My fingers curl around the strap of her tank top, sliding it to the side so I can kiss the soft skin of her shoulder.

I swear, I could live a thousand lifetimes with Callie and never get tired of this euphoric rush, the high that consumes me every time I'm near her. I never want it to end. I crash my lips against hers again, my heart beating wildly and uncontrollably.

I'm in love with you. I'm in love with you. I'm in love with you.

"I really should let you get back to work," Callie pulls away, breathless, though her head is tilted back, granting me me better access.

I kiss my way up the column of her neck, not ready to relinquish the feel of her skin underneath my hands. "Stay."

"As much as I want to, and believe me, I want to, I

don't want to distract you any more than I already have. Especially when you're already behind and super busy." She pushes me gently away. "You have to get back out there, Boss."

"Stay," I give her my best puppy dog expression, and she laughs.

"Stay here in the supply closet?"

"No, with me." I pick up her hand and place it across my heart. "Stay with me." It's not exactly what I want to say, but it's close enough.

Callie smiles sweetly, leaning in to give me one last kiss. "I'm not going anywhere."

I reluctantly open the door and lead her out into the hallway. We pass Frank, who's whistling along to the music and pretending very hard that he didn't just notice us emerge from the supply closet, hair all mussed and lips swollen.

We walk hand and hand back through the shop and out to where her 4Runner is parked on the curb. The wind has picked up and there's a loud rumble of thunder, closer than before. The clouds are moving rapidly across the sky, and it looks like the storm is going to hit sooner rather than later. I grimace thinking of how much work we still have to get done.

"I don't like the looks of that sky," Callie says. Her brows are scrunched as her hair whips around in the wind. "I saw on the news this morning that we're under a severe weather watch. Think it's going to get bad?"

"If it does, sounds like it will be north of here." I'm not an expert on storms, but we keep the local station on in the waiting room for our clients. "Your boyfriend's been on the air quite a bit today. He said the worst of it will probably hit Madison and Huntsville."

Callie swats me in the stomach with a laugh. "Well, in Jim Bann we trust."

I open the driver's side door for her just as fat droplets of rain begin to fall. "Are you heading straight home?"

"I was thinking of going to Mabel's. She's supposed to be getting off soon, and I've been promising her some hangout time. Why? Need something?"

"I was just going to ask if you could stop by the farm-house and check on Peaches? She hates storms and I try not to leave her alone if I can help it. But don't worry about it. We'll probably have to close up shop early, and she'll be okay until I get there."

"That's right, poor baby. You know what? Why don't I just go hang out with her? I can hang with Mabel another day."

"Are you sure?"

"I'm sure. Besides, I hear some hot mechanic might be getting off early and will be available for couch snuggling."

"I better get back in there then. I wouldn't want to leave Peaches without a couch snuggling partner."

Callie's laugh makes my own bubble up in my throat. I lean in and give her a quick kiss.

"I'll see you at home, then?"

Hearing her call my farmhouse *home* makes my chest tighten. She has no idea the effect she has on me, how much life she breathes into me. After four of the worst years of my life, she's made me whole again. I never thought I could have this, this overwhelming love that I feel for her, but because of her, I do.

And tonight, when I get home, I'm going to tell her.

"Yeah, see you at home."

Chapter 29

Callie

Jim Bann's suit jacket is still on.

Despite the darkening sky and the pink *Tornado Watch* banner at the bottom of the television screen, I'm not in panic mode—at least not yet.

A warm spring almost always means severe weather, so I've come to expect it. But even though I grew up riding out my fair share of storms in a basement with the tornado sirens blaring, I've never really gotten used to the feeling of being at Mother Nature's mercy. I'm not sure I ever will.

"Don't you worry," I say to Peaches, who's snuggled up next to me on Jensen's leather couch. "We're gonna be just fine." I know she can't hear me, but talking out loud helps distract me from the uneasy feeling souring my stomach.

Despite earlier reports that most of the

bad weather would be hitting north of us, the storm has shifted course and is now projected to hit central Alabama head-on. The local news has been broadcasting nothing but severe weather coverage for the last hour, and they keep showing a map of Alabama with various colors—green, yellow, orange, and red—indicating the projected threat. Dayton Springs sits smack in the middle of the red. It's not the first time that's happened, but still, it's unsettling. Peaches feels it, too. Ever since I walked in the door, she's been glued to my side.

I check the time. It's nearly four in the afternoon which, hopefully, means Jensen will be on his way home soon. Just the thought of seeing him again makes warmth rush into my cheeks.

The last few days with him have been some of the best of my life, and sweet magnolias, I've fallen so hard for that man I can barely stop myself from yelling it at the top of my lungs every time he smiles at me. We've been practically inseparable since the photoshoot at the waterfall, and ever since he opened up to me about what happened with Kase and Anna, it's like all the walls have been knocked down between us. Our initial connection is nothing compared to the one we have now. I didn't know it was possible to feel so close to someone, but when I look at Jensen everything inside of me screams "that's my person."

I have no idea what the future holds, but I want Jensen by my side—especially right now. I'd feel a whole lot better about facing whatever the weather is about to throw at me if he were sitting beside Peaches and me, his arms around us both. I can't imagine a safer place to be, but since that's not exactly an option at the moment, I'm just going to have to put my big girl panties on and deal with it like I've done a hundred times before.

"It's going to be fine," I say again, more to myself this time. "It's going to be just like every other time." Over the years, I've lost count of how many times I've been in instances like this, with Jim Bann on my screen and the sky howling outside. When you grow up in Dixie Alley, the South's equivalent to the Midwest's infamous Tornado Alley, it's just part of life. Tornado drills in school, monthly siren tests, and storms every spring that wake you up in the dead of night. You can almost time it—when the flowers start blooming and the pollen fills the air, it's a relief that winter is finally over, but it's also time to make sure your emergency supplies are stocked and your weather radio is still in good working order.

"Don't panic, be prepared," my father used to say whenever I was worried about a storm, and he always had our safe space ready to go by the time the first warning hit. Still, spring is my least favorite time of year and this is why. Thunderstorms in general make me a little jumpy, but a thunderstorm in April is a whole other matter entirely.

"We might as well try to eat something," I say to Peaches as she nuzzles up under my palm. "Are you ready for dinner, Sweetness?" I give her the sign Jensen taught me for "eat," and her ears perk up. "I take that as a yes," I chuckle, pushing the throw blanket from my lap. Peaches hops off the couch and trots over to her food bowl, waiting for me. She sits on her haunches, her eyes trailing me as I move over to the pantry where her food is kept. "I'm coming, I'm coming," I tell her, scooping out the correct amount to dump in her bowl.

The house shakes as a loud clap of thunder erupts overhead, startling me so much, dog food spills over the measuring cup in my hand. Peaches doesn't seem to mind that half her dinner ended up on the floor, but my "that can't be good" spidey sense is tingling. Outside the kitchen windows, the sky is getting darker by the minute, but it's still light enough to tell that the atmosphere is churning overhead. Angry, fast-moving clouds move across the sky and there's a haze to the air that gives it a weird color. Not quite gray, but not normal either.

"Green," I whisper, my heart rising in my throat.

If the sky turns green, a tornado is 'bout to be seen— the old adage pops into my head, each word like a booming bass drum, and when my phone starts ringing, I jump.

"Callie?" The tone of Mabel's voice on the other end makes my stomach flip over. "Where are you?"

"I'm at Jensen's house. Have you looked outside? The

sky's turning green. I'm kind of starting to freak out."

"I know, me too." There's a sharp intake of breath and then, "Sullivan called."

The sense of uneasiness churning in my stomach becomes a tidal wave. Mabel's ex calls frequently, but he's a meteorologist who chases tornadoes for a living. If he's calling on a day like today, it can only mean one thing.

"He called me yesterday, and I didn't answer," Mabel says, the quiver in her voice impossible not to hear. "But then he kept calling. Over and over. I just got off the phone with him. He's right outside of town, Callie. He's tracking it."

I swallow the fear rising in my throat. "How bad?"

"Nothing on the ground yet, but the radar doesn't look good. The storm is moving fast and it's strong. He said it could drop at any minute."

The words claw down my spine, and instinctively I look toward the TV. Even as I turn around though, I know what I'm going to see.

Jim Bann is still front and center on the television screen but somewhere in the span of me feeding Peaches to Mabel calling to now, the jacket has come off and his suspenders have made their appearance. "No, no, no," I hurry over to the couch, sinking down into the cushion as I turn the volume up.

"The storm is intensifying and we're now getting confirmed reports of rotation. We've issued a tornado warning for all of Jefferson and Clayton County. If you're in Clay-Chalkville, Trussville, or in the Dayton Springs area, you need to head to your safe space. Get to the lowest level of your home, a basement if you've got one. Otherwise, go to the center of your house in an interior room with no doors or windows."

The radar he's pointing to has changed, and red fills the screen. "This thing is coming right down highway 59 and it's moving quickly, so make sure you get to those emergency places in your homes."

Outside, rain batters the ground as a high-pitched keening slices through the air. "Sirens," I breathe into the phone.

"I know, I hear them." I can hear her rustling around in the background, I know my cousin is grabbing the emergency bag that she keeps in the pantry and heading for the hall bathroom. There's no basement, but the bathroom sits at the heart of the bungalow. It's the safest spot she could be.

"Alright, folks. We're getting reports of a confirmed tornado on the ground now, I repeat there is a large tornado on the ground, just outside of Dayton Springs. This is a tornado emergency, do not wait. Seek shelter now." Jim Bann's voice is calm, but urgent, and the giant screen behind him highlighting the pronounced, dark red hook that indicates tornado rotation makes my pulse spike.

"I gotta go, Mabel. I need to call Jensen." I end the

call without waiting for a reply and tap the screen to dial Jensen. The phone rings several times but there's no answer. I try again. "Come on, come on, come on," I whisper, as the sirens wail outside.

"If you live in Clayton County and you can hear my voice, you need to take shelter," Jim Bann's voice floats in and out competing with the sirens that demand me to move. "Go to the lowest level of your house. If you don't have a lower level, find a room in the interior of your home without any windows. We have confirmed sightings now that a tornado is on the ground. I repeat, we have a tornado on the ground."

"We gotta go," I tell Peaches, grabbing a bottle of water from the fridge and the throw blanket from the couch. I snatch Peaches' leash from the hook by the door and clip it to her collar. The farmhouse has a basement, but I have no idea if Jensen keeps supplies on hand for emergencies, and I stupidly never thought to ask, so I'll just have to make do with whatever I can grab in the next sixty seconds. I shove my feet into the tennis shoes I kicked off by the door and hurry to grab the flashlight Jensen keeps in the junk drawer by the fridge.

Outside, the battering rain morphs into a rattling sound that at first, I can't place, but as the sound intensifies, I realize that large hail is pounding the roof. It sounds like baseballs are being dropped out of the sky. It's so loud, I can barely make out the sirens anymore.

Peaches and I clomp downstairs and I look for a spot

to hunker down. There's a few egress windows on the far wall, but there's a small half-finished area that Jensen has fixed up for storage. There are a bunch of boxes stacked up and a large workbench housing a ton of tools, but there's a futon in the corner and it's as far from the windows as I'll be able to manage down here.

My phone is vibrating with emergency weather alerts and I quickly pull it out to tune into the livestream of Jim Bann's weather coverage.

" . . . don't wait. You need to be in your tornado safe place. We've got some new scans coming in as we speak and oh man, Dayton Springs, this thing is coming in right on top of you. It's going to cross Deertail highway and head right into the downtown area within the next two to three minutes."

"Oh my god." All I can think about is Jensen and Mabel—the auto shop isn't far from the main drag of town. Neither is the bungalow. Tears well up in my eyes, but I refuse to let them fall. I have to stay calm.

I pull one of the loose cushions from the futon and place it by my feet in case I need to grab it to cover Peaches and me. The lights flicker, once and then twice. The news coverage on my phone has frozen and I anxiously hit the side button of my phone, switching the home screen off and then back on again. I clear the weather app and try to pull it up again, but the storm must be interfering with the cell phone towers. I have one bar, but it's not enough for the livestream to come through again. I try calling Mabel and then Jensen, but neither call connects. "Dammit," I hiss, looking around for a weather radio, but if Jensen has one, it's not down here and I have no idea where to look for one.

My body shakes as wind and hail continue to batter the farmhouse all around me. The lights flicker again and go out for a few seconds before coming back on. "Oh please, please, please," I whimper, though I know the power isn't going to stay on for long. Not with the wind whipping the way it is. More flickering and then a few seconds later, the lights go out again for good. I switch the flashlight on, grateful for the small pool of golden light it supplies.

Fear, hot and raw, sinks its teeth into me as my brain begins to conjure up a dozen worst-case scenarios. *Don't panic, be prepared. Don't panic, be prepared. Don't panic, be prepared.* I repeat my father's words over and over like a meditation. Focusing on the words, I refuse to think about anything else. I'm as prepared as I can be, and I'm in the safest spot in the farmhouse. All I can do now is wait for the storm to pass.

"It's going to be okay, it's going to be okay." Peaches climbs into my lap, shaking like a leaf, and I wrap my arms around her and hold her tightly to my chest, murmuring a prayer into her fur. "Please protect them, keep them safe," I whisper, thinking of Jensen and Mabel, of our town and everyone in it. I squeeze my eyes shut. "Please keep us safe, too. Me and Peaches and—" My eyes fly open as a new horror rams into me. "Oh god, Ms. Dorothy."

I'd seen her that morning watering her flowers and we'd briefly chatted before I left to run errands. She'd told me she had no plans and intended to take it easy today, which means that it was highly unlikely that she'd gone to town. Which also meant that she was probably still in her RV at this very moment.

I shake my head back and forth, not wanting to even entertain the idea. Everyone knows that mobile homes aren't safe in bad weather. They fly like tin cans in tornadoes and anyone inside . . . nope, I can't think about it. Jensen and I talked about it once, that if the weather was bad enough, I should come down and shelter here at the farmhouse. Surely, he had the same arrangement with Mrs. Dorothy right? She would have come here. She would have known better than to try to ride out the storm in the RV, wouldn't she?

Now, my brain is spinning a dozen new scenarios, and I feel like I'm going to throw up. "What if she's outside?" I say to Peaches. "What if she's here and she's trying to get inside and can't or she needs help or something?"

I make a snap decision, pushing to my feet. "You stay here." I give Peaches the sign for "Stay" and tuck the throw blanket around her. If there's even the slightest chance Dorothy is outside and trying to get into the farmhouse, I have to help.

I hurry up the stairs and back out into the dark farmhouse. As I step into the living room, everything around me goes still. It's as if someone with a giant remote has pushed the pause button. For a single second, I can't hear the wind or hail. Even the sirens have seemed to cease their wailing. There's nothing but a heavy stillness as the air in the room changes. My ears begin to pop and my chest tightens from the change in pressure.

My feet understand before my brain does, and I'm hurrying back to the hall when I hear a strange sound. It sounds like the air conditioning unit kicking on, that low, constant hum, but then I remember that the power is out. As it gets louder and more menacing, I realize it's a sound I've been told about my whole life, but never actually heard myself. A sound I've feared for as long as I can remember.

It's the roaring of a freight train barreling straight for me.

I yank the door to the basement open. I'm halfway down the stairs when the entire floor above me erupts into a cacophony of pops and cracks, shattering glass, and splintering wood—all while the roaring, like a monster coming to claim me, grows deafening.

One second, I'm nearly at the bottom of the steps, my eyes on Peaches, standing on the futon, barking her head off, and then the next a battering ram slams into me from behind ripping my feet out from under me.

I'm spiraling in a vortex of color and sound as the thick smell of drywall dust floods my nostrils.

A scream, shrill and full of terror, erupts from my throat.

And the world explodes around me.

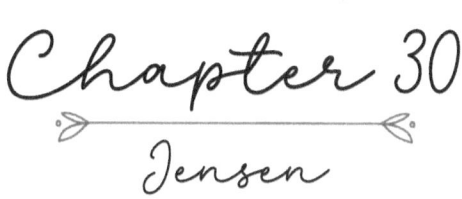

Chapter 30

Jensen

The garage doors aren't going to hold. The standard commercial steel isn't strong enough to withstand the tornado barreling down on Main Street, its thunderous battle cry a warning that there's nowhere to run. Nowhere to hide.

I make eye contact with Frank, whose wrinkled forehead is more creased than usual. He lifts his chin toward the front of the shop where the garage doors are violently shaking, creaking and groaning as if they're in pain. He knows as well as I do how bad this is. We're not in the center of town, but close enough to know we're in danger.

"We need to back up," I yell above the noise, pointing to the opposite side of the pit. When the sirens started blaring, I'd ordered everyone down here. Sarah, our receptionist, sits pale-faced on the floor next to Mrs. Barclay and her five-year-old son, Gatlin. Mrs. Barclay's check engine light was on and she'd come in right as we finished up with our scheduled clients for the day. Frank offered to do a quick diagnostic for her, but before he'd even had time to pull a single error code, the sky had turned from gray to green to almost black, and then the sirens sounded.

The safest place in the shop is the pits. They're below ground level, but the safety netting overhead isn't going to help us much. If the garage doors go, we'll have little protection from flying debris.

"As far back as you can," I urge Sarah and Mrs. Barclay, scooping up Gatlin to make it easier for his mom. The two women don't say a word as they hurry to the interior-most end of the pit, fear shining in their eyes. "It's going to be okay," I say, re-depositing Gatlin in his mother's arms. "We're going to be just fine."

Sarah nods, but tears well up in her eyes. Mrs. Barclay just wraps her arms tightly around her son, murmuring words in his ear, too low for me to hear above the whistling wind. It reminds me of Sutton and Ethan and their faces flash in my mind for a second, but I quickly shove the image away. I can't think about them right now.

I also can't think about Callie, even though every single beat of my heart is screaming her name, I can't let myself drown in the panic that threatens me every second I think of the woman I love. The army taught me that the most important thing is to stay focused on the task at hand. I have to do everything I can to keep these people safe.

Frank and I bunch in next to the women, all of us watching as the garage doors continue their battle against the wind. The overhead lights flicker a few times before going out completely, and my ears pop as the pressure drops. Gatlin lets out a little squeak of pain, but before I can say anything to comfort him, there's a low hum, a vibration that ripples through my entire body. The warmth leeches from my skin.

"It's coming," Frank yells, his voice barely carrying.

Only, he's wrong. It isn't coming. It's already here.

With a crash so loud it makes my ears ring, the steel garage doors crumple like empty soda cans, ripping off their tracks. The windows shatter, sending shards of glass flying through the air like shrapnel. Throwing myself over Gatlin and Mrs. Barclay, I do what I can to shield them, hissing as jagged fragments slice across my neck and back. Frank lets out a bellow next to me, but he's hunched over Sarah who's covering her ears, mouth open in a scream.

Dirt, bits of debris, hunks of insulation, and god knows what else clog the air. I squeeze my eyes shut to protect them, hacking out a cough as I press closer to Mrs. Barclay and Gatlin, trying to keep us as low as possible. Gatlin is wailing in my ear, his terrified cries mixing with the sounds of wood snapping, metal clanging against metal, and the whistling of debris hurtling across the shop.

Monstrous wind, ruthless and unyielding, unleashes itself on the shop, on *us* and there isn't anything we can do to stop it. With my own heartbeat thundering in my ears, time seems to slow down. It's as if I'm watching it all in slow mo—Frank grimacing against the pelting debris, Mrs. Barclay gripping her son tightly, afraid he'll be ripped from her arms, and Sarah clutching at the cross necklace she always wears, her lips silently moving in prayer. All while the storm rages over our heads.

It feels like ten years have passed before the roaring of the wind starts to fade. The air pressure stabilizes, and a heavy stillness falls over the shop. No one moves or even breathes deeply. It's as if we're waiting to see if it's really over or if the monster is only lurking in the shadows ready to come for us again.

I lift my head once I'm sure it's passed and do a survey of the pit. There's a thick, chalky haze in the air that smells like a mixture of damp earth, splintered wood, and something metallic. It stings the insides of my nostrils with each breath.

The emergency lights flicker to life, illuminating the shop in soft orange light. Scraps of metal, wood, and roofing material and more litter the concrete.

"Everyone okay?" I stand up and help Mrs. Barclay to her feet. She's covered in dirt and trembling, but otherwise unharmed. Gatlin clings to her with wide eyes and tear-stained cheeks, but he isn't hurt. Neither is Sarah, who is holding on to Frank, her lower lip quivering.

"We're all good, Boss," Frank wheezes. Blood drips down his arm from a sizeable gash in his bicep, but he waves it off when he sees me looking. "It's nothing, I'm fine. Piece of metal got me, but I'm okay." He points to my head. "What about you?"

It's then that I feel the warm, sticky liquid dripping down my neck. A jagged cut runs across my right temple. It stings when I touch it, my fingertips coming away coated in crimson.

"There's a first aid kit in the break room," Sarah pipes up. "Is it safe for us to go out?"

"I think it just side-swiped us," Frank says, twisting around to get a better look at the shop. He looks almost as surprised as I am that the place is still standing. "If we'd taken a direct hit . . . " he trails off. None of us needs him to finish that sentence.

I hop out of the pit, groaning as the movement sends stabs of hot pain down my back. Leaning down, I take Gatlin from Mrs. Barclay so she can climb out. Frank and Sarah emerge slowly, their heads on a swivel as they take in the damage.

Outside, several car alarms are going off and there's the faint sound of an emergency siren in the distance, but the storm is gone.

Sarah passes me, stepping over racks of broken equipment and scattered tools across the floor, heading for the employee breakroom.

I step through the gaping hole where one of the garage doors used to be. The ice cream store across from us is missing a chunk of its roof, and the glass doors are shattered. The locksmith two doors down is the same. The entire road is covered in chunks of drywall, tree limbs and branches, trash can lids, and crumpled road signs, but all the buildings on our street seem to be standing.

"Y'all okay?" I call out to the workers from the ice cream shop who have also come out to see the damage. When they nod, I head further down the road. At the corner, there's a pretty clear view of the main street. Stepping over debris, glass and twigs crunch under my boots.

"Oh my god."

Downtown Dayton Spring took a direct hit. The postcard-perfect image I've gotten so used to seeing as I drive into work every day is nearly unrecognizable.

Roofs and awnings have collapsed, and the majority of businesses have been stripped down to the framing. Telephone poles are snapped in two and low-hanging electrical wires are tangled together. Cars have been flipped on their sides between clumps of brick, roof shingles, corrugated metal, and the pink fluffs of insulation that clutter the sidewalks. There's even a child's bicycle twisted like a pretzel.

Sirens sound, but this time, the shrill wailing means that help is coming. Blue and red lights flash as emergency vehicles hurry to the epicenter.

Adrenaline jolts through me, and I run back to the shop. All I can think about are the people in those buildings. The people of this town. It may not have been where I grew up, but somewhere along the way, Dayton Springs became my home, and seeing it bleeding like a gaping wound, damn near rips the heart right out of my chest.

Sutton. Ethan. Callie. Sutton. Ethan. Callie. My brain, muddled and overwhelmed, is spinning with a million thoughts, all of them screaming for my attention. But it's the names of the people I love that are the loudest.

It was Sutton's day off. She's not down there. She's at home with Ethan. Callie is at the farmhouse. It's okay, they're not down there, I tell myself. It's hard, though, to shake the unwavering feeling of wrongness swimming in my gut.

"Frank! We need to get downtown. The tornado went right down Main Street."

Frank darts past me, needing to get a look for himself, while I look for Sarah, who's standing beside Mrs. Barclay, the first aid kit in her hand. "Sarah, come with me. There may be people who need help." I indicate the first aid kit. Sarah doesn't hesitate, just follows me as we rush back outside.

But something else is niggling at me, clawing at me, and I can't shake it. I reach for my phone in my back pocket, only to remember I'd left it to charge in my office.

A cop car is idling at the end of the road, and I recognize Jefferson Carmichael, one of Dayton's finest speaking with Frank through the open window. "You folks, okay?" He asks as we approach, eyes widening when he sees the blood dripping down the side of my face.

"It's superficial," I say. "We're fine. Mrs. Barclay and her son are back at the auto shop. They're okay, too. Can we help? How bad is it?"

"I don't know," Jefferson swipes a hand down his face. "We've got units responding, but it's too early to say. My job is to clear the outer streets. The damn twister waltzed right through Main Street like it owned the joint and then veered east and continued barreling down Route 3 without a care in the world."

Everything inside my body goes cold. "Wait . . . did you say Route 3?"

Jefferson nods. "We've got crews headed out that way."

Route 3. The very road I drive every single day, the road that leads me home to the farmhouse. Jefferson is still talking, but I can't hear what he's saying. My mind is only focused on one thing.

Callie.

Callie.

Callie.

Callie.

I run back toward the auto shop. I have to get home. Frank is yelling at me to stop, but I can't.

I beeline for a the first untouched vehicle I see, a big, black pick-up truck sitting in the parking lot. It's not mine, but I know for a fact the keys are sitting in the cupholder. I put them there myself after finishing a brake pad replacement a few hours ago. The truck is covered with hunks of building material and tree limbs, but thankfully, nothing that will prevent it from running. I fire the engine, yanking the gearshift into drive so fast there's a screeching sound, and whip it around and out of the parking lot.

I can't take my usual route through town, so I aim for the side roads, weaving around branches and downed telephone poles as quickly as I can. Once I'm out of the city limits, it's only a short drive before I hit Route 3.

Callie. I have to get to Callie.

I press down on the gas pedal, going as fast as I can. The trees on both sides of the road have either been bent in half or snapped in two confirming the twister's path. The sight of those trees, of the force it must have taken to leave such a trail of destruction behind sends terror through me like I've never known.

The road is practically impassable, but I pop the truck in four-wheel drive and keep going, finding alternative paths that let me pass. I don't let myself think about anything but the obstacles in front of me. I have to keep going.

I'm only a quarter of a mile from the turn-off that leads down to the farmhouse when I hit a dead-end. A massive pine has fallen, blocking the road, and there's no going around it.

I throw the truck in park, climb over the tree, and run.

I don't care that I left the truck's engine running. The only thing that matters is getting to Callie.

Please let her be okay, please let her be okay, please let her be okay.

The words spurn me onwards. I force my muscles to work harder, to move faster. My lungs burn in my chest, aching for more oxygen, but I don't care. I nearly wipe out on the slick asphalt as I hurdle over a piece of wooden fencing, but I keep going.

Please let her be okay, please let her be okay, please let her be okay.

The narrow lane opens up, and I look to where the farmhouse should be, but it's not there. It's just—gone. Only a pile of rubble remains. The brick fireplace and a single wall stripped down to the studs stand like sentries, while the remaining structure has been reduced to something unrecognizable.

The wraparound porch is crumbled into a mangled ball, and were it not for the cement stairs, I wouldn't even know where the front door used to be. There's no sign of the roof. It must have been ripped clean off, and it looks there's been some kind of massive explosion with pieces of the farmhouse scattered like confetti across the grass.

A strangled cry rises in my throat as I stumble, almost falling to my knees. "Oh my god," I wheeze, chest heaving. "Oh my god, Callie!" I scream her name, but the sound is hoarse and weak. "Callie!"

I throw myself into the wreckage, flinging aside hunks of brick and broken tile. I yank at whatever I can get my hands on, tossing it behind me, shoving away anything I can move. Broken nails and slivers of fractured pipes slice and tear at my skin as I dig, but I don't care.

"Callie! Callie, can you hear me?"

Fiberglass coats my forearms as I claw at soggy pieces of drywall. I ram my shoulder into a thick oak dresser, but it doesn't budge. Beneath my boots, the floor feels spongy, soft in places where it shouldn't be. I shuffle to the side, trying a different spot to tunnel through, but it's as if the pile of rubble has grown strong spindly arms to shove back at me, to keep me from getting inside.

"Callie! Callie!"

I keep digging, even though every muscle in my body screams in agony. My vision is hazy, clouded with sweat and dust, and every time I inhale, it feels like my lungs are filling with sawdust. The farmhouse, my home, my sanctuary has become a tangle maw of jagged teeth and crooked claws ripping me apart as I fight against it with everything I have.

"Please," I rasp. "Please." The word flows out of me like the blood dripping from my skin. I don't know if it's the house I'm begging or time or maybe even God, but that single word pours from my lips with every swipe of my arm, with every kick of my leg.

The farmhouse lets out a groan, the ominous sound grating against my spine like the scraping of fork tines against a ceramic plate. Whatever is holding what's left of it together is about to give.

A warped and cracked cabinet from the bathroom catches under my foot, and I fall face-first, slamming my knee into a twisted floor joist. I cry out, howling as spikes of pain shoot up and down my leg. Stars dance across my blurry eyes, but I push myself back up. I don't care if I break every bone in my body, if I lose every ounce of blood within these veins, I will find her. Even if it takes the very last beat of my equally mangled heart, I will not let this destruction win. I *will* find her.

Shep.

Kase's voice booms in my ear, louder than my panic. I slow down, chest heaving. "Kase?"

Shep.

Just my name again, nothing more.

"Please, Kasey. You have to help me. It's Callie.

She's—"

Shepherd. This time it's barely more than a whisper, but the urgency is loud and and clear. I stay still, breathing in and out slowly to still my heartbeat. I won't be able to hear him if I don't calm down. I have to be quiet, I have to listen, I—

A noise from just below me makes my pulse spike. It's not Kasey's voice, but I'd recognize that sound anywhere.

It's barking.

"Peaches!" I scream her name. "Callie? Can you hear me? I'm coming for you, baby. Just hang on."

I wait for some kind of response, but there's only Peaches. I limp closer to the sound, targeting the debris in that area, moving it as fast and as safely as I can.

"Come on," I encourage, even though I know she can't hear me. "Keep barking, girl." I have no idea how Peaches knew I was here or what made her bark, but it doesn't even matter as long as she keeps doing it.

I dig and dig, shoving my way through the remnants of my home, until finally, I recognize the stairwell leading down into the basement. I spot a flash of white and nearly begin weeping when my eyes land on Peaches, dirty, but unharmed, standing at the bottom of the steps and barking her precious little head off.

I fly down the steps, throwing my arms around Peaches who leaps into my embrace, her tongue lapping at the dirt and blood sticking to my forehead. I give her a quick kiss on the head and set her aside, my eyes darting around the room.

"Callie!"

The sound that comes out of my throat is guttural as I spot her lying on her back in a pool of blood a few feet away. Half of her face and neck are covered in blood, but I can't tell where it's coming from.

"Baby? Can you hear me?" Seeing her like this, so pale and unmoving, makes my stomach flip over. I run my hands along her body, careful not to touch her left leg which is twisted at an unnatural angle, and reach for the soft spot just below her jaw. Her pulse flutters underneath my fingertips, but it's very faint. She's breathing, though, and my own lungs nearly seize up with the realization that she's unconscious, but alive.

Over our heads, the farmhouse cries out, the snaps and groans a warning to me that we can't stay here for much longer.

It's risky to move her. I don't know how badly she's hurt, and if there's injury to her spinal cord, the worst thing I could do is jostle her around. But I don't have much of a choice. If I wait any longer, the remains of the farmhouse will crush us both.

Ignoring the throbbing, stabbing pain in my knee, I bend down and scoop Callie into my arms as gently as I can, cradling her to my chest.

"I've got you. Just hold on, okay? I'm getting you out of here."

Following the path I carved through the wreckage, I move slowly. Callie is limp in my arms and it terrifies me, but I stay calm, relying on my military training. I have to get us out of the house.

Peaches sticks close to my side and I talk to her as we climb, hoping she can at least pick up on my energy. "You're a good girl, Peaches. That's it, just follow me."

Digging my way to Callie felt like it took hours, but in what seems like only a handful of minutes, I'm stepping out into the night air with her in my arms.

Red and blue sirens illuminate the darkness as a police cruiser and an ambulance fly toward us, dust flying up from the tires.

"Over here!" I yell, trying to flag them down. "We're right here!"

The cruiser reaches us first. It's Jefferson Carmichael with Frank in the passenger seat. "When I saw you take off back there, it wasn't hard to figure out where you'd gone." Frank gets out of the car and hurries over to me. "How is she?"

"She's breathing, but we need to get her to the hospital immediately."

The ambulance pulls up next to the cruiser and the EMTs jump out, pulling a gurney out from the back of their rig.

"Her name is Callie Dawson. She's twenty-six years old. I'm pretty sure her leg is broken, but I can't tell where all the blood is coming from." I rattle off information I think will be helpful as the paramedics gently take Callie and lay her on the stretcher.

"I know I probably shouldn't have moved her but the house isn't stable."

As if to back up my claim, the farmhouse emits a mighty groan and the whole pile of rubble shifts, the entire thing collapsing in on itself, sending a plume of dust, dirt, and fiberglass particles into the sky.

I step back, swaying on my feet as the EMTs stabilize Callie for transport to the hospital. She hasn't moved at all since I brought her out of the house.

The adrenaline that kept me moving has waned, and my limbs feel as if they weigh a thousand pounds each.

"Callie," I call out her name, but it sounds like I'm speaking underwater.

Frank moves into my field of vision as black spots appear, blotting out his face. I think I hear him call my name, but it's distorted, muted. I try to reach for Callie, to tell her that she's going to be okay, but the world around me swirls, colors mixing together.

Callie.

Her face is the last I see before I sink into darkness.

Chapter 31
Jensen

Everything comes back all at once, like an electric shock to the system. My body jolts as my eyes fly open, and I gasp, blinking against the bright fluorescent lights overhead.

Callie.

It takes me a few seconds to realize I'm lying on a hospital bed that's semi-propped up in a small emergency room bay separated from the others by a thick blue curtain that's been pulled shut for my privacy. A bag of fluids hangs from a metal hook next to the bed and attaches to an IV in my hand.

My boots are sitting next to the bed, but when I swing my legs over and reach for them, the movement causes a burning pain in my neck and back. I reach around, feeling for the source, and find several of patches of thick gauze covering what I assume to be fresh stitches.

Gritting my teeth, I rip the IV out and stand up, wobbling as more pain shoots up my left leg. My knee has been wrapped in a thick black brace for support, but it still nearly gives out on me when I put weight on it. I'm not sure I can walk, but I have to try. I have to find Callie—even if it means I have to crawl to her side.

No one stops me as I shove the blue curtain aside and limp into a brightly lit hallway. Nurses and doctors buzz around, moving quickly from bay to bay as they tend to patients with injuries from the storm. I'm almost to the end of the hallway, close to the nurse's station, when the double doors open, and Sutton breezes through, her normally smiling face drawn into a tight line.

"Shep!" She nearly drops the cafeteria coffee she's holding when she sees me hobbling toward her. She hurries to my side, throwing my arm over her shoulder to help take some of my weight. "What are you doing? You're supposed to be—"

"Where's Callie? I pulled her out of the house, but I passed out and I don't know what happened after that. Is she here? Is she okay?" The words come out in one big breath.

"She's here," Sutton says, but the look she gives me is far from reassuring. My good knee starts to buckle and Sutton yelps a little as I sag against her. "We have to take you back to your room. You're still recovering."

"No," I shake my head. "I have to find Callie. You have to take me to her right now."

"Shep, I . . . " Sutton's eyes fill with tears. "I can't take you to her. They won't let anyone see her right now. Mabel's out in the waiting room. The doctor is supposed to come update her soon."

"I want to talk to the doctor," I say, taking an uneven step toward the doors.

Sutton looks like she wants to argue with me, but something in my expression stops her. She just gives me a little nod and wraps an arm around my waist to help me walk.

"Ethan?" I ask, trying not to wince at the pain in my leg as we walk.

"He's okay, a little shaken up, I think." Sutton lets out a breath. "We both are." She squeezes me a little tighter as we walk.

Out in the waiting room, it's practically standing room only. Half the population of Dayton Springs seems packed into the cramped space, all wearing identical expressions of exhaustion and worry. I spot Mabel in the corner, sitting with her head in her hands. A man I don't know, wearing a backward baseball cap, is sitting next to her, his hand on her back.

Mabel's head pops up when she hears us shuffling closer, tears immediately spilling over her cheeks when she sees me.

"Jensen, oh my god," she hops up and gives me a gentle hug, pulling back to look me over. "Are you okay?"

"It looks worse than it is," I wave away her concern. "Have you heard anything? How is she?"

"I don't know," Mabel's lower lip trembles as she swipes at her cheeks. "The last I heard they were going to set her leg and stabilize it, but it's not her leg they're worried about."

The image of Callie lying prone on the basement floor flashes before my eyes. The blood coating her face and neck. "Her head?"

Mabel nods. "They don't know what happened exactly, but they said it was some kind of blunt force trauma. They aren't sure how serious it is yet. They were going to run some scans on her, but their main concern is a possible brain bleed."

A brain bleed. The words make my stomach roll with nausea. "When will we hear something?"

"They said they'll update us once she's back from getting the CT scan." Mabel lets out a slow quivering breath. "That was a while ago though, and every time I ask for an update, no one will tell me anything. I'm just so worried and I—"

A wave of tears steals the rest of Mabel's sentence, and the man in the hat stands up, coming to Mabel's side. "I'm sure they'll let us know something soon, Mabeloo. It's all going to be okay."

"Is it?" Mabel snaps, though she doesn't push away

the hand he lays on her arm. If anything, she seems to lean in a little, using the stranger for support.

The pet name makes my eyebrows lift, and both Sutton and I share a look.

"Sorry, I didn't get a chance to introduce myself." The man holds out his hand for me to shake. "I'm Sullivan Rowe. Mabel's husband."

It takes me a second to recover before I can shake his hand. "Husband?"

"Ex-husband," Mabel pipes up, looking annoyed.

Sullivan gives her a wide grin. "Aw, honey, it's so cute when you say that."

"Ex-husband," Mabel insists, rolling her eyes. "I have divorce papers that prove it."

"Papers that require *both* of our signatures, darlin', and last time I checked, those papers were missing my John Hancock," Sullivan fires back, although his tone is more playful than anything else. Mabel, on the other hand, looks like she's two seconds away from junk punching the guy.

At that moment, a nurse appears, wearing light blue scrubs. "Callie Carpenter's family?"

Mabel's entire demeanor changes. "Yes, that's us. How is she?"

"The doctor will be stopping by to see you shortly, but I can take you to see her." The nurse eyes our little group. "There's a limit of two visitors in the ICU."

Intensive Care Unit. My stomach rolls over again. Every nerve in my body feels like it's on edge, like my skin is the only thing holding me together. I need to see Callie, need to lay my hands on her, hear the doctor say that she's going to be okay.

My lungs tighten, and for a moment, it's hard to breathe. *Intensive Care Unit.*

My old shadows start creeping out from wherever they've been hiding, slinking toward me. My heart begins to race. *Intensive Care Unit.*

Mabel and I follow the nurse through the crowded hallway of the hospital. I want to run, to beg the nurse to go faster, but I'm barely able to limp along.

When we arrive outside Callie's room, the nurse nods at the closed door. "You can go in if you want, but one at a time, please."

Mabel gives me a little smile. "Why don't you go first?" She points to a chair just outside the door. "I'll wait here for the doctor."

Despite how much I know she wants to see her cousin, she's giving me this time with Callie. I nod, unable to find the words to tell her thank you.

Grimacing, I push open the door. Seeing Callie in that bed, pale and unmoving nearly sends me to my knees. I limp closer, falling into a chair that's been placed close to her side and reach for hand. "Callie? It's me. Can you hear me?"

She's so pale, even her sun-kissed hair seems to have lost its usual luster and shine. There's a bandage above her left eye, and already the skin on that side of her face is beginning to turn a deep shade of purple. She doesn't respond to my voice and her hand is limp and clammy.

"Please." I lean in, pressing my forehead to her arm. "Please, Callie. You have to be okay. I need you to be okay. Please, just open your eyes."

A thick knot rises in my throat and I swallow once, twice. "Please," I choke out, barely above a whisper.

" . . . set the leg and put it in a temporary cast, but we need to wait until the swelling goes down to determine if she needs surgery." A deep voice floats toward me from outside in the hallway. "But, of course, the head injury is the bigger concern. Our initial scans show a localized brain contusion with moderate cerebral edema. "

"What does that mean exactly?" Mabel asks, her voice shaky.

"Your cousin has received a traumatic brain injury to her frontal lobe, and there's some pretty significant swelling. That's not uncommon for this type of injury, but so far the swelling hasn't responded much to medication—which is concerning. Cerebral edema like this causes pressure to build up in the brain, and if it doesn't resolve on its own, it has to be surgically relieved."

I can't move or breathe as I listen. My heart is in my throat.

"We've inserted a tiny device, an intracranial pressure monitor into her skull to help us track the edema.

The next 24-48 hours are critical, so we'll be observing her condition very closely."

Mabel sniffs, once and then twice, as if she's trying to keep the tears at bay. "What happens if the swelling doesn't go down?"

"Then there's a chance of herniation in the brain which would be . . . detrimental. There's no indication of that just now, but like I said, we'll need to keep an eye on things. Brain injuries can be quite unpredictable."

Fear, cold and sharp as a knife, slices through me. *Significant. Concerning. Critical. Unpredictable. Detrimental.*

Nothing the doctor said makes sense to me. How is it possible that just this morning, Callie was in my arms, laughing and smiling? I was holding her in my arms, kissing her in the supply closet at the shop, and now she's lying in this bed with a potentially life-threatening brain injury.

I run through the day's events, painstakingly replaying every minute, trying to understand how everything could go from blissfully perfect to devastating in a single day.

"I was thinking of going to Mabel's. She's supposed to be getting off soon, and I've been promising her some hangout time. Why? Need something?"

"I was just going to ask if you could stop by the farmhouse and check on Peaches? She hates storms and I try not to leave her alone if I can help it. But don't worry

about it. We'll probably have to close up shop early, and she'll be okay until I get there."

"That's right, poor baby. You know what? Why don't I just go hang out with her? I can hang with Mabel another day."

"Are you sure?"

"I'm sure. Besides, I hear some hot mechanic might be getting off early and will be available for couch snuggling."

Our last conversation rings in my head, playing on a loop.

"Oh my god."

I shake my head back and forth, not wanting to believe it, but the proof of what I've done is lying in the bed right in front of me.

My entire body starts to tremble. "It's my fault."

The words taste like sawdust on my tongue, and everything inside me recoils.

Callie was planning to go to Mabel's bungalow after she left the auto shop, but I asked her to check on Peaches. I'd sent her to the farmhouse.

She's here because of *me*.

It's as if all the air has been sucked out of the room, and I gasp, pressing a hand to my chest. Beneath my fingertips, my heart pounds.

What if I hadn't gotten there in time? What if the brain swelling doesn't go down? What if she...

I shake my head, refusing to let myself finish that

thought. But even as I force it away, willing myself to think about something else, anything else, a dozen worst-case scenarios spin to life in my mind, each once agonizing and unbearable.

"No, no, no," I murmur, gripping Callie's hand like my own life depends on it.

What if.

What if.

What if.

Those two little words seep into my thoughts like a poison. It spreads through my entire body until it feels like every muscle is contracted, pulled tight to its break-ing point. My body, rejecting those two words, strains as I fight the panic clawing its way up my throat.

The shadows swoop in, sinking their claws into me with such force that I gasp again, straining for air. The weight of what could happen, the possibility of those two little words bears down on me such force, it feels like a thousand boulders have slammed into me.

I can't move or speak. Everything is spinning. The room, my thoughts— I can't make sense of anything other than the sound of my heart pounding in my ears.

I drop Callie's hand. I can't touch her, can't be near her anymore. I doubt she'd even want me sitting here if she knew what I'd done. I shove away from the bed, standing on shaky legs, swaying as I try to find my bal-ance.

Callie's smile, her laugh, her touch. My brain is

hurling memories at me, like a spray of bullets, each one slicing me to ribbons. But then it's not just Callie. It's Kase's laugh thudding in my ears. It's the slap of his hand on my shoulder. His goofy grin.

All my fault. All my fault. All my fault.

I can't take it anymore. Tearing out of the room, I limp out into the hall, ignoring the agonizing pain in my leg. Mabel calls my name, but I don't answer her, and I don't stop moving. I can't breathe. I have to get out of here.

I take the elevator down to the ground level, hurrying to the main entrance, ignoring the concerned looks of those I pass.

The glass double doors slide open automatically when I approach and I step outside. It's nearly midnight, but the parking lot is still full of cars and people. The air smells like rain, but it's barely drizzling, and I don't even feel it as I step out from under the covered awning and shuffle toward the road.

It's slightly easier to breathe outside, but the thread that's holding me together is fraying fast. I bend over, placing my hands on my knees as I fight the anguish that has me in a chokehold. My vision blurs.

"Hey, you okay?"

I look up. There's a teenager in a hatchback idling a few feet away from me. "Yeah. Thanks."

He eyes me up and down and then nods at the hospital. "Are you sure, man? I can help you inside if you want."

"I just came from there." I start to wave him off, but this kid may be my only chance to get out of here. My truck is still at the auto shop. "Do you think you can give me a ride?"

The teen nods and leans over to open the passenger door. "Sure. Where to?"

I hobble over, grimacing as I lower myself into the seat. It takes me a second to answer him. I can't go home. I have no home to go to anymore . . . but I can't stay here.

I rattle off an address and lean my head back as the hospital disappears behind us.

Chapter 32
Jensen

The cemetery is cloaked in darkness, despite the sporadic street lights along the path. I've only been here a handful of times, but I find my way easily enough. Kasey's headstone sits at the top of a grassy hill in an area reserved for veterans. Two small American flags stick out from the grass, and there's a small, slightly wilted bouquet resting at the base of the stone, most likely left by Sutton on a recent visit.

The sight of those flowers, of the engraved letters spelling out my best friend's name makes my throat bob as grief wraps around me, squeezing me so tight it hurts. Shoving a hand through my hair, I swallow hard, aching to hear my best friend's voice. "I need you, Kase," I choke out the words. "I know I don't have any right to ask, but I need you to tell me that it's going to be okay. I need you to talk to me like you've done before."

If there's anyone that can help me make sense of things, it's Kasey. "Talk to me, please."

I suck in a breath and listen. A warm breeze rustles the leaves of the trees nearby, but there's no answer. No voice in my head, no whisper on the wind. There's only the still quiet around me.

"Dammit, Kase. You've talked to me before, and I need you to do it again."

I wait, desperate to hear him the way I have so many times before. "Please," I beg, my voice cracking. "I miss you so much and it's all my fault that you're not here. I'm so sorry." I can't keep the words inside me. "I don't know how to make it right. I wish it were me . . . it should have been me. I'm just so sorry."

I sink to the ground, my bad knee screaming with pain, though it's nothing compared to the feeling inside my chest.

"I've done it again," I whisper, tears rolling down my cheeks. "Callie's in the hospital right now, and I'm the reason she's there. I don't know if she's going to be okay and if I lose her . . . " A sob erupts from my throat, and I wrap my arms around myself as another follows and another. "I can't lose her, Kase. Please, you have to tell me it's going to be okay."

There's no answer.

It hits me then, the truth I've known but haven't

wanted to face for the last four years. My best friend is gone, truly gone, and there's nothing I can do to bring him back. It's heartbreaking and devastating and I let myself feel every single bit of it as tears rush down my cheeks. I cry for the man I've been the last four years of my life, for the way I tried to push Callie away and almost missed out on the best thing that's ever happened to me. I weep for the way there will always be a Kase-shaped hole in my life and for the future with Callie that I so desperately want but am terrified I'm going to lose.

I let myself feel it. *All* of it. The grief. The pain. The guilt. The regret. The joy. The hope. Every piece of it, I let it all out.

It's only when I'm completely spent, that the words float over me, the voice steady and sure. But it isn't Kasey's.

It wasn't your fault.

I straighten, swiping at my face. This voice is as familiar to me as my reflection. It's my own. Clear and unmistakable.

It wasn't your fault.

Instinct urges me to argue, but I can't. I hadn't realized until now that the voice I was most desperate to hear from wasn't Kasey's. It was mine.

It wasn't your fault.

It wasn't my fault.

That declaration settles over me, taking root in all the places were it aches, wrapping around all of those broken pieces inside me.

Finally, *finally*, I understand.

What happened to Kasey was a horrible, awful tragedy. An accident. One that I'll wish I could change every day of my life, but I can't carry this anymore.

I can't let the shadows keep me imprisoned forever. I can't keep punishing myself, not for what happened four years ago and not for what happened today. I have to let it go and move forward.

Callie told me I'd find it eventually, the strength of a river, like the ones that carve their way through the mountainsides, but I don't need that kind of strength. I just need her.

Whatever happens, no matter how much time I get by her side, it's worth the mountains and the valleys and everything in between. She's my home.

I inhale and exhale slowly, the breath moving through my lungs with gentle ease. "I have to go," I whisper, staggering to my feet.

Leaning down, I brush my fingers across the top of the smooth headstone and over the letters of Kase's name. "Rest easy, brother. And thank you, for everything."

My steps are lighter as I hobble back down the path, back to life.

Chapter 33

Callie

A low, rhythmic beeping echoes in my ears, pulling me from the warm darkness. My eyelids flutter, and I open them slowly, wincing a little at the brightness in the room. I try to speak, but the words come out in a garbled mumble.

"It's okay," a soothing voice says. "You're alright. You're in the hospital, and we're taking very good care of you."

A woman's face comes into view. Light brown skin, high cheekbones, and a gentle smile. I've never seen her before. "Callie? Can you hear me?"

I try to answer, but my body is heavy and everything is a little hazy. My eyes move around the room, taking in the details. The soft knit blanket covering me. The pale blue scrubs the woman is wearing. The machine in the corner that's beeping in time with my heartbeat. My tongue feels like it's coated in sandpaper, and my throat hurts when I swallow.

"Let's try a little water." The kind woman helps me sit a little more upright and places a small plastic cup of water in my hand. I lift it to my lips, and the cool liquid slides down my throat like a balm. I drain the cup.

"Would you like some more?" she asks.

I nod, the fogginess already clearing a little, though there's a dull ache in my head. I take a few more sips. "I'm in the hospital," I repeat, my voice raspy from not being used.

"You are." the woman nods. "My name is Camila. I'm one of the nurses who've been taking care of you."

"What happened?"

"You were injured when the tornado hit. Do you remember it at all?"

Like a key to a door, her words unlock a flurry of color and sound as it all comes rushing back to me. Peaches and the farmhouse. The sirens. Jim Bann's suspenders. The freight train.

Camila must notice the way my body stiffens. She pats me on the forearm. "You're safe now, Callie. You suffered a traumatic brain injury, but you're going to be okay."

I nod even though a dozen questions flood my thoughts. "How did I—"

"Callie?" Mabel cuts me off, standing in the doorway, with a hand pressed to her chest. "You're awake?"

I barely have time to blink before she flies across the room and flings herself at me. "Oh my god, I'm so glad you're okay." She's crying now, and even though I don't fully understand, I'm crying too. I wrap my arms around my cousin, squeezing her tightly.

"I'll go let the doctor know that you're awake." Camila gives me a little wink, shutting the door behind her as she leaves.

"Oh, Callie. I've been so worried about you." Mabel pulls back, giving me a once-over as if she can't believe I'm sitting in front of her. "Jensen and I both have."

Jensen. The monitor in the corner dings as my heart rate speeds up. "Where is he?"

"I sent him home a little while ago to take a shower and eat something. He hasn't left your side in three days, and I thought he needed a little break."

"Three days? I've been out that long?"

Mabel squeezes my hand. "When the tornado hit the farmhouse, you hit your head pretty bad. There was some swelling that the doctors were worried about. They kept you medically sedated for a while to give your brain some time to heal."

I can tell from the expression on her face that she's given me the CliffsNotes version. The dark circles under her eyes and her pale skin tell another story entirely. "I'm sorry I scared you, Mabs."

Tears well up in Mabel's eyes. "I'm just glad you're

okay."

"What about Peaches? Ms. Dorothy? I remember looking for her, worrying that she might be outside. Is she . . . " I trail off, scared to finish my sentence.

"She's fine," Mabel hurries to reassure me. "She wasn't home when it hit. She's been by to see you a few times. She brought you those." She points to a vase of sunflowers sitting on the small table by the bed. "And Peaches is okay, too. Sutton's been watching her."

"Oh, thank God." Relief surges through me. "The farmhouse?"

"It's gone," Mabel confirms. "Most of Main Street, too. It's too early to say definitively, but Sully says it was probably an F-3."

Bile rises in my throat. An F-3. The Fujita scale only goes up to five. "That bad?"

"Dayton Springs isn't going to be the same for a while." Mabel gives me a sad smile. "But the people here are made from tough stuff. We'll rebuild."

I swallow, letting the weight of her words settle over me. It's a lot to take in. "What happened after the tornado hit? How did I get here?"

"Jensen. He got you out before the farmhouse completely collapsed." Mabel squeezes my forearm. "He dug you out of the rubble with his bare hands."

"He did?" My throat aches as I process this. My brain is quick to conjure up an image of Jensen digging through the remnants of the decimated farmhouse to get to me, and it nearly cleaves me in two. It's all too easy to imagine the panicked look on his face as he tried to find me, probably thinking the worst. Bile churns in my gut, and for a moment, I think I'm going to be sick. After everything he'd been through when Kasey died, I can't imagine what must have been going through his head. My heart aches for him, for the man I'm so desperately in love with, I can barely stand it. "Oh, Jensen."

Mabel says something, but I don't hear her. The pain in my chest has spread, and the dull throb in my temple from when I woke up is now a mighty pounding. I have so many questions, but right now the only thing I want is Jensen. It's the only thing that can make me feel better, the only thing that can soothe the aching in my chest. I need to see him, need to feel his steady presence next to me. I rub at my temple and blink away the tears pricking the corners of my eyes. Relief, worry, shock, pain—all of it washes over me in waves. The overwhelming reality of what happened hits me with such force, it's almost hard to breathe.

"Are you okay?" Mabel asks, her brows knitting together. "Are you in pain? Do you want me to track down the nurse?"

I shake my head, even as the tears roll down my cheeks. "No, I'm okay, I just need—"

The door to my room swings open. I expect to see Camila and the doctor, but Jensen limps in, his hair still damp from a shower. He's leaning on a single crutch, wearing a light hoodie and a pair of jeans. His skin is pale, his brow creased with worry, but when his eyes find mine, they spark to life. "Callie?"

The sight of him standing there is such a relief, all I can do is cry as he rushes over to my side, dropping the crutch to reach for me. His arms go around me, crushing me to his chest, and his familiar scent floods my nostrils making me cry even harder.

He holds me for a long time before finally pulling back, his own cheeks wet with tears. "I was so worried about you." He cups my cheeks and leans in, pressing a kiss to my forehead, to both of my eyelids, my nose. When he gets to my mouth, he brushes his lips across mine so gently and tenderly, it makes me want to weep all over again.

I want more, so much more, but Jensen pulls away and takes a step back. I'm confused by the distance he's put between us. I look to Mabel, but she must have slipped out to give us some privacy.

"What's wrong?"

Jensen shakes his head, his face lifting with one of the most beautiful smiles I've ever seen. "Absolutely nothing. I just needed to make sure this was real and not some trick my mind is playing on me."

It's then that I notice the pallor of his complexion, the lines of exhaustion carved into his skin. "Come here," I whisper, reaching for him. He lets me tug him closer and sits down next to me on the bed. I take his palm and place it against my heart, beating so fast, I'm pretty sure someone is going to come running soon thanks to that stupid monitor I'm still attached to. "I'm here, and I'm okay. Because of you. Mabel told me you got me out."

A shadow crosses Jensen's features. "I blamed myself. I thought it was my fault you got hurt because I asked you to go check on Peaches. The whole time I was looking for you, digging for you underneath all the debris, I thought I'd never find you. And if I did, I thought you'd . . . " he trails off, anguish etched in his features.

"It wasn't your fault." I slide a hand up to his face. "You got me out, and I'm here. I'm okay."

"When they told me about your condition, it crushed me. All I could think about was the what ifs, and I knew that if I lost you, I'd never recover. I couldn't handle it, so I left." Jensen lets out a deep and heavy sigh. "But I realized that I have to stop punishing myself for things outside of my control. I don't want to spend my life full of guilt and regret. I don't want to run from the things that make me happy because I'm scared of losing them."

He leans in, pressing his forehead against mine. "So, I came back, and Callie, I swear to you, I'll never leave your side again. I'm so sorry that I left, so sorry that I haven't always been the man you needed me to be. If you'll let me, I promise to spend every day of the rest of my life making it up to you and showing you just how much you mean to me."

"You're already everything to me," I breathe out,

needing him to understand. "I don't want anything but you. I don't need you to be anything other than who you are. All the messy, imperfect, but wonderful pieces. I want them all. I want *you*, Jensen."

Jensen's lower lip trembles slightly as he reaches into the pocket of his hoodie and pulls out a small object, crumpled and encased in clear plastic wrap. "I bought this three days ago, and I've been carrying it around ever since." He opens my hand and places the item in my palm. It takes me a second to read the chunky red lettering of the label and to understand that it's a small apple pie. The kind you get out of the vending machines in the hospital lobby.

I must look more than a little confused because Jensen cocks a brow and gives me a little smirk.

"It's not homemade, but given that my stove is currently out of commission, I'm hoping you'll make an exception. Someone once told me that the best way to show how you feel is with pie. So, here goes. Callie, I'm in love with you. So desperately and deeply in love with you. From the moment I met you, you made me feel alive. You brought light back into my life when I was convinced I'd live in the shadows forever. I love you, and I don't want another day to go by without you knowing just how much. I was afraid to tell you before now, so afraid that if I surrendered to this feeling that it would ruin me, ruin us. But loving you isn't ruin, it's redemption."

Jensen's eyes go misty, and a single tear rolls down

his cheek as he lets out a shaky breath. "I don't care what this life throws at us. I don't want to face another day without you. Every thought I have is of you. Every single beat of my heart is for you. I'm yours, completely. Wholly."

A sob bubbles up my throat as tears drip down my cheeks. I clutch the little pie to my chest. Jensen doesn't rush me to respond; he waits, with so much tenderness swimming in those ocean blue eyes of his, I want to dive into them and stay there forever. This man, this beautiful, sometimes grumpy man who I never saw coming makes my soul sing. Even if I tried, I would never be able to paint this feeling, this love burning between us. I could try a thousand different color combinations, swirl together a million different textures and hues, but nothing would ever come close to this feeling of absolute weightlessness and wonder. This love he's offering me is one of a kind, a masterpiece in its own right. The kind of creation that artists try and fail to re-create because it's that remarkable, that life-altering, and it's ours.

"I'm in love with you, too." It's a pale comparison to what I feel flowing through my veins and pouring out of every cell in my body. There's so much more I want to say, so much indescribable love bursting from inside of me, I know I'll spend the rest of my life trying to articulate it. I settle for pulling Jensen close, my lips brushing his in a promise I intend to keep forever. "Fly with me, Jensen," I whisper against his mouth.

His answer is an all-consuming kiss that sets my entire body ablaze. As lips claim mine, his hands slide down to the sides of my neck, deepening the kiss. Slow and languid, he takes his time, and I memorize each caress of his lips, his tongue. I wrap my arms around his neck, pressing myself as close as I can. One of Jensen's hands slides down my back, bare thanks to the hospital gown I'm wearing, and shivers roll through me as his fingertips trail down my spine. I can't get enough of him, and I don't think I ever will. My pulse flutters wildly, as if my heart has sprouted wings and is about to take flight, which makes the makes the heart monitor in the corner go haywire.

An alert sounds, and Jensen and I jump apart as Camila comes bursting in, looking alarmed. Her eyebrows lift as she takes in the sight of us, wrapped in each other's arms, cheeks flushed. She lets out a little chuckle and props her hand on her hip as she eyes Jensen. "Well, that explains the alarm." She gives us a wink and walks over to turn off the monitor. "The doctor should be in shortly," she tells me, chuckling again before she shuts the door behind her.

Jensen's shoulders shake with laughter as he drops his face into the crook of my neck. I'm so deliciously delirious with happiness, I don't even care that we just got busted. Everything feels so right, so perfect. I wouldn't care even if the entire hospital staff came bursting into this room.

"I really should be more gentle with you." Jensen sits back, his hands trailing down my arms. "You've been through a lot. Your body needs to heal."

"So does yours," I say pointedly, eying the bruises on the side and back of his neck. I reach up and run my fingers along the ridges of the stitches at the top of his spine. He lets me examine him, pulling his shirt up to show me the various lacerations on his back. I eye the thick black brace covering his knee, and try not to cry at the deep scrapes and scratches that go all the way up his arms.

"It's nothing," he says, swiping a thumb across my cheekbone. Then gently, so gently, he takes my head in his hands and presses the softest of kisses to the thick gauze covering my wound. His hands move to my leg, and I try not to combust as he leans over and sweetly kisses the cast that starts just below my knee and wraps around my entire foot. Then he lifts my hands, kissing each of my palms.

I yank him closer needing to feel his lips against mine.

When we're breathless, I let him go, scooting over and patting the space next to me on the bed. Jensen hesitates only for a second before toeing off his shoes and sliding up next to me. Laying back, he lifts his arm and tucks me in close so that my ear is pressed to the spot just above his heart. We let out matching breaths, deep and long, and I lift my chin, studying his face. The worry lines have softened and though the dark circles are still there, there's a peace in his expression that makes me want to cry. I can tell he's fighting sleep as his eyelids droop.

"Rest now, my love," I murmur in his ear, pressing a kiss to his cheek. His arms tighten around me and I settle in listening as his breathing begins to slow into the deep rhythm of sleep.

"I love you," his deep voice rumbles, his long fingers wrapping protectively around my hip.

I snuggle in closer, my own eyelids growing heavy. "I love you."

The world around me starts to grow hazy, and the steady beat of Jensen's heart is like a lullaby, singing sweetly in my ear.

Chapter 34

Callie

Three Weeks Later

The long hand of the vintage singing bird clock hanging above our bed hits the top of the hour, and an eastern meadowlark begins chirping. I listen, amused, as the little bird finishes its song.

"Jensen." I gently shake his shoulder. "Did you hear it?" I shake him again. "Did you?"

"Uh huh," he mumbles, not bothering to crack open an eyelid. Instead, he uses the arm that's already slung over my torso to pull me closer, tucking me into his chest.

"The yellow warbler is next," I tell him, even though I know he's not nearly as excited about the clock as I am.

When Frank offered to let us borrow his RV while we figured out our next steps, he hadn't told us it was basically a time capsule. From the retro fabric of the curtains to the avocado green color scheme, the entire RV screams 1978, and I am absolutely obsessed with it. The bird clock is my favorite little oddity, and it fills me with absolute delight every time it sings.

I sigh contentedly and run my fingers along Jensen's forearm, tracing the colorful lines of his tattoos. Lying next to him in this bed feels like the most natural thing in the world. It doesn't matter that the mattress we're sleeping on is full of lumps and barely big enough for the two of us, or that Jensen has to hunch over just to get his head wet in the small shower. It doesn't bother me that the stove only works sporadically, the roof leaks in spots, and two of the windows are sealed shut. The man next to me is my home, and I'd live anywhere just to be with him.

I do miss the farmhouse and the airstream, but you don't survive what we have and still think of material things the same way. We lost a lot in the twister, including half the town, but houses and things are replaceable. It's the moments that matter. All the little pieces of our lives—the smell of the first flowers in springtime, a kiss beneath the autumn moon, laughing til your stomach hurts with your dearest friend, a warm, freshly-baked apple pie—those are things that matter. It's the experiences, the memories, the relationships. I survived an F-3 tornado, and I'm determined to live every day for moments like this one. Even if I never do anything else in this life, getting to spend every morning listening to a silly bird clock with the man I love is more than enough.

Something wet presses against my cheek, and I turn to find a pair of large brown eyes staring at me. "Good morning," I coo, scratching Peaches under her chin. "Are you ready for breakfast?" I sign "eat" and she leaps up, barking and wagging her tail.

Ever since the tornado, Peaches has been my little Velcro dog. She's never far from my side—a fact that Jensen jokingly bemoans. He keeps claiming that I stole his dog, but I see the way his eyes crinkle when Peaches and I are snuggled up together. Having children of my own has never been something I felt super passionate about, so the fact that Jensen and I may never have any doesn't bother me. I'm more than happy to play dog mom to Peaches, and I feel like our little family is complete. It's still hard for Jensen to talk about what happened with Anna, but I remind him every day that he's more than enough for me, and this life we're building is perfect just as it is.

Sitting up carefully, I ease myself off the bed. I hate how slow I'm moving, but the vertigo from my TBI is still pretty bad, and it's worse first thing in the morning. The doctors assure me it will fade with time, but for now, I have to take it easy. Bright lights can be tricky, and the headaches can be intense, but I'm trying not to get frustrated. I'm lucky to be alive, and I owe my body time to heal.

I pour kibble into Peaches' bowl and place it down

in front of her. The kitchenette area is tiny, and I have to step over the dog to start the coffee pot in the corner. I pull a small frying pan out of the cupboard and turn the nob on the stove. The burner clicks, but doesn't ignite. I try again. Still nothing. So much for making breakfast.

When I turn back towards the bed, Jensen's eyes are open, and he's watching me with an expression that makes my skin flush.

"Stove's out again," I say. "I was going to make omelets." I poke my lower lip out in a pout.

He laughs. "Let me try."

Flinging the covers off, he gets out of bed. He's shirtless in a pair of shorts that sits low on his hips, and sweet magnolias, the sight of him doesn't exactly help with the vertigo. I grip the counter for support and suppress a grin.

He fiddles with the burner for a few minutes before shrugging. "Stove's out again."

"Like I said." I laugh, giving his shoulder a shove.

Jensen captures my hand in his and yanks me close, wrapping his arms around me. I sink into his embrace.

"Morning, pretty girl," he murmurs, his mouth skimming the shell of my ear.

A warm shiver skips down my spine. "Morning."

Breath hitches in my throat as his lips travel down my neck, and when his teeth catch on one of my collarbones, heat flares through me. My head falls back and my eyes flutter closed as Jensen kisses my bare shoulders. One hand toys with the straps of my tank top, while the other stays anchored at my hip, holding me in place.

"You're so beautiful," he murmurs, taking his time as he moves back up my neck, pressing his lips to my skin before brushing his lips against mine. These sweet, gentle touches are enough to have me squirming in his arms, and I'm about to pounce when there's a loud knock at the door.

I groan, disappointment making my nose scrunch.

Jensen laughs at my expression and gives me a kiss that's over entirely too fast. "Later," he promises with a wink.

I'm half tempted to ignore whoever is at the door and turn "later" into "now," but a familiar voice calls out.

"Come on out of there, you lovebirds. I ain't got all day!"

I snort out a laugh. "Be right there, Ms. Dorothy."

We dress quickly, stepping out into the golden sunshine. It's early, but the air is already thick with humidity. Ms. Dorothy waits for us, leaning against the side of a new-to-her Oldsmobile. She's wearing a bright pink dress with flamingos and a pair of matching bedazzled sunglasses.

"Look at you." I beam, reaching to pull her in for a hug. "You're going to put all those native Floridians to shame."

Ms. Dorothy chuckles, squeezing me tightly. "Well, I figured, when in Rome." She pulls back, tapping me gently on the cheek. "I'm gonna miss you, neighbor."

I try not to cry as she gives me another hug. After both of our RVs were destroyed in the tornado, Dorothy decided to move in with her sister in Florida. She'd stayed long enough to get her affairs in order, but she was heading out today—something I could barely think about without tearing up.

She hugs Jensen next, sniffling. "You take care of our girl now, ya hear?"

"I will," he promises. "Are you sure we can't convince you to stay? I can work on getting another RV ready. Just say the word."

"Oh no, I think it's time to move on. Besides, I've decided I'm officially too old for tornadoes. I intend to spend the rest of my days on a beach with a good book and a drink in my hand. No more weather worries for me."

"Uh . . . " Jensen quirks a brow. "You know they got hurricanes there, right?"

Ms. Dorothy flashes a wide grin. "Sure, I do, honey. Whatcha think I'm gonna be drinking on that beach?"

We all share a laugh and another round of hugs. "Don't you worry about ole Ms. Dorothy. I'll be just fine." She reaches into her car and pulls out several Tupperware containers. "I made y'all some lemon squares and banana nut bread. It's a thank you for all you've done

for me."

A lump rises in my throat as I take the baked goods. "We should be thanking you, Ms. Dorothy. If it weren't for your advice, I'm not sure we'd be standing here."

"Nah, a love like what you've got always finds a way." She re-adjusts her sunglasses. "Well, I best be off. You two take care now."

Jensen wraps an arm around my shoulders, and we wave until Ms. Dorothy's car is out of sight.

I swipe at my nose and let out a breath. "So, what's the plan for today?"

Jensen points to the construction site behind the RV. We've already started clearing out the wreckage of the farmhouse, but it's a slow process.

"I've got a couple of guys coming to help clear the big stuff, but that's not til later. Oh, and your cousin is stopping by to take some photos for me. Insurance wants more documentation."

"Okay, how can I help?"

"You can go back inside and rest for a while." He gives me a pointed look. "Doctor's orders."

"I feel fine," I grumble, knowing this is not a battle I can win. "And I want to help."

"I know you do, but your brain needs time to heal. The more you rest, the faster that will happen."

I hate that he's right.

"What about your knee?" I challenge. If I have to take it easy, I'm determined that he's going to take it easy with me.

"Still hurts," Jensens confirms, "but my knee is hardly as precious or as important as this." He presses a kiss to my forehead. "Go rest, Callie."

I start towards the RV, but Jensen grabs my arm and whirls me around. "I love you," he says, cupping my cheeks.

Just like that, I feel a little better. "I love you, too."

The grin he gives me makes my heart pound, and I practically skip back to the RV. I didn't want to admit it, but the dull headache I always seem to have is getting a little stronger, so rest is probably wise. I lay down, snuggling Jensen's pillow and letting his scent lull me to sleep.

Mabel wakes me up a while later by plopping down on the bed, her camera bag crossed over her chest. "Wake up, Sleeping Beauty! Your favorite person is here!"

I wipe the sleep from my eyes and grin. "Jensen?"

Mabel purses her lips and gives me a playful slug in the shoulder. "You wound me with your words."

Laughing, I sit up and tuck my hair behind my ears. "How are things? I feel like I haven't seen you in a while."

"Sorry, I guess I've just been a little busy." There's a strange look on Mabel's face, and she won't look me in the eye. Whatever's been keeping her "busy" is not something she wants me to know about. I gasp as my Cousin Radar goes off.

"Mabel! You're seeing Sullivan."

Her eyes go wide. "What? No. I'm not *seeing* him. He's just here. I can't control where he goes, you know, and he's doing his work thing. Trust me, I don't want to see his stupid handsome face any more than I have to."

"Mmmhmm." I am not buying it. "And where exactly is he staying while he's in town?"

The answer is clear enough from the pink splotches that color Mabel's cheeks, and I burst out laughing.

Mabel rolls her eyes. "I'm not here to talk about Sully. I've got a job to do." She opens her bag and rifles around.

"That's right. Jensen said you were coming over to take pictures for the insurance."

She pulls a strip of cloth from the bag. It's the same bandana she used on me for the blind date photoshoot. "Not for insurance, Callie." Her expression has changed, and there's a softness in her eyes that I don't understand.

"What?"

"Just trust me." With gentle hands, she ties the bandana around my eyes and helps me up, leading me through the RV, out the door, and into her car. The drive isn't very long and when we park, I have absolutely no idea where we are. Mabel guides me forward, her grip steady until she suddenly stops—and I collide with something solid. Not something. Someone.

Jensen's hands are there to steady me, pulling me close.

"What's going on?" I ask, still not understanding.

He unties the blindfold, and I blink a few times as my eyes adjust to the light. We're standing in the exact same spot where we met during the first photoshoot, under the shade of a tall oak tree. A soft, denim blue blanket has been laid out atop the small hill that over-looks the river, glinting in the sunshine. There's a wick-er picnic basket on the blanket next to a bouquet of wildflowers, and framed photos of me and Jensen and from Mabel's photoshoots are placed between scattered rose petals. A Bluetooth speaker begins to play a soft, sweet song, and in the center of it all, Jensen stands with Peaches at his side. She's wearing a t-shirt that says *Mom, will you marry my dad?*

Tears well up in my eyes as Jensen reaches for my hands.

"Callie Dawson," he begins, his voice like a caress. "I'm in love with you, and I have been from the mo-ment I laid eyes on you in this very spot. I never thought I would find love like this—never thought it was even possible to love someone as much as I love you. I never thought anyone could love someone like me. 'Til now. 'Til *you.*"

Jensen's voice cracks on the last word, and I squeeze his hands, tears rolling down my cheeks.

"I was a broken man who didn't think he deserved anything more than pain and regret, but you brought my shattered heart back to life and filled it with such love, I can barely contain it. There's nothing I want more in this world than you, and I promise I will spend forever showing you how much I cherish you. It would be the greatest honor of my life if you would be my wife."

He bends carefully, moving slowly due to his injury, and gets down on one knee. "Will you marry me?"

"Of course, I will," I say, dropping to my knees in front of him.

Jensen wraps his arms around me, his lips crashing against mine. This kiss, this soul-searing kiss, brands itself on my heart. *I love you, I love you, I love you.*

When we pull apart, I spot Mabel crying her eyes out as she moves around us, snapping pictures with her camera. It hits me then, how this all started because of her, because of a photoshoot. I owe her a lifetime of Ben & Jerry's.

Jensen signs something to Peaches, who plops down in front of me. A sparkling solitaire glitters from her collar, and I have to swallow down more tears as Jensen carefully removes it and slides it onto my hand.

Falling or flying.

Falling or flying.

Falling or flying.

"Flying," I whisper against his lips. "Definitely flying."

Epilogue

@Jfroberg78: Did you see???? THIS IS NOT A DRILL! They're engaged! #Endgame #happilyeverafter

👍 👎 ❤️ REPLY   Just Now

@apagetoturn: OMG, STOPPPPP! I'm crying right now! Look at them!

👍 👎 ❤️ REPLY   Just Now

@bethanynorthpark: Talk about the butterfly effect! These two are GOALS. #heputaringonit

👍 👎 ❤️ REPLY   Just Now

@Lauradeets: I just knew it! So happy for them!

👍 👎 ❤ REPLY   Just Now

@Apuzzledreader: Those pictures are EVERTHING!
You can just feel the love!

👍 👎 ❤ REPLY   Just Now

@WoolLenn: Best. News. Ever!!! 🎉
Congratulations!!

👍 👎 ❤ REPLY   Just Now

@amieeloveschewie: OH MY HEART! Think they'll
invite us to the wedding?

👍 👎 ❤ REPLY   Just Now

Acknowledgements

Pablo Picasso once said, "Every act of creation is first an act of destruction." Man, I feel that in my bones, and honestly, it sums up my experience writing this book.

When I started my author journey, I imagined it looking a lot differently than it does now. I had a specific dream in my heart, and I was determined to make it come true. I'll spare you the details, but let's just say the door to that dream shut pretty firmly in my face. More like slammed, really. I won't lie, I was in the pit of despair over it for a long time. I didn't know what to do or where to go next. I struggled with that for years. Until finally, it occurred to me that maybe dreams don't actually die. Maybe they just evolve. Maybe you just have to be open-minded and willing to try a new way. Maybe you just have to pivot.

This book for me is my pivot. It was born from a place of destruction—I had to break down my own way of thinking and dreaming. I had to change my perspective and examine my own heart. I had to grow and learn and change— but now it's my favorite creation to date.

So, if you're reading this and you've been struggling with a dream that isn't coming true, please lean in. Sometimes dreams change. Sometimes they need to change, and in order for that to happen, we have to be willing to take a chance, to take a step into the unknown. Is it scary? More than you know. But it's also so incredibly worth it. Don't be afraid to pivot, my friends. Sometimes the new dream is even better than the original one.

Of course, as I'm reflecting on this book's journey, I have to take the time to recognize the amazing people who helped make it happen.

First, to my amazing cover designer, Emily Wittig. You absolutely blow me away with your talent. You brought my vision to life, and gave me the most beautiful cover anyone could have asked for. Thank you for being such a dream to work with. I hope we can continue making art together in the future!

To Sarra Cannon: Girl, if I ever meet you in person, I am going to hug the snot out of you. Not only has your Publish & Thrive course absolutely saved my bacon on more than one occasion, not to mention taught me everything I know about publishing, but you've also been incredibly kind and supportive to me over the years—going all the way back to my OG YouTube days. Thank you for being such a light in our community, and thank you for all you've done for writers like me.

To Tyffany Hackett: Oh sweet friend, how can I possibly express how grateful I am for you? Not only did you create the beautiful interior formatting for this book, but you've also been a huge cheerleader for me over the years. Whether it was a supportive comment or a beautiful picture featuring my books, you've always been so encouraging. You made me feel like my work has value, and I cannot thank you enough for that. You're simply the best. Thank you so much.

To my amazing beta readers, Jessica Froberg, Lenn Woolston, Laura Detering, and Bethany Gallahair: Thank you for your excitement and willingness to read this book, even when it was a hot mess. Your feedback helped tremendously, and your comments on the things you loved kept me going on the hard days. You're all rockstars!

To Amiee Couch: Snookie! Without you this book would have a whole lot more conjunctions in it! I love that we connect over books, and nerdy book talk on the phone with you is one of my favorite things ever! I appreciate all your help with making this book shine! You've always been in my corner, and I so blessed to call you my sister.

To Stephanie Smith: Thank you for being one of this book's earliest and most enthusiastic fans! Your excitement over my pages and our text message thread full of gifs gave me the courage I needed to keep writing. You have always encouraged me to step outside my comfort zone and promised to be the first one in line to buy this book. I'm so grateful that you're not only cousin, but my friend. Thank you for helping make this book a reality.

To Jessica Olson: Whether it's a thirty minute marco polo, a phone call, or a text message chain that's a million messages long, you're always there supporting me and encouraging me to keep going. Being a writer isn't for the faint of heart, but it's so much easier with friends. I knew from the moment I met you that we were destined to be best friends, and I was right! Thank you for being you and for always being there for me.

To Megan Addison. My real life Mabel, where do I begin? Thank you, thank you, thank you. You knew this book needed to exist before I did, and now because of you, because of all your prayers, encouragement and unwavering support, it finally does. Thank you for taking me to Sweetgrass and for showing me the possibilities, for believing in my dream even when I didn't. If I were standing on a battlefield, there's no one I'd want watching my back than you. Love you!

To Megan LaCroix: It's literally impossible to put into words how grateful I am for you. To put it simply, your friendship changed my life, and I will never stop thanking my lucky stars that you sent me that piece of "fan mail." You know these characters as well as I do. You've read every word I've ever written. You've talked to me on the phone for hours over plot holes and character arcs and more. You've held my hand through all the ups and the downs and everything in between. You are the reason I didn't quit. Thank you for being you. I love you to the moon and Saturn!

To my family, thank you for sharing me with the people who live in my head. I love you all so much!

And finally, to you, my dear reader: Thank you for taking a chance on me and this book. You are the reason I do all of this. I hope you love Callie and Jensen as much as I do.

About the Author

Kimberly Chance is a small town romance author who drinks way too much coffee and relates most to the little reindeer in *Frozen 2* who says, "I just *love* love!" When she's not writing kissing scenes or crying over her own characters, she spends her days teaching high school English. You can also find her re-reading her favorite books for the hundredth time, watching True Crime with her hubby, or playing soccer & baseball mom to her three incredible kiddos.

For more information about Kim or her books, be sure to check out www.kimchance.com

Want more Dayton Springs? Stay tuned for Mabel and Sullivan's story, coming in 2026!